ACCLAIM FOR *MAX-ARTHUR MANTLE'S* **BATTY BWOY**

"Max-Arthur Mantle's *BATTY BWOY* offers an engaging look at same sex desire from a Jamaican lens within an American context, which thankfully doesn't rely on stereotypes. His characters are fleshy, rough and rendered with complexity and profundity. Perhaps more than anything, *BATTY BWOY* pulls back the curtains on the terrors associated with pursuing self and desire. *BATTY BWOY* is a significant, yet haunting contribution to American letters. Quite a feat for a first-time novelist."

> - STEVEN G. FULLWOOD, *Black Gay Genius: Answering Joseph Beam's Call*

"Written in clean, precise prose, Max-Arthur Mantle, has shared a serious work that is both personal and still exquisitely lean in its rendering. Like all fine stories, the intimate world he portrays of a gay Jamaican man's journey is very specific, even as the themes of longing expressed paints a universal stroke."

> - L. MICHAEL GIPSON, author of *Collisions: A Collection of Intersections*

"With exacting detail, the author of *BATTY BWOY* bridges Jamaica and the U.S., through two generations whose search for freedom are oddly traumatic maps that followed with courage, guide the journey to fuller self-actualization and promise. Seeing the world through their eyes, hearing their hope through their tongue and dialect, offers authentic complexity to a narrative too often reduced to caricatures of victim and victimizer. Here the victims are also heroes: fragile, imperfect, and yet resilient as the Jamaican soil from which they came."

> - TIM'M T. WEST, author of *Red Dirt Revival, Flirting, and preldispositions*

"Truth-telling, even with the aid of poetic license, is cathartic, and healing. *BATTY BWOY* captures and unleashes much of the pent-up raw complexity associated with growing up gay in Jamaica, and in the Diaspora. There were many touching and familiar portraits of friends, as well as my own life-experiences, that made me consume the passionate telling of Mark's story. I rejoiced with his growing self-awareness, and groaned at the seemingly inevitable mishaps from an unshepherded sexual awakening."

- MAURICE TOMLINSON, Jamaican LGBTI and HIV activist

"*BATTY BWOY* is more than a bildungsroman about a black gay man dealing with the harsh realities of life in Jamaica and America. We meet a resilient, clever, and oftentimes hopeful male protagonist despite a young life filled with many hardships and struggles. He is an indomitable figure who seeks to create a third space for himself, free from the societal, cultural, economic, and racial stigmas that constrain him. This is the first of Mantle's trilogy series, and the reader will be sure to want to read the others. An eye-opening debut novel."

- SEAN FREDERICK FORBES, director of the Creative Writing Program at University of Connecticut

"*BATTY BWOY* is a beautifully written novel that documents a similar, but perhaps more harrowing lifestyle to that of the familiar. It reaffirms journeys I have had or communities I have worked with - homophobia, migration to foreign climes, educational crisis, racism, drugs, homelessness, hopelessness, and HIV are all themes I can identify with as an experienced community and youth worker. The protagonist is beautifully drawn with much scene setting that reveals the brokenness he is born into. *BATTY BWOY* is a social document that could find a home as a social work manual despite it being a work of fiction. The novel has echoes of *Cathy Come Home*

- an infamous and influential BBC docu-drama from the 60's, and *Push* - the debut novel by Sapphire which spawned the movie *Precious*. It is creative writing laced with personal reality. I cannot wait for the next instalment."

- DIRG AAAB-RICHARDS, Jamaican/British writer and LGBT activist

"*BATTY BWOY* touched a deep emotional chord. The book reveals so much more than a young black homosexual boy trying to find his truth in a wicked and perverse generation. I saw in the protagonist what I see in so many of the youths that I work with - broken, rejected, lost, struggling to find veracity and validation that eludes them. I was enthralled by Mark Palmer as he combat social stigma and struggled to gain acceptance."

- JANICE FLETCHER-BROOMES, Jamaican-born Canadian social worker and LGBT advocate

"I was captivated with excitement, waiting to unravel more of the story of Mark Palmer in Max-Arthur Mantle's debut novel *BATTY BWOY*. I was not disappointed."

- R. JIDE MACAULAY, contributor to *Black and Gay in the UK*

"Max-Arthur Mantle has debuted with a sure fire hit and soon to be considered classic novel. *BATTY BWOY* take the reader on a serious emotional rollercoaster ride that you secretly wish will never end. The characters will seem to become a part of your lives; so much so, that you may find yourself talking to them out loud, asking them why or exactly what the hell were they thinking? Written with vivid detail, *BATTY BWOY* ranks amongst the top best sellers such as *B-Boy Blues*, *Invisible Life* and *Come Sunday Morning*."

- KIRE SENOJ, *Callaloo Literary Journal*

BATTY
BWOY

Max-Arthur Mantle

First Edition: April 2015.

ISBN   978 – 0 – 578 – 16016 – 0

For more information please visit www.maxarthurmantle.net

This book is for anyone who is different. Stay different.

"There is no greater agony than bearing an untold story inside you."

- Maya Angelou

"Not everything that is faced can be changed, but nothing can be changed until it is faced."

- James Baldwin

"None but ourselves can free our mind."

- Bob Marley

Daphne felt defeated. For six weeks, she had been holed up in a cold jail cell - somewhere in upstate New York - after a failed attempt to cross the border. She was conned out of a meager savings by relatives who promised to smuggle her to Manuel, her husband in Hartford. She never made it. Instead, she was deported to Jamaica.

The news of Daphne's unexpected return quickly spread through Bonnet. She kept to the house to hide her humiliation. Her father, Nathan, a gentle, slow-moving, illiterate farmer, advised her to trust in the Almighty God and soon she would receive His blessings. He called her Queenie, and she was his favorite of his seven children. He raised them with a strict hand, but was partial to her. The other children were regarded by how useful they were on the farm. Daphne knew he loved her more, and she never forgot to let them know it. She was welcomed back when other siblings would have had to tough it out on their own. There was nowhere she could have gone and be treated so special.

Daphne was a woman of undetermined means and limited wit. Her gravelly voice belonged to someone taller than five feet three. Her dark skin was covered with scars, and veins shot up her arms and down her legs like aimless tributaries. Short plaits crowned her head like unruly weeds. Her eyes showed too much white in the middle of her pear shape face. Her wide nose cast a shadow over a meaty mouth - the under lip always wet. A long root incisor anchored two rows of dentures. She never wore makeup because it failed to evoke a feminine mystique. She had realized at a young age she would never be called beautiful. She knew she had her father's cossetted love. If she had no other reason to flatter herself when she looked in the mirror, at least she had those incandescent teeth.

Daphne's family had been poor for generations. It was a way of life for country folks. You were considered fortunate if you lived in Kingston. Indoor plumbing and electricity were amenities that never made it to the village. Washing by the river was as normal as walking barefoot to school and wearing *tear-up batty* pants. Clean, mended garments were reserved as Sunday best. Her family never thought their lives were less because it was the only life they knew.

They survived on basic subsistence. Nathan was a good enough farmer who kept them contented. They never went hungry nor were close to borrowing, and they always had a little more than the neighbors. He cultivated acres of sugarcane, banana, and other cash crops, and raised chickens, goats and pigs. A donkey he called Tally doubled as a mute friend and a means of transportation to the market. When Daphne grew older, her family prospered after Nathan built a shop in the front yard.

The whitewashed, three bedroom house rested on cement blocks on a steep hill in St. Catherine's farmlands. The front of the house leveled with the red dirt road that meandered up the hill. It had never bothered Daphne to share a room with three sisters when she was a child, but returning with two daughters became a discomfort she grew to tolerate.

The cramped room had a lumpy mattress that was wedged in a corner, next to a table with a kerosene lamp and clothes spilling out of cardboard boxes. Her brother, Berris, and his son occupied a smaller room. In the third room, Nathan and the children's mother, Sylvia, slept on the same bed since they had been married for thirty-six years. A busted bureau stood by their window, trapping sunlight. Now, as then, family photos faded, plastic flowers gathered dust and Sylvia's scented powder box collection increased when she had a birthday.

A passageway separated the bedrooms. The front door was left ajar in the daytime for the breeze to drive out heat and mosquitoes. They bathed in a zinc pail and relieved themselves in a pit toilet behind the house. Cooking was done in the yard on a coal stove. The used wood when there was no money for coal. They ate outside at a metal table surrounded with logs refashioned into stools. When the tropical rain came, they gathered their plates and sat on the veranda. In the yard, vines weaved on an overhead grill and created a cool shade from the severe heat. Red blossoms matured into gummy fruits, attracting tropical birds. Hibiscus hedges bordered the road and pressed against wood beams which led to the shop.

Daphne assumed the role of shopkeeper to escape housework and the constant pestering from her daughters. The shop became her refuge. After breakfast, she perched her angular body behind the counter, draped in a starched apron, ready to service her customers - the neighbors. They came throughout the day to buy a daily ration and to gossip. It was the business of everyone to know everybody's business. Gossip was traded like Bible scriptures. "Let mi tell yuh dis" filtered through the shop with eyes glaring and lips drawn close to ears, after being sworn to secrecy. Gossip reserved for the steps of the Baptist church as villagers entered to worship their Lord and Savior.

Daphne was not a regular churchgoer. She only went when she was invited to a wedding or funeral. She preferred gossiping in the shop. Behind the counter, she had the liberty to say whatever she pleased, whereas in the house of the Lord, she was expected to act as His humble servant and keep her mouth shut.

She was not happy the latest gossip was about her. She dismissed the gossip, and said she had missed her daughters and decided to come home to be with them. The neighbors rolled their eyes with disbelief and the gossips continued. They said she had missed the opportunity for a better life for her family because young people didn't have a promising future in Bonnet. She made up stories about America, a place she saw from a jail cell. No one knew any different since she and Manuel were the only ones to travel outside Jamaica and he had not returned. She remained busy in the shop and feared he was making a life without her.

While Nathan was a devoted father, Sylvia had no maternal instincts. She liked being pregnant. It made her feel worthwhile and superior to women who couldn't have children. Everyone catered to her when a new baby was expected. Nathan massaged her limbs when she complained of aches. The children brought water from the standpipe and heated it for her bath. Neighbors visited with compliments and treats from the market – a piece of crabmeat, a yeasty drink to increase stamina or the preferred jerked pork. When the babies came, she could not put up with changing their *nappies*, wipe running noses and quieting their tantrums. Nathan's preference for Daphne made Sylvia feel like her rival. She encouraged Manuel when he showed interest in Daphne because she thought marriage would get her out the house.

Daphne's feeling was mutual. She thought Sylvia was too emotional, always crying for reasons she never understood. She also resented that Sylvia would conspire with Pastor Franklin to get her to church. She spent more time with her father in the shop and on the farm, and never wished

4

she had been dear to her mother.

Nathan entered the shop after dusk. Leaning on his cane, he lit the kerosene lamp. Daphne's smile left her face and her fretting eyes were fixed on him. He was ailing from the pain in his chest he received when he fell off the donkey. Had he been a younger man, he would have simply taken two painkillers and walked it off, but he spent more days in bed and less in the fields. Each breath was a stitching pain. It made bending and raising his hands agonizing. Sylvia tried with no success to appease his mood by piling food on his plate.

Nathan was worried about Daphne's future. Seeing her toiling away in the shop for two years, biding time for Manuel to come home dampened his spirit and questioned his faith. He thought God would have shown up sooner with His blessings. The farm was in neglect because he was ill. He thought Berris and his grandson would have been able to maintain the produce, but they were worthless farmers. Without a fruitful harvest, closing the shop was inevitable. He would have no surplus or money to take care of Daphne and her children.

Nathan browsed the shop to see what remained. Daphne felt the urgency by his silence and waited for him to say something.

"Queenie. Wah yuh nuh guh stay wid Manuel madda inna Kingston. Yuh cyaan just set up inna de shap a wait fi de bwoy. Him nat cuming back!"

It was not what she wanted to hear. She tried to change the subject.

"Ou yuh feel papa? Yuh waan fi guh a de docta again?"

"Yuh hear wah mi sey? Yuh betta aff a Kingston. Fine wok ar guh a de embassie ahn guh a Manwel. Mi cyaan tek care a yuh ahn de pickney dem."

"Mi cyaan live wid da ooman deh. Shi cyaan tan ah bone inna mi!"

"Yuh haffi luk bout yuh fuecha."

5

Daphne waited two weeks for an appointment letter to arrive from the US Immigration. She realized if she wanted to see Manuel again - save the marriage or what was left of it - she had to go to him. She didn't want to be a burden to her father and going to live with her mother-in-law was the last resort. Nothing good would come from living with Inez because her daughters would suffer more than her. While she could defend herself against a difficult woman, who regarded her as a nuisance, her daughters had no choice but to suffer whatever abuse they faced.

A brisk two-mile walk down the hill took her to the main road for the bus to Kingston. While she waited, she exchanged greetings with familiar faces. When the bus arrived, she paid the fare and moved down the aisle to a window seat. A girl jumped before her and stole the seat. Daphne gave her a mean look. The girl sucked her teeth before retreating to the back row and curling her skirt between her legs

A woman Daphne knew squeezed into the seat beside her to gossip. Daphne hushed her when she mentioned the immigration, fearing bad luck. She also didn't want her business to get back to the neighbors. To divert the conversation, she asked about Marse Powell's new granddaughter and if Pastor Franklin caught the person who put the out-of-order letter in the suggestion box.

The bus conductor shouted, "Guh dung inna de bus. Smal' up yuh self. Spanish Town, Half Way Tree, New Kingston, nuh skoolas!" The passengers watched each other settle into the tight seats to begin their journey. A woman from the Baptist church who Daphne knew, told the passengers that Jesus loves everyone. When they gave her an obligatory nod, she took out a dog-eared Bible for an impromptu sermon. She warned, He was coming soon like a thief in the night.

The drive to Kingston was long and bumpy. The bus buckled under its weight and dallied around potholes on narrow, two-lane roads. The passengers were nervous when it veered on a shaky bridge and crossed a dried-up river filled with rocks. The sun blazed and sweat poured from their disgruntled faces. They fanned themselves with newspapers and poked their head out the window. The loud radio drowned out chatter. Higglers on their way to the market looked over their shoulder at the oncoming bus threatening their space on the road. Rowdy youths walking to school stuck their tongue out to the passengers for their amusement. Farmers over yonder waved and grinned like actors in a "Come back to Jamaica" commercial.

The hilly, tropical terrain gave way to a sea level cityscape. Through the windows Daphne saw the Marcus Garvey statue in Linstead and the colonial building in Spanish Town where she got her daughters' birth *cerfitickets*. In Kingston, large concrete houses dotted the hills. Cars congested the powerline streets with pedestrians disappearing into air-conditioned offices. When the bus arrived in New Kingston, Daphne got off and hastened her pace to the US Immigration and Naturalization Services.

An armed guard sat in a Plexiglas booth before a circling crowd waiting to enter the building. Daphne pushed through the crowd and stood before him. He looked at her sideways as she stared back at him.

"Yuh hab identifikation?" The guard asked. "Ahn yuh appintment letta?"

She reached between her breast and brassier then took out the letter and her passport. He was warmed by her smile in the picture and loosened his manner as he flipped through the pages.

"Twenty-five?" he asked. "Yuh luk olda."

"Mi know," Daphne said. "Wi cuntrie gal grow fass."

The guard wanted to smile, but decided not to.

Inside the building, she got a number and waited. When the number was called, she handed the appointment letter to another guard, who told her to listen for her name. Daphne patted down her wig, wiped her forehead, ran her tongue over her teeth then cupped her fingers to smell her breath. She straightened her clothes and checked in her mind if she had on clean underwear. She wasn't sure why she needed to know this. She wanted to be prepared for anything.

A baritone voice echoed in the office.

"Miss Daphne Winifred Mabel Palmer!"

Daphne darted in the direction of a grossly fat woman motioning her to enter an office. An amused murmur settled when she closed the door behind her. The woman took her passport, but kept her gaze on a typewriter. She tucked the appointment letter in a file, shifting the fatty layers hanging from her waist and scrutinized Daphne.

"Wat is yuh perpus fah goin' to America, Miss Palmer?"

Daphne's chest tightened.

"A waan fi si mi husban ma'am."

"Yuh husban?"

She glanced at the passport.

"Oh, a beg yuh pardon, Mrs. Palmer."

Daphne flashed her teeth to no avail. The woman's aloofness was chilling. Daphne peered at her fat ringless fingers clicking at the typewriter. She thought the woman believed she was better than her because she had a decent job and lived in Kingston, but at least she had a man, or proof of having a man.

The woman asked a series of questions. Daphne's monosyllabic answers were inaudible and suspended between frowns and eye-rolls. She shifted on the chair and looked at the ceiling. The questions about her deportation made her feel cornered. She tried to explain and the woman listened with fascinated disgust, enthralled by the terror in Daphne's eyes. She gloated with the power of her job. She knew Daphne and the people waiting to see her were circumscribed by poverty and ignorance. Their lives would be drastically altered if she granted them a visa to America.

After hearing Daphne's story, she told her she should have used a better judgement. She scolded Daphne like she was a disobedient child. Daphne felt humiliated. She feared returning to Bonnet without good news. She imagined the kind of life she and her children would have if she decided to live with Manuel's mother. Nathan was the only person who cared about her. She wanted to cry but was consoled by a stamp in the passport. It was the answer she was looking for.

"Mrs. Palmer. Mi granting yuh a one-year visa."

A string of saliva hung from Daphne's lip when she opened her mouth in surprise.

Fi nuh more dan a year."

Daphne cried, but they were different tears.

"Mi a waarn yuh. Nuh overstay yuh visit."

Daphne bowed her head.

"Tank yuh Jesas."

The grossly fat woman looked up and cleared her throat.

"A mean tank yuh ma'am."

Daphne felt exonerated. The gossips stopped. The neighbors spoke highly of her great expectation. She felt relieved walking down the road and being seen because they no longer thought she was a failure. They believed she was on her way to riches in a country where the streets were lined with gold.

9

Nathan organized a party the night before Daphne's departure and invited everyone from the village. It was an all-night affair that felt like a holiday. Everyone was happy Daphne was going to America. A goat was slaughtered - the meat curried and the bones boiled in a spicy broth called mannish water. Six chickens were killed and roasted with jerk seasoning on an open grill with cassava and sweet potato wrapped in foil. Ackee with salt fish simmered in a *dutch* pot beside a frying pan with fritters. Sister Gordon from the Baptist church and some of the neighbors brought a little something wrapped in brown paper bags to make the festivities merrier.

Between the eating, talking, laughing, and playing dominoes, the villagers drank and stumbled around dancing to Byron Lee and the Dragonaires. They swung their hands and gyrated their hips in the fashion of the Ska dance. The children played into the twilight. Their bellies were filled with bulla and beef patties. They sucked on chicken bones and chewed sugarcane with the juices sliding down their cheeks.

Daphne left after breakfast for the bus to the airport. She wore a new dress purchased at the craft market. Manuel's auntie gave her two bottles of Wray and Nephew white rum. Nathan saved a fruitcake and salted codfish from the party, things he said she would miss eating. She looked away when her daughters held onto their grandmother and cried. It did not deter her. She warned them to mind their manners and do what Granny Sylvia said. She gave her father a gentle hug as her mother looked on with reclaimed content. She walked down the hill, clutching her *dulcimina* with a subdued smile, relieved and excited about what was to come.

On the plane, she fumbled with the seat belt until it clicked. She bowed her head and whispered the only prayer she knew - *God is good. God is great. Tank him fi dis meal, Aw men.* She rolled her eyes at the flight attendants demonstrating what to do in case of an emergency. She didn't believe anything those *stoosh*, nice looking Kingstonians said. Oxygen coming out of a face mask sounded like a magic trick. Why did she need a face mask if the plane crashed? It seemed ridiculous the seat was a flotation device, whatever that meant.

A few hours into the flight, the plane rattled through a pocket of clouds. She woke up from a light sleep, her nerves unsettled. The seat belt sign was illuminated and the pilot advised of more turbulences. Her stomach turned. She wanted to vomit, but nothing came up. She asked for water, and gulped it down after pouring some in her palm to pat her forehead.

The plane dipped again like it was falling out of the sky. She clenched her teeth and shuck her head. The passenger beside her raised an *Air Jamaica* magazine over his face to ignore her. Her ears began to ache. She shoved bubble gum in her mouth and swallowed her sweet spit to ease the pressure. She calmed when the plane leveled and the pilot instructed the staff to prepare for landing.

Daphne opened her eyes when the plane screeched onto the asphalt. Everyone clapped. She wasn't sure why they did, but she followed because through the windows she saw America. She smiled at the flight attendants' sing-song goodbyes, and bolted to the main concourse to retrieve her luggage before there was a line at customs. She felt queasy standing before the immigration officer. She shifted her weight on one leg and thought about the last encounter - being carried away to a backroom for questioning. When the immigration officer stamped her passport and welcomed her to America, she flashed her teeth and headed out the airport.

The passengers on the train from Grand Central to Hartford differed from those on the subway. There were no long-haired men in leather jackets and tight pants with loud girls in mini-skirts and platform shoes, running through the cars. They were replaced by taciturn men in suits with their legs

11

crossed and glasses on the tips of their noses, quietly reading *The Wall Street Journal.* There were delicate women in designer dresses with their hair pulled back so tight their eyes flared. They cradled their purses and guarded shopping bags at their feet while glaring at magazines.

The trained zipped out the city and headed north through the wealthy Connecticut suburbs. Faraway mansions hinted at a life in America where everything was possible. Daphne's mind was filled with wishful things and what she would accomplish. She loved America immediately - at least the idea of America.

When she arrived in Hartford, she sat in the waiting area with her *dulcimina* by her side, her ankles crossed and arms buried between her legs. She rocked nervously back and forth, flicking her eyes at moving cars, waiting for her husband. It had been almost three years since she has seen Manuel. It seemed like ages ago.

Part One

Chapter One

It was the summer of 1969. Free love and let the good times roll were perpetuated by Hollywood picture shows. Glossy magazines advertised color televisions as status symbols. The Jackson 5's "I Want You Back" was rising up the charts. Elvis returned to the studios, making a comeback with his pirated black swag, and Neil Armstrong made a giant leap for mankind with a single step on the moon. The house in the suburbs with the white picket fence, 2.5 kids with mommy and daddy at the dinner table was a *Leave It to Beaver* American fallacy.

The reality of soldiers returning disenfranchised, some in body bags from an unpopular war threatened the propaganda. Celebrations were overshadowed by civil unrest. A nation divided. Men felt emasculated. Women burned their bras and men dressed like women rioted at the Stonewall Inn. Woodstock seemed like a rainy weekend festival for pot-smoking hippies in the east, and Manson and his deranged disciples went on a rampage, spilling blood in the west. An era of hope and hate.

Hartford was removed from it all. Her inner-city woes never made the national headlines. The French-Canadians and Puerto Ricans were rioting, but no one cared about the blacks living in semi-depressed walkups that quarantined them in a life of poverty. A concrete jungle populated with illegal immigrants on extended stays. Men working dead-end jobs and their women bused to the suburbs as domestics. Transistor radios blasted songs

17

reminiscent of home to soothe their anguished fates. Apartment doors with multiple locks and grilled windows offered false security from the vicious cycle of impending doom. Garbage littered the allies and bred another outbreak. Mange mongrels roamed abandon lots. People sat on weathered porches waiting for the postman to deliver their monthly welfare checks. Neglected children played in trepid water gushing from rusted fire hydrants. Young mothers gripped babies to their shaking hips, abandoned by futureless men, ill-equipped to be fathers.

Daphne's eyes flooded with tears when Manuel drove to the train station. He had grown delicate, heavier, and a shade lighter with new lines around his eyes. He looked older than being twenty-eight. His afro and platforms heightened his five feet ten frame. His smile met hers with an awkward hug, spinning her like a schoolgirl. She seemed peculiar as well. He would have to return to behaving like he was married a man. He propped his hands on the steering wheel and grinned like he was making it in America. He would take care of her. As they drove down Albany Avenue, Daphne studied his face, searching for something familiar.

Manuel remembered when they met. He saw her when he passed the shop. She wasn't like the pretty girls at the market, who never returned his stare. She wasn't under Pastor Franklin's vigilance and his weekly Bible study. She was worldly and outspoken. She wanted more than a life in the country. She occupied his mind. His timid "Howdy" became determined, until he mustered the courage to ask her to the church social. He was surprised she said yes because he had never seen her at church.

Daphne hated the church social. She felt the inquisitive eyes of the church folks scrutinizing her, but she enjoyed Manuel's company and agreed to go with him to play bingo the following week. Every weekend

18

thereafter, they were inseparable. They picnicked by the river and read Miss Lou stories. He came by the shop in the evenings and they talked for hours, gazing at the stars and counting *peeni walli*. She wore his work jacket on chilly nights, and he cherished the little wire ring she made for him. A year or so later, they told their families they wished to marry because Daphne didn't want to bring a bastard in the world.

At twenty-two, she was pregnant again and living up the hill with Manuel in his auntie's house. Manuel farmed and sold the produce at the market in Linstead while she made an effort to be a wife and mother. She wanted to start a new life in Kingston. Manuel couldn't afford to move to their own place. They would have had to live with his mother, a woman he hardly knew. He wanted to go to America. His dream was realized with a farm worker's visa. When he left Jamaica, he had planned for Daphne to follow with the girls, but things got complicated.

Their reunion was bittersweet. Time grew them apart. The excitement of being together cooled, and they barely spoke to each other. Their lives became mundane in Manuel's third-floor rented room on Edgewood Street. Their dreams of a better life were curtailed by circumstances. Manuel's income was only enough for rent and food. It strained their relationship. They evaded feelings. Manuel lost interest and came home from work smelling of alcohol. Daphne grew bored from watching soap operas all day. The only thing they had in common was a twin bed with split personalities. She liked her side firm, placing two-by-four planks under the mattress while he preferred a softer sleep with an extra blanket.

The marriage was a disappointment for Manuel. When he came to America, he worked on a tobacco farm in Virginia. The minimum wage in American dollars when converted was more than he ever made selling produce from the farm back in Jamaica. He decided never to return. When his visa expired, he boarded a Greyhound bus to Hartford to live with relatives and found work cleaning the streets. He saved money to rent a room and waited for Daphne. When she was deported, he assumed the life of a single man. No one knew about his wife and children in Jamaica. The marriage became disposable. Their separation justified his infidelity. It was a credit to his virility, a test of his manhood like other Caribbean men. Daphne made herself believe whatever he was doing in America was all right. She never questioned his faithfulness in their letters.

Daphne coming to America curbed Manuel's sexual pursuits. It was convenient having her in his bed. He no longer needed to go on the prowl, out all night, chasing skirts, spending money he didn't have, looking for a woman to release his pent up frustrations. Sex was something like a ritual they did after *American Bandstand*. Manuel got home from work, washed up, ate supper, got in bed and Daphne followed. He groaned and trembled on top of her, then rolled over to sleep. Unfulfilled, she left the room to fix herself another serving of fruit cake.

Manuel was a letdown. Reading his letters and waiting all those years, soared Daphne's expectations. Manuel wasn't the man she remembered, nor was he the same man in his letters. He didn't seem like someone dependable. The two years he lived in Hartford, he worked as a security guard, a parking lot attendant, a delivery driver, and packed boxes in a factory. He could never hold onto a job. He either quit or was fired. His job as a shoemaker's apprentice with intentions of owning a shop seemed farfetched. He said it was a secured craft that would never be obsolete. Daphne had doubts. She thought no one in their right mind was repairing old shoes when discount shoe stores were popping up at every strip mall all over the city.

Daphne was tired of depending on Manuel. She hated being alone in the room. She wanted to live the kind of life she had hoped. She wasn't sure what she wanted, but she knew it wasn't what she was doing. She had heard how life was good in America. What she was doing wasn't close to her dreams. She wanted to write home and let her father have something to be proud of, something to tell the villagers. It didn't feel like she was in America living the life and receiving God's blessings.

She wanted something more. She saw the women on Edgewood Street going to work in the suburbs, returning with shopping bags, their hair and nails done, sporting new outfits, and going out with their men. She envied them. She wanted something similar. It was the only life that seemed possible, more attainable than Erica Kane's. She wanted a job. She pestered Manuel to find her something under the table that didn't require working papers. It took weeks, but her spirits brightened when he told her about the woman in West Hartford.

Daphne showered and lubricated her skin with shea butter and painted her lips with Vaseline. Her afro wig was bouncy and shiny. Under her gabardine winter coat, she wore a jersey wrap dress with a sweater draped around her shoulders. She was pleased with her reflection in the window. It took some effort.

She boarded the bus on Albany Avenue and glanced at passengers exchanging early morning small talk. She knew soon she would be doing the same. When she arrived in West Hartford, she walked down North Main Street, crossed at Farmington and headed to Arlington. The house was at the end of the street next to Fairview Cemetery. It was the home of the woman looking for someone to care for her willowy old mother.

A Mercedes was parked in the driveway. Daphne realized it was Miss Crown's house when she noticed her initials on the letter box and on a sweater on the back seat of the car. She pressed the doorbell and was startled by a stir inside. A small dog ran to the door and jumped at the screen.

"Just a minute."

A white woman peeped out the window. Her puffy made-up face deflated when she saw Daphne standing at her door.

"Can I help you?"

Daphne cleared her throat.

"Mi is Mistress Palmer ma'am. A cum 'bout de jab."

Miss Crown arched her brows and walked away from the window. She motioned for Daphne to go around to the back door. Daphne followed a narrow trail with pine trees shading a swimming pool and waited.

"Sorry about that. I just had the carpet shampooed."

Miss Crown fidgeted like she was talking to someone behind the trees.

"Manuel's wife?"

Daphne nodded.

She searched for something clever.

"Oh! Mitchel said he's a good fellow, doing swell."

Daphne nodded again.

"It must have been a long trip … coming from … the city?"

Daphne nodded for the third time.

"Come in out of the cold. Take a load off."

Daphne stepped inside the house and looked around. The living room was filled with pictures. In each picture, Miss Crown was smiling and in the arms of a different man. She looked at Daphne with uncertainty. She ran out of things to say.

"Mother! The new girl is here."

Ten years before and a few pounds lighter, Miss Crown would have been considered a strikingly beautiful woman. She had big blue eyes, blonde hair cascading down her back, voluptuous breasts, and a body that encouraged a stare. Her mother and people of her generation thought she was flawed because she never married or had children.

She spent her time with generous middle-aged men, who came in and out of her life, on their way to finding themselves. She signed up for anything considered exciting amongst her lady friends at the country club. She went wine tasting to Napa Valley with Ronald, whale watching in Alaska with Darren, and to Cancun with Wilson. Adventures gave her something to do and talk about, having never worked a day in her life. When her mother fell in the bathtub and broke her hip, her bedridden dependence cramped her style.

Miss Crown took Daphne's coat and walked her to the den, smiling at the way the sweater hung around her shoulders. She thought it becoming how black gals like Daphne caught on to habits, doubting she ever played tennis. She joked with Daphne about her experience taking care of moody old people. Daphne said she was a fast learner. She grew up minding farm animals and was kind and gentle. Miss Crown smiled. She asked about Manuel. Daphne said he wasn't making good money and she needed a job because she was tired of watching Erica Kane. Miss Crown smiled again. She told Daphne that Mitchell spoke highly of her. He said she wasn't like the other illegal aliens that came to the country expecting a hand-out. Daphne smiled.

23

Daphne learned about Miss Crown's rules set for black folks from another time, only updated. She wasn't allowed to enter the house from the front door, and Miss Crown's bedroom was off limits. When she had what she termed *gentlemen callers*, Daphne was to remain with the old woman in her room. Daphne bit her lip when Miss Crown asked her to wear a uniform. They agreed she wouldn't because she wasn't the maid.

Despite Miss Crown's ways, Daphne like going to work. At the end of the week, she had money. She looked forward to the 6:30 am bus commute. Miss Jean from Barbados came on the bus two stops after her on Vine Street. She also worked for one of the women at the country club in West Hartford. She spoke in exclamations. She like to gossip about Miss Crown. Miss Farley, a nurse's aide from Georgia, got on at Bedford Street. She talked about the hospital, using medical terms like she knew what she was talking about. Miss Sanchez from El Salvador spoke very little English. She sat in the middle seat, her head bobbing side to side, stuttering "Como" like a broken record. Miss Jean said Miss Shirley, the cook at the country club, said Louis, the gardener, heard strange sounds coming from Miss Crown's bedroom. She thought, *har man dem a heat anda two foot table*, alluding to a sexual act her Christian way didn't permit her to describe in details.

The old woman liked Daphne's company. She thought she was strange, but amusing, especially the way she spoke. She liked to listen to Daphne's tales about her island country life. Daphne endured the old woman's difficulties and tried to remind her she wasn't her maid. Her job was to serve meals, give her a bath, and make sure she took her medications. She was at her beck and call, listening for the little bell by her bed to ring when she left her alone. The old woman didn't see any difference in Daphne's job with that of a maid, but she didn't let her know it.

On sunny days, Daphne sat her on the screened porch next to the pool while she watched her soaps and nibbled on something sweet or greasy. The old woman filled those days with stories about her dead husband next door at the cemetery and petted her hyperactive dog. She listened to Dinah Shore eight-tracks and romanticized about meeting Mickey Mantle. She spoke about a time when decent Christian white people didn't feel threatened by what was going on around them. Daphne didn't know what she was talking about. The most fun she ever had was dancing with the *Belly Woman* at the *Jonkonnu* street parade during Christmas.

On paydays, Daphne rode the bus up Albany Avenue to the hair salon to touch up the roots of her recently pressed hair. Sometimes she got her nails polished with a bright red coat. She went to the G. Fox store on Main Street for an egg salad at the lunch counter on the sixth floor. One week she came home with shopping bags and she felt like she was on top of the world. Manuel asked if she got anything for the children. When she gave him a leather wallet the following week, he stopped scrutinizing the way she spent her money.

Daphne felt like a new woman. She ran around the room singing James Brown's "Say It Loud, I'm Black and Proud," feeling good about herself. Manuel liked her independence, but he resented her changed behavior. She pressured him about moving to a one-bedroom apartment in the fixed up triplex Miss Farley lived at on Bedford Street. Some nights she never cooked. She and Miss Jean, who actively recruited men to keep her bed warm, stayed out all night at different bars on weekends. Although she left Manuel as she pleased, she thought herself a respectful married woman and missed the way he once looked at her.

Manuel passed the time listening to the Major League World Series on the radio. Daphne joked it was in pretense because all he knew growing up in Jamaica was football and cricket. He hated being alone at nights in the room, but pretended everything was fine, covering up his jealousy when she came home laughing with alcohol on her breath. He never asked if she was with Miss Jean and the men she befriended. They were the men who called out to women on the streets even if they knew they were spoken for.

Manuel was miserable because their bed was cold. He began to crave her because she became the girl from the shop he had lusted for, and not the complaining bitch he felt trapped with. One night, as she entered the room, he pulled off her clothes and took her to bed. No words were exchanged. His act seemed desperate, but it was what Daphne wanted. He made her feel like a natural woman.

It seemed like the passion was back. Manuel waited every weekend for Daphne to come home half drunk and giggling. Sometimes they went out together and shared a meal at a diner, or dancing at Club Caribe. It was like that for a couple months until Daphne missed her cycle and began throwing up in the mornings.

She knew what was happening to her and she wasn't happy. Her visa was about to expire and the thought of staying in America illegally was frightening. She told Miss Crown she was quitting. She smiled and gave Daphne an extra fifty dollars with her last pay. The old woman thought Daphne's replacement from Trinidad was funny, especially the way she spoke.

Manuel wanted her to return home because she was difficult when pregnant. Daphne wrote to Nathan, expecting a homecoming party, but when she received a letter from Sylvia instead, she collapsed and wept. Her father was three months dead.

Daphne showed up in Kingston, not barefoot, but very pregnant, to live with Inez, Manuel's eighty-year-old mother. She couldn't bear living with Sylvia and be reminded of her father's grave in the backyard. She thought people would understand if she complained about a mother-in-law as opposed to hating her mother.

Inez lived alone in a large house in Waterhouse, a low-income area in Kingston which was prone to violence. The rooms were rented not because she needed the money, but for the house to appear active to discourage thieves. Inez opened her door and saw Daphne on the street looking bewildered, teary-eyed, and swollen like a drowned corpse.

In a letter, Manuel begged Inez to take in Daphne. He said it was something a mother would do. Inez hadn't heard her son call her mother in years. It reminded her of the boy she left to fend for himself, being passed around to relatives while she tried to be the woman she thought she was and would never become.

She agreed for Daphne to live in her house because it was an attempt to make things right with her son. She had no reason to hate Daphne; she just never got close enough to loving anyone. She preferred people to mind their business. Everything and everyone displeased her. It was her nature to squint her beady black eyes and criticize rather than utter something kind. On Daphne's wedding day, she said she wasn't fooling anyone wearing a white dress because country gals grew up fast, they only acted like they were stupid.

Daphne didn't blame Inez for being cantankerous. It was the life she lived that made her bitter. Inez traded a life in the country for a series of failed marriages that ate away at any dream she ever had. She married abusive men who died on her. When her third husband was killed by a

27

drunk driver on Washington Boulevard, her years were confined to her house, supported by life insurance checks.

She spent her days pulling up weeds in the garden and yelling at hooligans who took short cuts through her yard on their way to Mr. Barnaby's shop. At nights, she was contented being alone, watching her little black and white television. The kids sung at the playground *Ole Miss Inez stuck inna har way, if yuh fuck wid har, shi wi put yuh inna yuh grave.*

Daphne gained forty pounds her second trimester. She ate everything in sight, slept the days away, and was in a constant mood. The pregnancy brought her back to Jamaica to a life she thought she had given up. She missed Miss Jean and their times spent cavorting in bars. She missed Miss Crown's condescending smile and the wiry old woman prying into her personal life. She even missed Manuel's humdrum love making. Being pregnant and Inez's bad mouthing tested her nerves.

Within weeks, Inez regretted having Daphne in her house, and used every opportunity to provoke her. She hoped it would send her back to St. Catherine, where she thought she belonged. She was perturbed that Daphne remained civil during her tireless jests.

Daphne was patient because it was just a matter of time before Inez succumbed to one of her ailments. Inez complained about headaches and joint pains, but put off going to the doctor and relied on homemade potions. She believed *cerasee* tea was the cure for everything, like adding scotch bonnet pepper to improve a meal. She stayed in bed, buried under a blanket, coming out only to relieve herself or roam the kitchen for food.

"Gal! tun dung de nize. Mi head a hat mi!"

Daphne shut her room door and turned down Barbara Gloudon on the radio. She found solace in her talk show. It spoke to ordinary people that

28

were in far worse situations than her. She heard Inez whimpering for a few hours then the room was silent. She never heard from Inez again that night or any other nights. The doctor said a blood clot in her brain was the culprit that killed her. Manuel responded weeks after her funeral like she had gone out for milk.

"Wah did de lawya seh bout de ouse?"

Daphne and Manuel were the sole beneficiaries of Inez's most valuable asset. Before rigor mortis crept in, Daphne was busy making changes to her inherited house. The bedrooms were cleared of any reminder of Inez - the walls washed with *Jeyes*, the mattress turned in the opposite direction, linen burnt and replaced, and all Inez's personal belongings thrown in the trash or given away.

She posted a sign on the front gate to advertise that the two spare rooms were available for rent. The house received a fresh coat of paint and the old broken toilet seats were replaced. She wanted to do more, but the money ran out. Berris brought her daughters from their grandmother and built a coop in the backyard after she purchased fowls to breed and sell eggs. Some neighbors complained about the foul smell drifting into their bedrooms. Others sympathized because she was going on her third child, unemployed, and they didn't believe there was a husband in America.

Chapter Two

Mark was born on the fifth of July. Manuel was restless in his room. He lay in bed with his heavy eyelids sliding up and down. He stared at the ceiling in the dark, trying to unravel his thoughts. He was hung-over and tired from drinking, caught up in the independence celebration, trying to feel good about himself. He forced a smile, wondering what his son would look like. He wasn't sure what he felt being a father again. He thought the two girls must have forgotten about him, and now there was a son he didn't know how to father.

It was after midnight and the surge of heat had not let up. The backless hospital gown stuck to Daphne's body like loose saturated skin. She gesticulated like she was having something terminal removed. When she pushed the baby out, she sucked her teeth and sighed. The infant rested between her breasts like a helpless bundle with a vacant look on his face. Her water had broken, the cord was cut and a bond was never initiated. She was determined to leave the hospital and get on with her life.

Mark was frail and dehydrated. He was kept at the hospital for observation. When Daphne brought him home a week later, he seemed normal. The neighbors were surprised he looked nothing like his mother. He resembled the picture they saw of Manuel. His complexion was lighter. He had a narrow face, almond-shaped eyes, and a constellation of freckles sprinkled across his cheeks. A switch at birth they declared.

31

He was so quiet, Daphne sometimes forgot he was there alone in his crib. Unless he was crying for his bottle or was hot and bothered from soiling himself, she paid him very little attention. The baby reminded her of a deferred life. She watched him grow, anxious to return to America. His seven-year-old sister, Eileen, was elated she had a little brother. She volunteered without protest. She gave him baths, changed his *nappy*, held his bottle, and spoke to him like she did to her dollies. Daphne felt reassured Eileen would attend to him without her having to raise a finger. Winsome, the five-year-old, made no attempt to disguise her contempt. She bolted from the room when Daphne brought him home, crying that she was no longer the baby.

Daphne rented the two spare rooms to a couple with three children. It made the house noisy and busy. The only break she got from their relentless quarrels was when the man disappeared for days. It left the woman and her children depending on her for food, depleting the little she had for her children. When the rent was late and the chicken eggs went missing, she told the woman to leave. She rented one room to a single woman with a child the same age as Winsome, and the other room to a man who worked late at nights.

She was not a good landlord. The woman threatened to withhold the rent when there was a problem. When the pipes broke and the water dripped all night, Daphne said the plumber was called, but he never came. There wasn't money to hire help to repair things broken in the old house. She relied on idle men in the neighborhood. When one wasn't a thief, he had his eyes on Eileen who looked older than her age.

The man who worked late at nights didn't pay his rent and couldn't be

32

found. Daphne felt cheated. She complained to the housing authority then posted an eviction notice, but he never returned for his belongings. His supervisor said he no longer worked for the company. He said he was caught doing something taboo with another man and fled Kingston to save his life.

The room was rented to a lady named Beatrice who had a penchant for gossip when Daphne fed the chickens. It was what they did in the evenings before the mosquitoes came out. They shared a cigarette and gossiped. Beatrice said Miss Lindsey, who sold clothes from a spare room in her house, gave sexual favors to the butcher on Penwood Road and received the best cut of meat for free. Mrs. Davidson had been to an obeah man in St. Thomas to keep her husband, and Angela, the teenage dropout was pregnant again and didn't know who the father was.

They rarely spoke about the men except the ones who cheated and beat their spouse. Bernard was different. He was a secret wish for every woman on Barbados Road, whether they were married or not. A man's man who knew how to handle a woman and keep her satisfied. Being a bad boy with encounters with the law, they found appealing. His tall, stocky, screwed-face presence was intimidating yet sexy. Daphne envied and criticized the women he slept with. She wanted to be one of those women. She wished for someone like Bernard to make her feel good - real good. Manuel's letters were not enough.

Bernard made a quick impression. There wasn't anything he could have done that would not have brought a smile on Daphne's face. She was open for him. She anticipated peering through the kitchen window and seeing him at Mr. Barnaby's shop, when he came to buy *Craven A* cigarettes and *Red Stripe* beer. She gave him some teeth hoping for a conversation. He flirted with made-up reggae lyrics that made her blush. One afternoon, he saw her at the supermarket and they left pushing their carts side by side. They exchanged compliments, expressed interest and confirmed a date. It didn't bother Bernard that Daphne had three young children, or that he was her junior.

Bernard arrived at Daphne's house later that week for the promised home cooked meal. He met the children. Eileen called him Uncle after dinner, and he was invited back the next evening. He quickly became a part of their lives. It seemed like nobody remembered a time when Bernard wasn't at the dinner table. The children saw him in the mornings leaving their mother's room on his way to work at the warehouse. His dirty clothes were mixed with theirs, and his work boots were always at the front door. Daphne stopped writing Manuel, and Bernard moved into her heart.

Her pressed hair was chemically relaxed, and she discarded house dresses for tighter clothes that showed off her fullness. Bernard saw a cheerfulness in her that came with giggles. Manuel's letters were left unopened after a flick of the wrist to check for money. The little he sent was an incentive for Daphne to acknowledge his existence to the children. When no money came in the letters, Manuel remained a figment of their imagination.

All was not well with Manuel. He got his paper, but he was collecting unemployment checks. He frequented bars, and got drunk on anything cheap. It numbed his loneliness. He never told Daphne about the DUI arrest and six months in jail. She never missed his letter while in the custody of the Connecticut Department of Corrections because she was busy rewarding Bernard for having served his purpose - keeping her broken house from falling apart and satisfying her carnal needs. She never knew about Delores, the woman he met at one of the court-ordered AA meetings.

She was from the Bahamas and attended a Pentecostal church on Albany Avenue. She invited him to church and filled the void because he soon saw Jesus' relevance in his life. He found work as a janitor and his letters stopped. Daphne found substitution raising the rent and selling chickens and eggs.

One afternoon, Daphne left her bedroom to answer a knock at the front gate. It was Miss Lindsey asking for credit on six eggs. She said she fell out with the butcher. Daphne didn't press for an explanation. She figured if she gave her the credit some friendship would develop and the details revealed in future laments.

Their idle chatter was interrupted by Mark's screams coming from somewhere in the house. She waited for Eileen to quiet him, but the girls were at school. The sound was terrifying. She raced to the kitchen and found Mark lying on the floor with a frying pot of hot oil splattered over his body. He was lifeless in her arms. His skin bubbled with boils. She cried violently, pleading to God not to let him die on her.

At Bustamante Children's Hospital, a nurse wrapped Mark in a towel and rushed him to the doctor. Daphne paced the lobby fearing the worst. Her thoughts raced. How could that have happened? Why wasn't Eileen back from school to watch him? What was he doing in the kitchen? She had many unanswered questions floating in her head. She never asked herself why she wasn't there keeping an eye on her son. While she filled out the hospital forms, she overheard the nurses accusing her. She didn't respond. She wiped away the tears and fixed her face on the forms.

Mark's third-degree burns weren't as severe as Daphne thought, but he was transformed into a restless boy in distress. His body trembled like a freezing cat. The bandages cocooned him in a constant state of unrest.

Daphne made weekly visits to the hospital for updates from the doctor. The girls heard stories about his recovery. They were warned not to play in the kitchen because they could end up in the same predicament. The doctor said the burns would leave permanent scars. Daphne thought he should be grateful to be alive.

The nurse that attended Mark became a familiar face. Her voice was soothing, her touch recuperative. She was always there when he was miserable. He called her "Mama," which brought a smile, but saddened her because he didn't realize she wasn't his mother. When he came from the hospital, his sisters didn't recognize him. Winsome thought he looked like a monster. Daphne left him in the crib with a fan over his head while Eileen made an effort. As he recovered, his energy was restored.

The neighbors said Daphne was sleeping with the local gigolo and her neglect almost killed her son. They called her an unfit mother. She wanted to get away. Bernard stopped coming around, staying clear of sneers and losing the interest of other women. She returned to the US Immigration and was relieved to receive a four-year visa. She wrote Manuel and was distraught when she read his letter. She pushed the suitcase back under the bed and bawled. Manuel said he was tired of being alone. He told her about Delores. He wanted a divorce.

Daphne hurled the wedding plates on the wall and walked around the house foaming at the mouth. She wanted to hurt Manuel. Everything that reminded her of Manuel – his letters, the cards and anything he sent her during the holidays – she threw in the trash. The children heard her crying and ran into the kitchen.

"A wah Mama?" Eileen asked.

"Him gaan!" Daphne said. "Yuh fadda, him gaan!"

The children had heard those words before when their grandfather had not returned from the hospital. It meant watching frantic adults throwing themselves on a coffin being lowered into the earth.

"Wi fadda?" Eileen asked. "Ah who dat?"

Daphne stayed in bed the rest of the day. She ignored Beatrice's calls. Eileen kept Mark in their bedroom. Winsome played on the veranda. The house was silent. They ate left-over corned beef and cabbage with white rice, and washed it down with *sugar water*, then went to bed. The next morning Daphne looked drained. She sat in bed writing letters and plotting. Beatrice returned and they talked for three hours in the bedroom. Her outbursts became controlled sobs. Her mood was peculiar the entire week. The children weren't sure whether she would lock herself in the bedroom or break something. Beatrice's visits gave her an audience for the dramatics.

Manuel's cousin, Beverly, agreed to put Daphne up when she returned to America. Beatrice became the children's guardian. The girls cried when she left. Four years seemed like forever for a child.

Daphne was grateful to Beverly. She was one of Inez's relatives that were never invited to the house. Daphne supported Beverly during her fights with her baby-father, and she remained loyal. She respected Daphne because she was decent and didn't judge her because she wasn't.

Beverly was like family, but Daphne disliked her ways. She was what people called a *butu* - a vulgar girl. She hung out on street corners with the boys drinking beer and smoking ganja. She dressed to tempt older men. Her hair was dyed red or bleached blond, and her curling fingernails were painted like a rainbow. She was always in a fight with other girls over their boyfriends, and no one was surprised she carried a knife. She was the girl the neighbors warned little girls not to become.

Beverly was all those things, but she loved those she considered family. She lived in Hartford with Marvin and her daughter, Tamara, and found a stable life that had eluded her while growing up in Jamaica. She received a cosmetology certificate in night school and opened a beauty parlor next to Marvin's jewelry shop.

Marvin made custom jewelry for flamboyant dancehall artists and crafty drug dealers. He started with cheap silver rings, selling them from a suitcase at intersections downtown. Word spread about his unique designs, and he later received pricey orders for gaudy gold chains with diamond and other expensive stones. He rented a storefront on Albany Avenue and moved his family to a four-bedroom house overlooking a lake. Beverly was his walking billboard. At the dancehall fetes, she wore gold from head to toe - gold pins in her hair, yards of necklaces, rings on every finger, bangles up to her elbows, and broaches, anklets and toe rings. When she grinned, a piece of gold sparkled in the center of her mouth.

When Daphne arrived, she became the mediator for their fights. Beverly challenged Marvin. Why was he working so late when she wanted him in bed? Who was he meeting at the strip mall? Who was that gal that said, "Big up, nuff respect," at the dance? Sometimes her jealous rants drew him closer - made him feel loved by a protective woman - but when he wanted to conceal an affair, her questions made him feel like an overgrown boy.

They always fought, but made up and got it on. An accusation and malice evolved into a mumbled apology with dinner at a restaurant, followed by clothes being thrown on the floor, doors slamming, moaning in the bedroom, and Jesus' name being called in vain. Tamara listening in bed, hugging her pillow, ecstatic her parents were making a little brother or sister.

Daphne helped Beverly in her salon. She made a little money while she waited to hear from the agency that staffed nursing homes. She adjusted to the changes. Miss Crowns told her she didn't need her services because the old woman was dead. She lost contact with Miss Jean who had moved to Bridgeport. She also no longer saw Miss Farley on the bus because she had a car. She heard Miss Sanchez was deported.

She wanted to confront Manuel, but she hadn't met Delores and didn't know what kind of woman she was. She feared a quarrel might turn against her. When Marvin told her Manuel ordered a ring for Delores, she could barely contain her rage. She telephoned Delores, pretending she was Marvin's assistant calling for a fitting.

Delores drove up to Marvin's shop with Manuel sitting next to her in the car. Daphne's impulse was to run outside and rip his head off, but she remained calm and watched them from behind the window. She didn't contest the divorce, having lost feelings she once had for Manuel. Her anger slowly diminished. It wasn't the picture of a happy couple she had expected. Manuel looked flustered and Delores was shaking after what must have been a fight. She went out to the car. Manuel was alarmed to see her. He didn't know she had returned. Daphne curled her lips like she was going to spit on him. She thought seeing him she would have exploded, but Delores' pitifulness severed the lost. She whispered with scorn, "Duppy know who fi friten," then went back inside.

Mark was enrolled in Mrs. Dubois' basic school on Barbados Road like every other child in the neighborhood. He was a small and nervous four-year-old, a little too skinny for his size. The haircut he'd been given the day before was too short and there were scratches on his scalp where the clippers had nipped him. Eileen walked him to school every day for the three weeks he attended. The first day he came home wailing he hated Mrs. Dubois because she was a scary monster. Eileen laughed because she remembered her first day had gone the same way.

Everyone feared Mrs. Dubois. She was a remarkably tall woman from Haiti with blue-black skin that stirred suspicions. The children said she was a voodoo woman. Her dialect was different and she wore long free-flowing dresses with beaded head wraps. She looked like a revivalist. She taught with a strictness that created timid students, afraid to be called on. Parents were pleased with the results she achieved, as she stomped out rudeness. The pupils dreaded crossing her because they would be at the mercy of her beating cane.

Mark was petrified by the rumor that Mrs. Dubois' husband was the fabled black-heart man. The children said he looked like a pirate - broken teeth, cobwebbed hair, torn dirty clothes, and was cursed with a black heart because he was pure evil. He went from town to town kidnapping small children, ripping out their heart and burying them in shallow graves. Anything bad that happened at the school was because of the black-heart man. When Johnny fell off the monkey bar and gashed his knee, it was because of the black-heart man. When it rained and bull-frogs mated in the gulley behind the school yard, it was because of the black-heart man. When Mrs. Dubois canceled the school trip to Hope Gardens, it was because of the black-heart man. They said he was on his way and nothing or anybody could stop him. Mark's heart raced when he heard the stories.

During lunch, he picked at the black-eyed peas served with chicken and

40

rice. He hated black-eyed peas. Mrs. Dubois threatened another serving the next day if they didn't clean their plates. None of the children wanted black-eyed peas again, and if he didn't clean his plate, he would be pinched or shoved by the school bully.

Sweat covered his forehead when the school bell rang for dismissal. He tightened his sour stomach and dashed to the toilet. He froze when he saw Mrs. Dubois standing at the bathroom door. He tugged the hem of her dress to get by. She looked at him with upturned lips like she smelled something foul. Mark opened his mouth, but nothing came out. His stomach twisted in pain. Something wet slid down his legs. Mrs. Dubois pointed to his soiled shorts and shook her head with disappointment. All the children laughed. Mark cried all the way home.

He never returned to Mrs. Dubois' basic school after Beatrice's threatening words. He stayed home for three months. Daphne arranged with Mrs. Mills, a first-grade teacher at Balmagie Primary, for him to sit in her class. He wasn't officially enrolled because he was too young, but he excelled.

Although the older children picked on him, he found security in Mrs. Mills because she treated him like her child. She loved children and they worshiped her. On Teachers' Appreciation Day, he wrote a poem, *De lov inna mi hart jus a bwoil up fi yuh*. He beamed when she reciprocated. The other teachers were also kind. They saw Mark as the shy, little boy who made faces and needed to be nurtured because something wasn't right at home.

Daphne returned home a changed woman - forty pounds heavier with a double chin, breasts like cantaloupe, and buttocks full as the moon. Her Jheri curl, the new look seen in *Ebony* magazine - dripped on her collar, left wet spots, bred blackheads, and looked like steel wool if not moisturized. Her face had hard lines too soon for a woman in her thirties. She looked tired and matronly.

It was a time of increased violence in Kingston because of an upcoming election. People feared for their lives. Waterhouse was the center of the turmoil. Candidates canvassed neighborhoods with a truckloads of supporters. Guns were illegally issued to criminal allies and they started mini wars in the streets. People kept their political affiliation a secret to avoid attacks from opponents. Ringing a bell publicized support for the Jamaica Labour Party and risked a bullet wound from someone making a fist, in support of the People's National Party.

Gunshots echoed through the streets while Mark and Eileen played on the veranda. Neighbors shut their doors, mothers cried for their children to come inside, and people ran down the streets ducking for cover. The neighborhood became silent. A strange, harried man scaled the front yard fence and ran passed Mark and Eileen, heading down the passageway. Eileen pulled Mark next to her and they trembled. The man ran to the back of the house and kicked open the back door, looking for a place to hide.

Two policemen with guns pursued. They fired at the man as he jumped the back fence and ran down the lane. Eileen cried for her mother. Daphne ran out of the shower, pulling a towel over her breasts. One of the policemen remained in the house to calm Daphne and her children. He promised to return to make sure they were safe, when Daphne said she lived alone with her children and didn't have a man to protect them.

Corporal Russell Seymour was slender - neither short nor tall - with hooded eyes and a thick horseshoe mustache which made him look sad. His hair thinned at the top with gray sideburns. He was defined by his uniform. When on duty, he was an honorable member of society, bestowed with a modest amount of respect.

He was proud to be a police officer, his life ambition, going on twelve years, although many of his colleagues advanced to higher ranks in far less time it took him to make corporal. He was assigned tasks other officers shunned - delivering the prisoners' food, and stocking hygiene supplies in the rat infested jail. He wasn't the first pick when the Jamaica Constabulary Force needed manpower.

When Daphne met Russell, she was divorced and in the process of selling the house. She liked Russell's company, but he wasn't sure how to gauge her temper, so his interest stalled. He supported her as she struggled to sell the house. She worried that without Manuel's consent she didn't have legal rights. A lawyer advised her to take Manuel to court for child support and contest ownership of the house since Inez's will stipulated she was a beneficiary only through marriage.

At her case brought in family court, the judge granted her ownership on account that Manuel had never paid a dime in child support, and since it was impossible to enforce payment while he was living in America, she was awarded his only asset in Jamaica. Within three months she accepted an offer on the house, and made a down payment on another. When Manuel returned to appeal the judgment, the house was sold and Daphne was packed and ready to move her family.

Manuel stood at the front gate with three parcels, looking like a used car salesman in his boxy polyester suit and sweating in the August heat. Daphne heard Eileen calling and her face soured when she saw Manuel.

"Wah yuh doin' here, Manuel?"

"Mi cum bout de ouse. Fi seckle tings between us, ahn fi si de pickney dem."

"De ouse sell a-ready!"

"Wey fi mi share deh?"

"Fi yuh share?"

Daphne screwed her face and glared at Manuel.

"Yuh evah send money fi de pickney dem? Yuh a talk 'bout fi yuh share."

"A mi madda ouse."

"De juge gimme it."

"But …"

Daphne slammed the door behind her and retreated to the bathroom.

"Hey Eileen, Winsome, baby Mark," Manuel said. "Mi bring unno presents."

Eileen batted her eyes. She thought she was too old to play with dolls. Winsome grinned at the brown skin dolly smiling back at her. It felt like Christmas morning when Mark held his fire truck, fished out from some Toys R Us discount bin.

"Ah who yuh is?" Mark asked.

"Yuh madda nuh tell yuh bout mi?" Manuel asked. "Mi ah yuh daddy."

Mark knitted his brows. His mind was flooded with questions.

"Wi daddy? Yuh a wi daddy fi real? Yuh cum back fi wi?"

Manuel was speechless like something got caught in his throat.

"Weh yuh was? Mama seh yuh lef wi. A wah wi duh mek yuh lef wi. Mama sey yuh lef fi gud. Yuh cum back fi wi? Wi ah guh be a fambily now?"

Manuel felt stressed by Mark's relay of questions. He stood beside Mark hoping for an embrace and to shut him up. Mark didn't move. Manuel cupped his fingers under his son's chin and raised his head to look in his eyes. He saw in Mark the little boy he had been - the abandoned child passed around by relatives with no sense of what it meant to be loved. He realized he was no better than his phantom father, the mystery man who showed up on his way through Bonnet or days before Christmas. He didn't want to be like that man anymore. It wasn't too late to act like a father. It wasn't the children's fault. They were caught in the crossfire.

"Wa'ppun to yuh?" Manuel asked. "Weh yuh get dem mark pan yuh 'and fram?

"Him bun-up inna hat aile," Eileen said. "Bout five year now."

While Manuel inspected Mark's scars, Daphne stormed through the front door with a bucket. She threw the bucket of piss at Manuel. The piss splashed all over his suit. She slapped him in the face and jumped on him. He tripped and fell on an overgrown *Shame Ole Lady* bush. The children screamed. Daphne's obese body pinned him into a choke hold. Manuel saw his life flashing before him. The woman he had loved - the mother of his children - was trying to kill him. He pushed her away and ran through the gate. He bolted down Barbados Road and disappeared for almost two decades.

Chapter Three

Mark was nine years old and glad he didn't share a room with his sisters. There were no tenants sending him on errands, no chickens pecking his feet, and he didn't hear gunshots at night. The only ruckus was a preacher wailing "Halleluiah! Glory be to gad by de blud ah Jesas" from a makeshift church resting on the *gully-bank* dividing Duhaney Park from Washington Boulevard.

The rooms were smaller than those at the house on Barbados Road, but living in a two-story house was a novelty. The living room, dining room and kitchen were built on the ground floor, with three bedrooms and a bathroom located upstairs. Noise traveled through the thin walls, exposing the adjoining neighbor's business. The front door opened to a dirt veranda and driveway with a small front yard. Some houses were under construction with verandas and driveways leveled by cement. Some verandas were opened, others were enclosed with protective grills and decorative awnings. After the down payment, Daphne had no money to make any improvements. Russell paid a man with a truck to level the driveway with white gravel from the bauxite company.

As families moved into Cooreville Gardens, Mark watched through his bedroom window, eager to meet his peers. The neighbors on the left were the Masons. Mr. Mason worked at the soft drink company. His wife was a quiet woman, who spent most of her time sewing in a bedroom. She was rarely seen outside their house. They had two sons and a daughter called Little Nicky. Across the street was Mr. Lebert, a single father, and his three daughters, Bernadette the youngest. Mr. Lebert worked at the water company. A few doors down the street were the Henry's and their son, Levi. Mr. Henry drove an old Mercedes Benz and owned a minibus that took passengers to Mandeville. His wife worked for the telephone company. Miss Miller, a teacher at Holy Childhood High School, lived with her parents next door. Up the dead-end street, Everton, the local trouble-maker, lived with his mother, who worked at a supermarket.

Chosen Few Avenue had its fair share of working class residents who acted like they were better than their neighbors because they had government jobs as teachers, nurses, or policemen, and were able to improve their house by building an extra bedroom or could afford an economy car. Mr. Crawford was also a police officer like Russell, but he was not a friendly neighbor. He lived next to Mr. Lebert. He left early in the morning in his sergeant patrol car, and closed his door when he returned home late in the evenings. No one knew what went on in that house with his family. The Seventh Day Adventist family up the street, kept their nose in the air when they passed. The nurse that lived next to them boasted about her job and car. She warned her son to keep away from the wayward neighborhood boys.

The children mimicked their parents. If the adults were feuding, their children held a malice. Daphne's neighbor on the other side from Mr. Mason, built the wall between the yards and she demanded half of the cost. Daphne couldn't pay and it created a rift between their households. The neighbor never spoke to Daphne again. Mark was not allowed at their house and their child would cut her eyes whenever she saw him. Mr. Mason didn't ask for money when he built his wall. His daughter, Little Nicky, was the first to say, "Yow," instead of the bruising, "Go suck yuh madda."

She was an impressionable little girl with darting eyes, floppy ears and teeth too big for her mouth. Her bony body and knock knees were the first things the kids teased her about. When she walked, her *bottom* stuck out higher than she intended. Mark's first impression of her was that she was feisty with a wit for insults. She thought he was inquisitive. She shouted, "Weh yuh a luk pan mi fah?" when he gazed at her from his window, then crossed her eyes and stuck out her tongue to seal the beginning of a new friendship.

They played *Dandy Shandy* and Jacks. With enough kids loafing in the yard, they played Red Light and Simon Says. Mark liked *Dandy Shandy*, a game of dodge ball reserved for little girls. The bigger, rowdier boys in the neighborhood sometimes joined the game only to laugh at themselves and show off their athletic agility, but usually stuck to playing soccer and cricket. Mark showed no interest in sports. He wasn't like the rest of the boys.

He frequently hopped the wall to visit Little Nicky. She was his only friend, although he was a few years older. After homework, she was always engaging and willing to waste time to chat and play games. She had a quality he adored and needed. Being her friend gave him a chance to bask in her father's kindness. Mr. Mason was full of fun and jokes. He spent time with Little Nicky and taught her things she found fascinating. On Sundays, they took joy rides to the country. She would call to Mark from the front seat, grinning and waving like a beauty queen. Sometimes Mark was invited and Mr. Mason gave him an impression of a constant father.

49

Russell lived in the house, and although he fathered four children raised by mothers somewhere in St. Thomas, he wasn't someone anyone called daddy. When he was out of his uniform, he regressed to a sort of brute, incapable of expressing his emotions. He looked bottled up and constipated.

At the dinner table, he loaded his mouth with food, slumped in his plate and chewed with his eyes closed. He raised his head only to gulp down Daphne's sweet concoction. He never said a word to the children unless he was drunk and passed out in the bathtub. Those times he strung incomprehensible words together, shocking them if he remembered their names. He made Mark tense.

On a Sunday in June, Daphne and Russell came home dressed in their finest threads, and displaying more than their rationed affection. The children were curious when she told them to have a seat on the plastic covered floral couch which no one was allowed to sit on.

"Wi jus a cum fram de justis a de peace," Daphne said.

The children looked at each other, unblinking, unsure how to react.

"Wi marrid!"

Mark sat scratching himself. Russell got up and went to the bathroom. Daphne grinned and made a show of adjusting the wedding band on her finger.

"Marrid?" Winsome asked.

"Wah yuh tink bout dat?" Daphne asked.

"Suh wi fi call him daddy now Mama?" Eileen asked.

"Mi nuh know. Call him wah yuh feel fi call him."

Russell remained Mr. Seymour to the children and whenever he wanted their attention he uttered a grunt.

Bernadette was a big girl. Everything about her was big. She had big bones, big eyes, big teeth, big lips, big hands, big feet, and a big appetite. She was the only girl on the street that went over the boys' house in the evenings before her father came from work. She liked to play hide and do it with the boys - hiding in the backyard behind a tree, waiting to be found, and rewarding the lucky boy with a feel of her breasts or more. She sat before the television with her legs *wide-open* for the boys to poke her vagina as she giggled and pretended to watch *Charlie's Angels*.

She was responsible for letting the boys on the street lose their virginity. The neighborhood's sex education crash course without reciprocation. She was their introduction to the birds and the bees without the awkwardness of a parent. Her talent was attracting the boys for sex games. She didn't possess qualities they liked in a girlfriend. She wasn't pretty with long hair and light skin. Her yard clothes weren't fancy. She wasn't smart. She didn't play sports. She was friendly with an available vagina. She taught them what a girl's breast felt like, how hard the nipples got when the right boy touched them, and how wet a vagina got when fondled. They learned about the pleasure caused by the milky liquid squirting out of their erect penis.

Bernadette enjoyed the attention she got from the boys. They made her feel what she lacked from an abusive father. Being promiscuous gave her pockets of affection from the neighborhood boys that made having a loveless father bearable. While she feared her father when he was volatile, nothing mattered to her than to make him happy. When he was in good spirits, they played house. She served his dinner, washed his clothes, cleaned the house, and raked the leaves under the *guinep* tree. She did whatever she could to keep his wrath at bay.

She never knew her mother. She bled to death two days after she was born. Bernadette was convinced she killed her mother because her father told her so. She was ignored by her sisters, and it didn't matter what she did they never loved her.

She found an improbable version of love when she opened her legs for Donovan, Levi, and Lamont. For that brief moment when they touched or entered her, she felt they cared because they were always willing. While the boys saw her as nothing more than a slut, they had a fondness for her she never received from her father.

Mark's first sexual experience was with Bernadette when he was eleven years old. He wasn't her favorite. He was merely the lucky boy who found her first hiding in the backyard. When he was rewarded with poking his finger in her vagina, he did so with all the eagerness as the other boys, but his reaction was different. He frowned. He said he didn't like the foul fishy smell. Bernadette felt rejected and later chose who she wanted to play with. Mark was never invited back. Instead, he sat on the wall festering a nervous desire to stare at adolescent boys with erections chasing her.

The neighborhood boys said Mark was soft and expelled him from their activities. They called him the dreaded "sissy." He felt ostracized. Rolling his eyes in protest only ignited their pestering. When he came home from school and switched passed them on the sidewalk, they jeered "Sissy bwoy. Sissy bwoy." It tested Little Nicky's loyalty because her brothers were amongst the tormenters.

When the boys congregated at the wall, he never left his bedroom. He closed the window and escaped in a world where he was not ridiculed. Listening to Barry G and Casey Kasem's Top 40 countdown on the radio, dancing with a towel on his head, pretending it was long hair, kept him entertained in his solitude. The name-calling persisted because he wasn't aggressively masculine. He knew he was different from the other boys. He pacified their rejection by assuming his soft, effeminate nature was the trait of someone refined. He felt removed from them as if he was something better than them, and at the same time he felt less than they were. He disqualified them as not being worthy of his friendship. He thickened his skin and learned new cutting words in his defense. Words more inflicting than responding, "Get last!"

Daphne saw two ladies walk up Chosen Few Avenue and bang on the neighbor's gate. No one came outside to greet them. The neatly dressed ladies, with briefcases in hand, approached Daphne's front gate and smiled like they knew her. She smiled back. They stood waiting for her to invite them in. She wondered who they were. They were not familiar. None of the women on the street went out of their way to speak to her. They usually waved in passing to avoid being rude. Daphne patted her hair and walked to the gate to greet them.

Other pairs knocked on gates and slipped pamphlets in mailboxes. Mrs. Crawford peeped through her window and waited for the ladies to leave before she came out to retrieve the pamphlet. She read it, sucked her teeth, and threw it in the trash. Mr. Lebert's dog barked viciously and they skipped his mailbox. Daphne thought they were selling encyclopedias. She rolled her eyes when she realized it was religious.

The women introduced themselves as sisters from the Kingdom Hall of Jehovah's Witnesses, and wanted to share their message. Daphne was irritated, but they seemed like nice ladies. She didn't mind a break from the housework. She decided to listen to their presentation, accept the pamphlet or whatever they were giving away, and bid them goodbye. As they spoke, she liked their disposition. She admired their sophisticated manner and felt obliged to let them talk as long as they wanted. She offered them a glass of lemonade.

They had a magazine called *The Awake*. The cover had a picture with families of all different races. The caption asked, "Are you one of the chosen that will inherit paradise on earth?" Another magazine, *The Watchtower*, had a similar picture of people dressed in biblical attire. It asked, "Who are the one hundred and forty-four thousand that will rule beside Jehovah in heaven?" Daphne cleared her throat. She was nervous. She dreaded the fire and brimstone sermon. She remembered her mother trying to persuade her to go to the Baptist church, and how she felt tormented by the scrutinizing eyes watching her and Manuel at the church social. She wanted nothing to do with a church.

However, these ladies were different. They said the Kingdom Hall wasn't a church. Daphne wondered if it was a cult. They told her about serving Jehovah and living in paradise on earth. Daphne thought people who were saved went to heaven when they died. She had never heard anything at Sunday school about living forever on earth in paradise, or maybe she wasn't listening. She was curious about what they believed. She didn't challenge their beliefs because she had none of her own. When they invited her to the Kingdom Hall, it felt like she was being initiated into their sisterhood.

The next Sunday, Daphne woke Mark to attend the Kingdom Hall meeting. To his dismay it became a routine. She stopped smoking and swearing and began reading a bible called the *New World Translation of the Holy Scriptures* - a modern version of the outdated biblical language. The Jehovah's Witnesses' ideology occupied her mind.

Whenever she invited the ladies to her veranda to read from their religious magazines and recite verses from their revised bible, the closer she felt to being part of their group. She was never close to her siblings, and when they called her "Sister Daphne" it appealed to her. She spoke about her life growing up in St. Catherine, traveling to America, and the sacrifices she made for her family. The pleasant ladies listened noncommittally while reverting to scriptures and anecdote that worked like therapy. They were a source of friendship and their religion was a part of the package she agreed to.

Mark was anxious to take the *Common Entrance* test to be promoted to high school. His sisters had passed on their first attempt, so he was expected to do the same. He had another chance in the sixth grade, but he was eager to move on. Ava, his classmate, *batter-bruised* his face when he didn't pursue her interests, and told everyone he was a sissy. He feared another year at Pembroke Hall Primary would lead to students treating him the same way the boys in the neighborhood did. He hoped to attend Calabar High because it was a good school, and girls weren't allowed.

When the results were published in *The Gleaner* newspaper, every student on the island searched thousands of names looking for theirs. The task was tedious. Students traded pages in silence in the classroom, until someone yelled, "Mi fine mi name," followed by a congratulatory cheer. Mark was disappointed he didn't see his name under Calabar High. He looked under his second choice, Jamaica College, then the third, Kingston College, and fretted. Pain shot through his stomach. He raised his hand to be permitted to go to the restroom. His eyes watered. He wet his face to recuperate from the sickening feeling. When he returned to the classroom, he was surprised when the teacher called his name for Meadowbrook High. He was so happy he wanted to run all the way home.

Mark looked forward to graduation although he knew his mother wouldn't be there. She sent twenty dollars in a postcard to substitute for her absence in his life. When he changed the money into Jamaican dollars, being alone didn't feel that bad. He bought black dress pants, a tuxedo white shirt, and a navy blue tie to wear on graduation day. The shirt sleeves were too short. The arms stopped above his wrists. He pulled them down, but the shirt wrinkled across his chest and tightened over his shoulders. He tried to ignore it, but the burn scars on his hands disturbed him. They had faded into his complexion, but were still visible. They became apparent at times when he didn't want to be reminded that they were there. They came to the surface whenever he thought of his mother. He didn't miss her when he saw the scars because he thought she was never there when he needed her.

Mark stood up and cleared his throat before singing "If I Had a Hammer" during the graduation ceremony. He was demoted as one of the lead singers of the boys' choir when his voice cracked. He was disappointed, but the sprout of hair around his genitals and under his armpits excited him tremendously.

The summer before high school, Mark shot up two inches and lost interest in playing yard games with Little Nicky. He spent time with Eileen's boyfriend, Ronnie, the track star who attended the College of Arts, Science and Technology. Ronnie dared him to swim - pulling him under in the deep end of the pool. Mark thought he caught his death. Ronnie held him to the surface as he stroked and paddled like a frog. He was proud when he learned to swim. It was something to brag about.

Ronnie was an excuse to leave the house on Saturdays. Mark feared his rough play, but liked that he never called him a sissy. Ronnie made sports interesting. Mark liked swimming and tennis because they weren't hooligan sports like soccer. He liked any attention he got from Ronnie because he was always training for a track meet. Ronnie's hope for a scholarship to an American college was becoming a reality with every 100 meter victory. Recruiters were looking for track stars for the Olympics.

At the end of summer, the boys and Bernadette gathered next door to *run-a-boat*, and watch Bruce Lee karate movies. They fried chicken back and scourged the refrigerator for whatever they could find. The event marked the return of a new school year, or as they joked, "yuh free paypa bun."

Mark listened to their idle chatter from his bedroom. He feared their jeers would evolve to being called a "batty bwoy," and the consequences of that were more detrimental.

Chapter Four

Mark's first day at Meadowbrook High was a two bus commute from his manufactured working class neighborhood with cluttered row houses, washed clothes hanging on wire lines, chickens and pigeons nesting in coops and shirtless boys with their ribs sticking out, running barefoot, to a neighborhood with tree lined streets, two car garage houses with swimming pools, manicured lawns, satellite dishes channeling American programs into carpeted homes manned with washer and dryer, and children wearing shoes and socks playing with Fisher-Price toys.

His new peers were from a diverse socio-economic background. They were rich kids living on the hills, exiting luxury cars, waving goodbye to smiling parents. The poor ones, who lived in houses that sat on captured land along gully banks, walked to school or rode the minibus. They were unified by the school's uniform. Boys wore khaki pants and short sleeves shirts with blue and green epaulets. Girls wore pleated shift dresses of the same pattern. They all wore black shoes and dark socks. Girls grew out their pig-tails and sported crimped and flat-iron pressed hairstyles. The boys sported budding mustaches and walked with a kick in their steps, intoxicated with puberty.

Mark sat in the third row of the classroom. The teacher's pets and smart kids coveted the front row. He nodded his head as he walked through the aisle to his desk. No friendship was initiated, but he spotted Anthony whom he recognized from primary school. His was the only familiar face, and he no longer felt alone. Anthony gestured something to the girl who sat behind Mark and she packed up her school books and traded seats.

"Mi nevah know seh yuh pass." Mark said.

"Eehee mi pass," Anthony said. "Blousenawt! De skool yah hab nuff prettie gal."

Out of habit, Mark pursed his lips and rolled his eyes.

The noise settled when the teacher entered the classroom. She dropped her textbook on the desk and rested her handbag on the back of the chair. She wore a purple floral jumpsuit, drowning her petite frame. The elastic waist pulled up too high gathered under her drooping breasts. She heard whispers as she scribbled on the blackboard, and turned around to assert her authority. Her legs were spread wide to keep her balance and her toes hung over the shoes. Her eyes twinkled.

"My name is Miss Peart. I am your Principles of Business teacher."

The solemn faces in the classroom looked passively at her and busted out laughing. Miss Peart glared at a girl in the front row who whispered to her. She felt humiliated like the time she walked out the restroom with a trail of toilet paper stuck to the bottom of her shoes or when she sat on a whoopee cushion in the crowded auditorium. She banged her fist on the desk and shouted to settle their amusement. The classroom busted out in another roar of laughter. A student in the back row fell out of his chair. The girl in the front row pointed at her.

"Teacha, dem a lawf haffa de lipstick pan yuh teet."

Miss Peart found a compact in her bag, saw the purple stain on her front tooth, and smudged it with her finger then continued scribbling like nothing happened.

Anthony told Mark about the popular students in the class. Dale was one of the most attractive boys at school. His mother dropped him off in a black BMW. He lived in Cherry Gardens, a wealthy neighborhood near the hills. His father was a record executive who had produced a Bob Marley and the Wailers album, and it made him rich. His mother had entered the Miss Jamaica beauty pageant. She was half white, which explained Dale's light skin and what everyone called pretty hair.

Brian was charismatic and liked by everyone. He lived in Orange Grove, beyond the hills. His father owned an industrial company in downtown Kingston and was a self-made millionaire. Brian had rich dark skin with dreamy hazel eyes they called *puss eyes*. His bow legs and athletic frame made him the first pick on the soccer team, and a favorite amongst the girls.

Everyone wished they sat next to Dale or Brian, they wanted to be next to Gillisa, the prettiest girl in school. Her light complexion and long hair suggested she was also mixed. Her eyes, nose, and lips were delicately placed on her heart-shaped face. She had a thin body that hinted at firm breasts with womanly curves under her private school girl fashioned uniform. She aroused the boys when she crossed her legs because they hiked her hem above the knees. When she flicked her hair, popped gum, or licked her lips, her playful flirt had the boys at full attention in their pants.

Neither Dale nor Brian got the chance to sit beside Gillisa. Before they picked a seat, her court of girlfriends - acting like little ladies in waiting vying for her favor - had already chosen seats that kept everyone on the outskirts. Dale carried her books one week and they sat after school sucking on snow cones. Brian gave her his Michael Jackson jacket and she styled her hair like Sandy from *Grease*. She toyed with their affection, but nothing ever developed. Brian settled to the back of the classroom and Dale somewhere in the middle.

Mark sat the closest to Gillisa, but she barely knew he existed. He positioned himself to be in her favor by befriending Georgette, one of her ladies in waiting - a title she wore with pride considering she looked like a featherless turkey next to Gillisa's swan-like features. She was Gillisa's most trusted friend because they lived in the same neighborhood and they copied each other's homework.

Mark liked Georgette because she made him feel relevant. He stuck to her when Gillisa was preoccupied with Dale and Brian. She protected him from the boys who called him names and threatened to beat him up after school. He waited for her when she played netball and carried her books when they walked home to the bus stop. He made her feel as popular as Gillisa.

Mark thought if he befriended Gillisa's he would become Brian's friend, but he ignored him. Brian was only interesting in Gillisa and varsity soccer. Mark knew he had no shot at being on the soccer team, but if he was selected to tryout during the physical education class, it was an opportunity to be around Brian.

He felt ridiculous in the soccer uniform because his skinny legs were exposed. His face reddened when the classmates laughed. He wanted to run back to the locker room. He was too old to cry. Their laughter averted to Nicholas. It was the funniest thing the boys saw all day. Nicholas tucked his jersey into his shorts and pulled the waist up to his chest.

Mark joined in the mockery and Nicholas retaliated because he was the only boy he dared to fight. He kicked Mark to the ground. His banged his head on the concrete. Mark stood up and clobbered him. His busted knee was less severe than Nicholas' black-eye and swollen lips. His heart skipped a beat when Brian brushed the dirt off his back. He sat in detention daydreaming about Brian.

The next day Mark sat in the back of the classroom with Brian. He bragged about his detention with the cool kids and reveled in Brian's new interest. They became fast friends. Mark followed him everywhere. They ate the same lunch. Whatever Brian liked or disliked, Mark copied. He sat close to Brian, carried his books, and wore his Michael Jackson jacket. He knew his feelings were different, but there was nothing he could do about it

For two weeks, they rode the bus after school to the video arcade in Half Way Tree. They played Ms. Pac-Man and Galaxy. Sometimes Brian beat the high score or Mark got an extra player. Each coin Mark dropped into the video game, bought time with Brian - chances to brush his hands against Brian's when they held the control stick, chances to lean against him and smile, and chances to hug him because he was his special friend. He longed for something more than friendship.

Mark's fantasied coupledom with Brian was interrupted when the boys wanted to be break dancers. Brian loved break dancing. He practiced with Dale on the shiny tiles in the school's auditorium. They did head stands, the helicopter, and the shoulder freeze. Art of Noise's "Beat Box" blasted from Dale's boom box. Mark attempted a head spin, and fell on his back. The pain scared him from trying again. He was kept in Brian's group to change the cassettes or lower the volume when a teacher approached. When *Breakin'* was released on video, Brian invited Dale to his house to watch the movie. Mark wanted to go because he was anxious to see the house where he lived.

They took a crowded bus out of Kingston and got off on a hilly slope in

St. Andrews. Beyond the hill was a gated community of mini mansions with swimming pools, luxury cars and satellite dishes. Brian's house was the biggest and best looking house Mark had been in. His family had a maid that wore a uniform. The living room's plush tan carpet looked like it was never stepped on. The spacey room had white sofas around a mahogany coffee table. Framed Carl Abraham prints decorated the white walls. An Edna Manley sculpture sat on a marble pedestal. It was free of the typical market scene and animal figurines Mark saw in his neighbors' homes.

Brian's house had the largest color television Mark had ever seen. Electrical cords connected it to a satellite dish on the front lawn. The patio in the backyard housed a tropical pond with large goldfish circling for food. It was next to a kidney shaped swimming pool. A formal dining room on the other side of the house contained a glass top dining table with eight tables and a tall cabinet stocked with crystal glasses and china. A gigantic kitchen lead to the garage that stored two luxury cars. On the other side of the house, four bedrooms were connected to two bathrooms.

The boys paused and rewound the video to repeat the dance moves. Mark listened and laughed when they did. He wished the movie would never end. He wanted to drift away and wake up in Brian's life. When Brian's friends visited, he feared the usual torments. He was relieved he wasn't put on the spot, dared to do something impossible, or called a sissy. It was the first time he felt comfortable and not picked on by boys his age. He didn't want to leave Brian's house. When he returned home, he resented everything about his neighborhood and the people living there. He bragged to Little Nicky how interesting his life became when he left Cooreville Gardens. She listened wide-eyed with fist under her chin as he told her about his special, rich friend, Brian.

It was after midnight. Mark forced his frail, slender body through his bedroom window. He climbed down the grill and scaled the wall to meet Anthony at the corner of Chosen Few Avenue. Daphne and his sisters were asleep. He didn't want to wake them by going down the stairs and opening the front door. He scaled the wall because the gate also squeaked. They planned all week to go to the Stone Love street dance. Anthony, who lived in Duhaney Park, wore black jeans ripped at the knees and a red shirt painted with graffiti. The neon green thick laces in his high-top sneakers matched his baseball cap. Mark wore blue stone-washed jeans with a faded yellow polo shirt. He slipped on his only pair of dress shoes and wore them without socks because it was cool to do so.

They walked down Maytals Crescent towards the vibrating sound system at the intersection of Bob Marley Boulevard where a rowdy crowd gathered. People danced in the blocked street like it was an open nightclub. Boys sat on the curb smoking cigarettes and drinking *Red Stripe* beer. They called to girls who showed off vulgar dance moves - kicking up their legs with the crotch of their panties winking. Men roamed the crowd looking for available women to fondle. Women stared at each other, criticizing what they wore and did to their hair. They peeled the greasy skin off jerk chicken bought from the sweaty man turning meat over a smoky steel drum. Rasta men with knotty white beards peddled sugarcane and *ital* peanut. *Swatty* women sat over boiling soup pots with crab claws sticking out. The crowd cheered the deejay's selections, Shabba Ranks' "Mr. Loverman," "Tinga-Tinga-ling" and "Trailer Load a Girls," banging street signs and lighting firecrackers. Neighbors who saw themselves as upstanding citizens, slammed their front door in contempt.

Anthony saved five dollars from his lunch money for peanuts. Mark had fifteen to buy jerk chicken and sugarcane. They walked through the crowd reveling at the antics. The unknown faces from other neighborhoods invaded theirs. Mark saw Levi with a cigarette in one hand and a beer bottle in the other. He *skin him teet* and went over to talk to him.

"Yuh madda gwaan skin yuh alive if shi fine hout sey yuh deh yah," Levi said.

Anthony took Levi's cigarette, blew the smoke through his nostrils, and puffed circular clouds in the air. Mark shrugged when he gave him the cigarette, but the boys staring at him compelled him to put the wet butt between his lips and inhale. He swallowed the smoke and coughed violently. The boys laughed.

"Bumbowclaat! Yuh fi blow hout de smoke," Levi said. "Nuh swalla it."

"A him fus time," Anthony said. "Him wi learn it."

Levi saw Cynthia and whisked her away for a dance. His hands tightened around her waist then slipped down to her meaty buttocks. He pinned her against a speaker and grinded between her legs. She raised her leg behind his back and wined into him, bobbing and weaving, her hair falling out of the hairdo she had piled on top of her head. The speaker vibrated her body into his and their hips dipped to the rhythm. She buried her face into his chest while he rested his chin on her head. Mark watched Levi's penis growing in his pants, rubbing against her crotch. It excited him. Cynthia saw him staring and he quickly looked away.

Levi was the unofficial leader of the neighborhood boys. He was respected because of his family's status in Cooreville Gardens. His father was the only one on Chosen Few Avenue to drive a Mercedes Benz. He attended Campion College, took courses in French and music, and the way his yard clothes were better than the boys Sunday best was evident that he was a little privileged for that area of Kingston.

His popularity as a *gallis* - having many girlfriends and future baby mothers – made him more experienced with girls that went beyond playing hide and do it. Girls from other areas in Kingston journeyed on weekends to sit on the sidewalk and chat with him outside his house, waiting to be invited to his bedroom. He had far more opportunities than the other boys and he was regarded as a *Don*.

He liked Eileen and often stood outside Mark's front gate when he visited Little Nicky's older brothers, Lamont and Roger. Eileen liked his attention, but she and Winsome hadn't reached the age where girls began wishing for a boyfriend. They were reserved when it came to boys, who they had little contact with because they attended a strict all-girls high school.

Levi was confident and acted more mature than the other boys, but most of his actions were to gain their approval. When Eileen ignored him, Cynthia became an easier target. Bernadette was always available, but she wasn't a challenge, and no one saw her as a way to earn cool points.

Cynthia lived on Maytals Crescent. She the only child of a woman who kept to herself. When Levi visited, it was clear he wasn't invited beyond the front gate. Cynthia often met him on the side walk and lingered when he was hanging with the boys. She tolerated the boys immature nagging for the sake of having time with Levi. When she came next door, Mark knew Levi was close by.

At these times, he engaged Little Nicky at the wall to tete-a-tete about mindless and useless things to keep them occupied so it wouldn't be obvious when he stared at Levi. It was the only thing he could do and not raise hostility. When Levi spoke to Mark, it was usually in a condescending or teasing manner. He showed no fondness. The only difference between him and the other boys was that he never called Mark a sissy. Mark thought if Levi was given the opportunity, they would become friends. He never got the chance because the other boys were always around.

Daphne's visa was renewed with a permanent status. She was free to travel to America as she pleased without having to return to the embassy. She liked living with Russell's family in Norwalk. It was a sleepy town with hints of the bordering wealthier towns and a different standard of living from what she knew in Hartford's inner-city. Russell's brother, Ralph, lived at the top of the hill on Bayview Avenue.

The house was far better than what Daphne was accustomed to. It was a modest suburban three-story with an attic and basement, front and back decks, and a large yard with apple trees and friendly white neighbors. However, Ralph was not wealthy. He was a custodian at the country club in Westport. His years of service gave him the means of getting a piece of the American pie on credit.

The house was deserted in the daytime. When its occupants returned from work and school, it was transformed into a busy home filled with activities. Ralph's living quarters occupied the top floor which lead to the attic. He had a private entrance in the four-car garage, he used to bypass his family.

Daphne had a small room on the ground floor and shared a bathroom with Ralph's mother, whom they called Aunt Kitty. Ralph's girlfriend and daughter had adjoining rooms on the second floor. The living room was crowded with couches overflowing with cushions and an oak coffee table with dusty *National Geographic* magazines and wooden wildlife figurines.

The walls were covered with framed coin collections, vintage maps and photos of the family at different stages of their lives. The living room led to a large TV room with open bay windows looking out onto an overgrown apple tree. Outside, the American flag danced in the wind on a lush green lawn.

Aunt Kitty's bed was never made. She was almost ninety years old and her day started at four in the morning. She got out of bed when the house was snoring and fumbled in the kitchen for pots and pans to prepare her three meals before sunrise. Daphne found her peculiar. She pretended that she was hard of hearing, but complained to Ralph about everything everyone said before she went to bed after the six o'clock news. She spent the afternoon sitting alone in a rocking chair on the deck, knitting and talking to herself. She had finished two sweaters for her grandchildren which took three months, and was working on a blanket for the winter.

Ralph's biracial half-sister Geraldine and her two adult sons, Carl and Allen, had rooms on the second floor. Carl sneaked his dates into the house late at night. He played cricket with other Caribbean men and fished on Long Island Sound, spending more time guzzling Budweiser than catching anything. Allen was divorced and repaired old cars, lining them on the street, using the garage as his work station. His two sons, Brandon and Christopher, visited from their mother's house down the street and sometimes spent the night.

Russell's Americanized family was polite and civilized. Everyone was cordial and a raised voice was never heard in the house. They had long migrated from Jamaica and assimilated into what they thought being American was, but kept their patois, jerk chicken and reggae music when it was necessary at their monthly cookout. They treated Daphne like family.

69

Ralph's girlfriend and daughter were like the sister and child she never had. Daphne completed a caregiver course at Norwalk Community College. She was hired by a family of another old woman in Westport, after a favorable response to her twenty-five word ad placed in the employment section of the local Jewish newspaper. Living in Norwalk guaranteed a higher pay because of its location to Westport, one of the wealthiest towns in America. Residents held the biggest piece of the American pie and maintained a watchful eye on their dying parents to secure their birthright. Caregivers were hired for twenty-four-hour assisted living to put their minds at ease as they waited for their parents to expire with dignity.

Little Nicky waited for Mark to finish reciting his latest Brian episode.

"Mi hear seh yuh a guh a farin."

Mark wanted it kept a secret until he was certain. He was disappointed the previous summer. His passport was stamped with a visitor's visa, but he still wasn't sure. That summer after tenth grade, a letter from Daphne arrived containing a plane ticket. He jumped the wall to share the news as Little Nicky cut her eyes, filled with jealousy.

"Wen yuh cum back yuh a go twang ahn gallan like yuh betta dan mi."

He couldn't sleep the night before his trip to America. His clothes hung from a nail behind the door over his brown shoes. He was restless, thinking about the stories he had heard about America. They all seemed too good to be true. In the morning, he was dressed hours before Russell drove up in his police jeep to take him to the airport. Little Nicky watched him fidget in his three piece suit. His shoes ached around the toes, but the discomfort was bearable. Eileen took photos to document the occasion. Winsome only cared about the ocean view drive to the airport.

When Mark arrived in America, Jamaica seemed like a generic version of everything. America being a first world society was newer, bigger and better, and whiter. Jamaica's majority was black. All others were unified by the "Out of many one people" motto, along with their patois and island culture. Although race was a factor in Jamaica, its relevance was mixed up with class. Being black was celebrated, but the upper crust of society were often mixed and white-looking. Having blue eyes and blond hair with a little nigger in their blood didn't make them outcasts like those confused Americans who felt neither black nor white enough.

In Jamaica, they were the ruling class with wealth like whites and the admirations from blacks who saw them as better versions of themselves. They won political offices and beauty pageants, lived in mansions on the hills, drove Mercedes automobiles, and owned businesses in the private sector. They were the Bob Marleys and Michael Manleys of society - the privilege ones. Nevertheless, the Jamaican whites seemed inferior to their American counterparts because of their third-world status. For a nation dependent on tourism - rolling out the red carpet to foreigners who had saved their paycheck looking to rekindle some lost groove, the upper crust islanders were not the real deal.

Mark arriving in America in the mid-eighties, during the excess of the Reagan era, in an affluent Connecticut town, instilled in him the belief that America was everything one could imagine. The streets weren't lined with gold as rumored, but it seemed believable that at one time they were. From the simplest things - a warm bowl of cornflakes for breakfast and not the ridiculed egg and bread, to clean streets, large air-conditioned shopping malls, beautiful parks and nice talking white people who thought he was funny and easy going, it seemed like the Promised Land.

Mark realized how it felt to live like Brian, and because he was experiencing this upgrade in America and not some carbon copy version in Jamaica, he felt privileged. He saved all these pleasures in his mind to later brag to Little Nicky.

He was amazed by the many television channels unlike JBC, the only station in Jamaica that signed on in the afternoon and ended its broadcast by midnight. He didn't need a pricey satellite dish like Brian to watch *The Price is Right* or *Big Bucks*. He was fascinated with the Olympics and kept a scrapbook with sports stories collected from *The Hour* newspapers. The spirit of the Olympic Games promoted an image of America as a nation of winners, all getting along and thriving in a modern, sophisticated world. Mark wanted to be a part of that world.

He cheered Mary Lou Retton and Greg Louganis and sat on the edge of the couch when Carl Louis won the 100 meter race, wondering if Ronnie might one day do the same. He liked the synchronized swimming and rolled his eyes when Allen said the male swimmer was gay. It was the first time he heard that word, but he knew by the layer of sneer it was coated with, it was a euphemism for batty bwoy.

When Daphne worked on the weekends, she didn't mind missing the Sunday meetings at the Kingdom Hall, but not the time and a half pay. Her boss, Miss Post, lived with her mother in a modest house by Westport's standards on Compo Beach Road. It had three bedrooms with a library and den. The swimming pool overlooking the beach was on a manicured lawn with shaded flower beds and a forested backyard.

After Miss Post left the house and her mother was fed and wheeled to the porch, Mark came downstairs. He was amazed by the luxury. It looked better than Brian's house which was his only reference of a proper upscale home. Everything in the house looked expensive. It had an open feel, designed with wall-to-wall French windows and thick stain beams. The hardwood floor was covered with plush tan and white area rugs. A vase filled with sunflowers was the only color besides its white and tan motif.

There were three coral printed chaise lounges filled with over-sized white cushions. The kitchen met the living room, separated by four high top wicker bar stools set against a narrow granite countertop. A stone fireplace merged with the white walls. Tables were decorated with fossils and corals next to contemporary furniture. Large abstract oil paintings hanging on the walls appeared more sophisticated than the small island landscapes in Brian's house. The surfaces were sparsely decorated with lifestyle magazines and leather-bound books.

It looked like a perfect beach house, prepped for a photo shoot for the pages of an upscale home interior magazine. Across the street, beyond the white picket fence and groomed azaleas, was Compo Beach. Mark wrapped a sweater around his shoulders like a preppy rich kid and went outside to sink his feet in the sand.

Westport's Compo Beach was where its wealthy residents came for a day off from their busy productive lives and catch up with their neighbor's activities. Women spoke about their husband's company, their children graduating the top of their class at Greens Farms Academy and being accepted to Yale, Harvard, or Princeton. Men spoke about summering in Europe or their vacation home in Martha's Vineyard or The Hamptons.

Their children showed off the luxury car they received for their sixteenth birthday, and made plans to drive to the city for a shopping spree on Fifth Avenue. No one went in the water. They lounged on Williams-Sonoma canvass chairs under matching umbrellas and browsed magazines that reflected their upscale lifestyles. They nibbled on little sandwiches prepared by brown maids and sipped on tall glasses of iced tea.

Mark sat at a picnic table under the pine trees. He was the only black person at the beach that wasn't on someone's payroll - pushing a stroller or nursing an elder. He admired the muddy shoreline and murky water brimming with seaweeds.

A group of teenagers sat aimlessly at a picnic table, smoking Marlboro Lights with a radio blasting Prince's "When Doves Cry." A blonde girl kissed one of the boys and they laughed like it was the coolest thing. The other boys hooted. They seemed at ease in their carefree world. They had everything they wanted at their disposal with a swipe of their parents' black American Express.

One of the boys threw a football to Mark, hitting him on the head. They snickered as he collected himself. Embarrassed, he saw the accident as an opportunity to meet real American teenagers.

"You're to catch it dude," the blond boy said.

"Mi nevah know yuh was trowing it to mi."

His accent was thick. The all laughed again.

"What? Where are you from? You talk funny."

"Jamaica," Mark said.

"Oh, the islands. Like no problem mon. Irie."

Their unapologetic laughter made Mark self-conscious. It felt like they were laughing at him. One said his housekeeper was from Jamaica. They asked if he knew Bob Marley, had every smoked marijuana or lived by the beach - all stereotypes festered by ignorance. They played a UB40 cassette and asked him to show them how to dance to reggae music.

Their flattery felt like ridicule. Mark was awkward in their company. He realized how different his life was and suddenly felt ashamed. Although he felt better than his neighbors back in Jamaica, he thought he was far from being like these American teenagers.

Daphne made her favorite Shake 'N Bake chicken. She settled on the bed to watch *Wheel of Fortune* before sticking pink rollers in her permed hair. She then read a few pages of *The Watchtower* before falling asleep with the magazine in her hand. Mark watched the beach goers depart, hoping to see the teenagers again. He knew he didn't look or dress like they did and wasn't even on their level, but he could learn to speak like they did and they wouldn't make fun of him. He watched *Family Ties* to imitate the white characters, picking up a few words that felt pretentious.

Mark's vacation days rolled along with normalcy and very little excitement, but everything that was ordinary seemed extraordinary to him. His trips to Pathmark supermarket with Daphne were like a mini episode in an on-going saga about the circus of her life. She loaded shopping carts like she was feeding a family of eight. He wished his mother was like the white women in Westport.

When Daphne returned home, she came like Santa Claus, shipping barrels of clothes, food, and appliances. After Beatrice moved, she hired a helper and treated her with contempt. Mark thought she was no better because her job was similar, the only differences being the American currency and white employers. Daphne didn't wash and clean like her helper, but he thought she was nothing more than the help.

Daphne was content with her life and didn't expected much as far social mobility. When she wasn't working, she was busy knocking doors and handing out magazines to clock her forty pioneer hours. After completing the caregiver course, her plans for a nursing degree was stalled. The sisters at the Kingdom Hall kept her in a semi-illiterate state with the promise of inheriting everlasting life on earth. They weren't concerned about the times she read scriptures and the messages were lost in translation because they explained it the way they wanted her to understand.

When Mark returned to Jamaica, a cloud of insecurity was lifted from over his head. Although he felt inferior to the rich white kids in Westport, he acted superior to the boys in the neighborhood because he was the first to travel to America. It seemed he crossed the ocean and moved up a class. Little Nicky noticed. He ignored their jeers that he pretended to be *highty tighty*. It felt better than being called a sissy.

The neighborhood boys envied his clothes. Gone were threadbare shirts and pants cut at the knees refashioned into shorts. They were replaced by new comfortable clothes like what Brian and boys in America wore. He had Reebok sneakers - a brand every boy in Jamaica coveted - Polo shirts, Levis jeans, a brand new bicycle and roller skates.

With his new sense of self, he identified his less masculine traits as a sign that he wasn't a *butu* - a vulgar person of a lower class. Brian's life was no longer his ideal. He felt like his equal. It was unsettling to Little Nicky how Mark evolved from a sissy boy, who found refuge in her friendship, to a stuck-up teenager who discarded her. She called for him to peep through his bedroom window and talk at the wall, but that ritual was over.

Katelin was Daphne's so-called godchild. She needed a place to stay in Kingston before starting teacher's training college. Daphne agreed for her to stay in Eileen and Winsome's room since they had migrated to live with Manuel. Katelin promised to help around the house like the helper.

She was a genuine country gal. Living in Kingston with electricity and indoor plumbing amazed her. She opened the refrigerator door throughout the day to check the light inside, pondering if it went off when the door was closed. She used the toilet then ran downstairs to open the sewage in the backyard to look at her stool, dumbfounded how it got there.

The neighborhood boys tried to coerce her for sex, but she always said, "Mi gwaan te-te-tell yuh madda." Mark despised her. She was more masculine than he was. Her country manner made him feel refined. He showed off around her because he wasn't only a Kingstonian, but had been to America. His snobbery got her to do things no one would put up with. Although he regarded her with contempt, she was the only one besides Little Nicky that gave him validation.

One evening they were alone, he rented an X-rated movie. When Katelin heard the moans from the television, she came out the kitchen to investigate.

"Mi gwaan te-te-tell yuh madda!"

"Fi wah?"

"Wah kinda naw-si-si-si-ness yuh a watch?"

"Yuh nevah si a blue movie?"

"Yuh nuh ole eenuf fi a watch dat. Tek it hout."

She stood before the television, condemning the nasty things white people did. She glared at Mark's trousers undone at the waist, his hand squeezing his penis.

"Wah yu-yu-yuh dween?

"Noting. Yuh waan fi touch it?

"Tou-tou-touch wat?!"

"Mi ting."

"Yuh to-to-too nawsie!"

She left the living room and went upstairs. Mark waited for her to return.

"Mark! Tun it aff ahn be-be-behave yuh self!"

"Cum here ahn luk at dis!"

She came down the stairs like a curious cat. Mark lay on his back.

"Cum rub it."

He pulled down his pants and cover his erect penis with a towel.

"Mi gwaan te-te-tell yuh madda."

"Eef yuh nuh touch it, mi a guh tell maa bout yuh ahn Lamont."

"Yuh a ji-ji-jinal."

"Jus rub it a lickle."

She was apprehensive. She walked behind the coach and pulled on his penis.

"Nuh suh hawd!"

"Yuh tink m-m-me a one a dem dutty gal dem?"

"Jus tek it easy."

"Like de-de-dis?"

"Rub it slowa."

She adjusted her strokes.

"Like de-de-dis?"

Mark was aroused by the naked men in the movie.

"Dweet fasta, nat hawd."

He could feel himself changing inside. A creamy fluid shot out his penis.

"Ah wah wrang wid yuh?"

Mark looked at the wet towel and frowned. He thought he was becoming a man.

Daphne arrived at Mark's high school graduation, baffling his teachers and peers. No one knew who she was. She was never seen at a PTA meeting in the five years he had attended Meadowbrook. People in the auditorium stared at her dress. It looked homemade and ostentatious for the occasion. The shiny gold and black dress stopped at her thick thighs and was covered with red leaf patterns. The cut-out sleeves looked vulgar and the bodice was too tight. She looked out of place standing next to the other women, who were dressed in elegant and conservative dresses.

She stood up, pulled down her dress, and clapped as Mark went up the podium to receive his diploma. He rolled his eyes when he heard her cheer He was so embarrassed he hoped Brian and the rest of his classmates had not noticed.

Mark became disaffected with Daphne's new rules. They were imposing. After all the years of being in and out of his life, she showed up claiming her mother of the year award. He thought she didn't have any right to tell him what to do. He stopped going with her to the Kingdom Hall meeting on Sundays and the Thursday night Bible study. He began to smoke cigarettes. He drank beer with Anthony and stayed out late at night. Everything he did challenged Daphne authority. She was always ready to explode, and he rebelled without apology.

The night Daphne reached for a belt and seventeen-year-old Mark raised his fist daring her to hit him became the turning point. Counseling from the elders at the Kingdom Hall could not salvage their relationship. She put down the belt and raised her fists. She threw anything at him that was in close range. She pushed him against the wall, and challenged him to fight her.

Mark remembered that Eileen and Winsome endured branches from the

Morning Glory tree laced across their backsides and flower pots grazing their head at the slightest insubordination. Daphne inspected their clothes before they left the house and if she thought it was too tight or short or didn't meet her idea of what was decent, they had to change or it was ripped to shreds. She threatened to kick Mark out of the house, all in attempt to control a young man that was growing up before her and rejecting her life.

Chapter Five

Mark stood in line trembling as he waited for his *O'level* results. He avoided Roger, Little Nicky's brother, who was ahead in line. They had grown up together attending Meadowbrook High, but Mark stopped talking to Roger when he returned from America. Roger studied the sciences, was on the School's Challenge Quiz team, and played sports. He was oblivious to Mark's snobbery.

When Roger got his result slip, he knew he had passed all seven subjects. Mark waited for him to leave the office. Of the six subjects he sat, he passed two - History and Principles of Business. He went to the restroom to cry, then reemerged like his world hadn't been shifted from under his feet. Repeating wasn't as terrible because he was younger than the average fifth-year student, but the shame of being at the same school as Roger advanced to sixth form was unbearable. He dreaded going home. Daphne would berate him, call him a failure, and ridicule him for pretending he was better than Roger. Little Nicky would call him a dunce.

Gillisa and Georgette were also not happy with their results. Gillisa decided to repeat the fifth form at Meadowbrook. Georgette wasn't sure she wanted to be in Gillisa's shadow anymore. No one was surprised Dale had failed. He decided to go to Excelsior Community College with other repeaters, and when he explained to Mark, it seemed like the answer. That night at home, Daphne quarreled, but after Mark's tears and pleading, she agreed to pay the tuition for him to repeat the subjects.

Exed had three programs that supported its multi-million dollar fiscal year. It wasn't keen on attracting the brightest scholars, but rolled out its red carpet to those who could afford their exorbitant tuition. The ICEP program, for repeaters, had the largest population on campus. It attracted wealthy repeaters as far away as Montego Bay.

It was an Americanized fifth form with a liberal agenda. Anyone new to campus could spot who was enrolled in the ICEP program. They dressed like new face models in a fashion show. They spent the day sitting on the library steps and under the shading trees smoking cigarettes and listening to dancehall music. Some went to classes, but most were time wasters.

Mark was bunched in with the ICEP stereotype. The recent graduates from teacher's college didn't expect much from him, but every day was a reminder he never wanted to feel the way he did when he didn't pass. It fueled an ultimatum to take his studies seriously. It was a year of avoiding Roger and his sixth form friends. He learned to ignore Daphne's, "Why yuh nuh smart likka Roger?" and Little Nicky's, "Yuh suh dunce!" At the end of the year, he passed the other four subjects. It was a reason to celebrate he had endured a year of feeling like a failure.

He decided to progress to the *A'levels*. Daphne asked why waste another two years. Mark wanted to go to the University of the West Indies, and passing two or three *A'levels* was a prerequisite. Daphne paid his enrollment in the Pre-University program before returning to America. She wished him luck, but doubted success. She recommended a file clerk job with the government because the neighborhood boys had similar jobs. Mark rolled his eyes and said he was better than that type of work.

Mark befriended schoolmates who didn't criticized his effeminate ways. There was something about Tessa. It wasn't just her name, Melissa Tessa Rachel Scott, but the way she looked and behaved. Her light complexion got her ahead in the black line. She had Rastafarianism in her blood. Her long and curly, sandy brown hair was natural, with a single dreadlock down her back. She wasn't from the group of *rastas* who squatted on captured land, selling peanuts and sugarcane. She came from a line of white settlers and Rastafarian copulation, who came up in society by being artists and musicians. Her mother was a sculptor with a permanent exhibition at the National Gallery. She was the closest thing to Bob Marley Mark knew.

Tessa had an amiable quality that also made her beautiful on the inside. Her white features were only on the surface. When she opened her mouth, her blackness came out. She was down to earth and that surprised Mark. He thought looking like her would give him a legitimate reason to act like he was better than the dark skin majority because it was what people like that in Jamaica did.

Tessa was aware of her effect on the boys. She spoke frankly about men and sex, which made her seem more mature than her peers. She was the liberated voice for the girls who weren't as experienced. She dated men twice her age who had options beyond the boys' reach.

Tessa's mother, Cedella, was an older version of her. Their relationship was unusual compared to mothers like Daphne, who didn't know how to treat their adolescence with respect. Her laissez-faire attitude gave Tessa choices and not ultimatums. They smoked marijuana together. Sometimes she baked laced cookies for Tessa and her friends. They cooked together - exotic dishes that surpassed the typical oxtail and jerk chicken. They got in bed together, braiding each other's hair and talking all night about sex, their men, and their lives. She was the coolest mother Mark knew. He looked forward to seeing her when he visited Tessa's home.

Cedella was a mystery. Mark loved everything about her, except the way she kept her house. The first time he visited the spacious four-bedroom house at the foot of Mountain View, he thought they were still unpacking from a recent move. When he returned weeks later, the cluttered mess made him realize Cedella wasn't as perfect as he thought. Her sculptors made with found objects - old tires, car doors, barbwire, street signs, steel chairs and large metals - were mixed in with clothes, linen, shoes, and other miscellaneous objects that made the house an active junkyard. She worked from a couch in the living room. Oil painted canvasses were stacked in corners - some were new, but most were in a state of decay. She never complained when Tessa left her clothes on the floor. The disarray of the house was the only fault Mark found.

Tessa's artsy style was reflected in her attire and personality like the way she called out any boy who thought he was too cool. She wore tie-dyed MC Hammer pants with off-the-shoulder blouses exposing her belly button. Sometime she wore men's clothes. At those times, she had spent the night at a boyfriend.

She never wore dresses on campus. She preferred the freedom pants gave her. She could sit on the steps with her legs open without attracting the boys' wandering eyes. She wore her *rasta* sandals with pride. When Mark saw her at her mother's exhibition in New Kingston with her hair pinned up in a chignon, wearing an evening dress and high heel pumps, he knew what everyone saw in her. Tessa was spellbinding.

Tessa's circle of friends grew up together in Montego Bay and reunited at Exed. They possessed her qualities – being beautiful and down-to-earth.

They invaded campus hangouts and made admirers. Tessa zipped in and out of her classes, sometimes missing days, but showed up when there was a test and aced it. She flirted with Mr. Nwosu, the Sociology exchange teacher from London, like he was another school boy waiting to carry her books.

Mark felt like one of the chosen few she befriended. He saw her on weekends away from the unavoidable pretense on campus. She always had time for him when he visited unexpectedly. She never nagged that he was effeminate or hung around too many girls because she understood without making an issue of it. When he saw her on campus, he knew she would offer a kind smile or a compliment which made his day a little better.

As Mark progressed in the Pre-University Department, his peers changed from the popular time wasters to the smart kids. He began to assert himself although his flamboyance made the students cringe. If he wasn't around the camaraderie of a handful of classmates, he was subjected to ridicules and threats. He found security in excelling in his courses.

In the History class, he debated with Beulah, the born-again Christian, supporting Anne Boleyn's court of men suspected of being homosexuals. It was the first time homosexuality was discussed without the customary anti-gay hysteria. Beulah made references to God's punishment on Sodom and Gomorrah and the class supported her. They thought George Boleyn and the men beheaded by Henry VIII's orders deserved to die because of their ungodly, perverse acts.

The subject arose in the Literature class when James Baldwin's *Giovanni's Room* was read. The students objected that the novel was included in the syllabus. They thought the book should have been banned. Mark argued

James Baldwin was a great American writers. Beulah asked if he died of that homo disease, "like de ress ah dem."

In Mr. Nwosu's lecture, he was tactful in his support of Mark. He told the class homosexuality wasn't a psychological disorder. His views were different because he was British and he was more tolerant. He said it wasn't his place to judge or condemn someone that was homosexual. Beulah asked if he would have a friend who was homosexual and he said he wouldn't hold it against anyone.

Mark's interest soon shifted to Mr. Nwosu. He came at a time when Mark needed someone to look up to. He was different from the other teachers, at least a decade younger. He was bi-racial with a Nigerian father and white mother. He was attractive and his British accent elevated his appeal to movie star status. Unlike the typical suit and tie worn by most of the male teachers, he wore jeans and polo shirts to his lectures. He looked like he played football in college and kept his body conditioned. The girls got lost in his sultry, light brown bedroom eyes. His curly hair had a scholarly, receding quality. The most attractive thing about him was his friendly disposition. As far as he was concerned, he was away from his family for a year, on an island he described as a tropical paradise, and teaching a class of infatuated students. His topics challenged the status quo and made references to homosexuality without quoting Buju Banton's, "Boom bye bye, batty bwoy fi dead."

Mark made him his personal Jesus. He never missed a lecture and sat in the front row. His Sociology text was the only book he pressured Daphne to buy. The other books, he made copies of chapters as the class progressed or borrowed from the library. He held onto every word Mr. Nwosu said like it was gospel. When he spoke during the lectures, it was like Mr. Nwosu was the only person in the classroom.

Tessa also liked Mr. Nwosu. She saw him after school in the apartment he rented at the back of Maya's house. Maya was Cedella's roommate from art school. She was a professor at the university. When Cedella visited, they entertained each other with lengthy discussions, consuming bottles of wine and a well-cooked meal. They ranted about art, politics and anything else on their minds. They ended the night with updates about the men in their lives and how great the sex was.

Tessa showed up for these dinners to peek at Mr. Nwosu, shirtless in his apartment. When he joined the dinner parties, their relationship was upgraded to a comfortable first name basis. She wasn't embarrassed to rub her leg against his under the dining table or stop by his apartment to share a joint.

Mark daydreamed about Mr. Nwosu. He was excited to be his pupil, but frustrated when he was alone in his office, second guessing what he said. Mr. Nwosu realized Mark's infatuation, but didn't encouraged nor dismissed the attention. Mark knew his feelings would not be reciprocated, but he hoped for a friendship.

He wrote Mr. Nwosu a letter lamenting about his fatherless life and overbearing, absentee mother. He told Mr. Nwosu he was his role model. The letter read like the unsolicited desires of a young man with an intolerable crush. Mark feared being chastised, and hid behind platonic ideals of respect and admiration. Deep inside, he harbored raw lust and an unbearable urge to do unspeakable things.

Mr. Nwosu was accustomed to letters of that type from girls, which he reciprocated and offered his bed and body, but with Mark it was different. He decided to steer Mark in another direction.

Mr. Straps was the head of the Pre-University Department and a friendly uncle to the students. He and Mr. Nwosu were drinking buddies. One evening, they decided to go have a drink and invited Mark. He knew it meant a night out stopping by at least two strip clubs. Mark saw it as an opportunity to socialize with Mr. Nwosu off campus and be regarded as an adult. They wanted to expose Mark to women.

They drove to a club on Constant Spring Road. A young girl, made-up to appear younger stood at the entrance and declared the admission was a two drink minimum. Mr. Straps nodded like he was way ahead of her and ordered four rounds of beer. Mark ordered rum and coke, the starter drink of choice for cocky teenagers. Mr. Straps suggested a Dragon Stout, advising it would put hair on his chest. Mark complied, took a sip, dismissed the bitterness, and visualized hair follicles germinating.

After the third round of beer, Mark and his teachers were laughing like old chums. Mr. Nwosu told them about the girls on campus who liked him and tried to pry into Mark's fondness for Tessa. Mark said they were just friends. Mr. Straps argued men and women couldn't be just friends because there was always sexual tension, unless the man was homosexual. It felt like an accusation. Mark felt uneasy. He looked at Mr. Nwosu to change the conversation. Mr. Nwosu said the two sexes could be platonic if there wasn't any attraction, and the man didn't have to be gay. During his drunken slurs, he said he loved women - always had and always would. Mr. Straps wasn't sure about the relevance of the comment, but Mark knew what he meant. If he wasn't as drunk, the silly smirk on his face would have been reduced to tears.

The club of horny men clapped feverishly when a cheerful voice announced the night's entertainment. Under a spotlight, a skinny, wide mouth girl stood with her legs apart. Her black satin blouse opened with a red brassier supporting breasts the size of oranges. Black panties peeked under her miniskirt, its tightness blended with her dark skin. Her sweat loosened the grease slicking back her hair and dripped down her face. She held a beer bottle and puffed on a cigarette between a painted grin.

The spotlight followed her to the center of the bar with eyes fixed on her wiggling out of the blouse. The deejay scratched the record and shouted, "Cease ahn cum again!" She sat on a chair and bent her legs over her head. Mark's eyes popped when she slipped off her panties and stuck the cigarette in her vagina. The men roared and threw dollar bills at her feet. "Needle Eye Pum Pum" played as she puffed the cigarette with her vagina. She smiled at her captivated audience. Mr. Straps and Mr. Nwosu nodded at Mark and sipped their beer. Mark felt like an impostor.

Mark's crush developed unbearably. He saw Mr. Nwosu receiving lap dances in dimly lit clubs and girls leaving his apartment with their clothes unraveled. The more privy he was of Mr. Nwosu's exploits, the greater his fantasies became. At the end of the school year he was upset Mr. Nwosu would return to London. He visited his office more frequently, wishing he told him how he really felt. He hoped with time the feelings would become platonic. They never did. They were merely suppressed.

Everyone on campus made plans to attend Reggae Sunsplash in Montego Bay. Mark had never been and he knew Daphne wouldn't allow it. She started quoting the Bible at opportune times to condemn him and his recently acquired social life. She warned him about the drugs consumed during the event. He decided he was going without her consent when his favorite teacher invited him.

89

On the way to Montego Bay, they stopped at Fern Gully and ate grilled food from street vendors. They climbed Dunn's River Falls and Mark stared at Mr. Nwosu swim trunks. He bought Mr. Nwosu a braided belt and he gave Mark a pocket knife. Mark asked if he deserved the award for "Best All Round Student" in Sociology and he told him although Beulah got higher grades, he was by far the best "All Round." Mark blushed and he realized it was the closest he would ever get to Mr. Nwosu - his perpetually straight, womanizing, demi-god - and it was enough.

Reggae Sunsplash was the highlight of the Jamaica's entertainment calendar. Commercially successful reggae and dancehall artists were the headline acts with American Hip hop artists. The week-long event was a twenty-four-hour music festival. The long days of unknown artists transformed into longer nights of celebrated stars. Craft vendors sold Bob Marley memorabilia and anything Rastafarian with offerings of every imagined island food. A crew from MTV filmed the event and Mark was excited when he was asked to introduce a music video. He curtailed his accent to something American viewers would understand.

There were cloud puffs of ganja everywhere. The music was as intoxicating as the cold beer during the day, and the white rum that kept the revelers warm at night. Mark took a turn at the *ganja* being passed around. He saw Tessa and the two drank without inhibitions and danced in the afternoon rainstorm.

It was a good year for Mark Palmer. He passed the three subjects and was accepted to the University of the West Indies. He received news that his father began filing for him to live permanently in America. Migrating seemed like a better option, so he declined admission and found a job. He also wanted to have money, independent of Daphne's strings attached generosity. He became the newest and brightest employee at General Accident Insurance Company. His desk was in the center of a newsroom styled office. With his first paycheck, he purchased a small wardrobe. He beamed in the mirror each morning to work. The picture had changed from a frail nervous baby and insecure bullied youth, to a promising, assertive young man.

Mark's acquaintances at home dwindled to Suzie and Little Nicky, who only answered to Danicka, now that she was in high school. Suzie moved into the neighborhood to live with her father on Miss Lou's Avenue. Mark noticed her at the video rental shop built on the side of her father's house. They met when she visited Exed. Suzie was still in high school, but when she stripped out of her uniform and stepped on campus in tight jeans, cropped T-shirts and released her hair from its ponytail, she commanded the same attention like the community college girls.

She didn't speak to anyone in Cooreville Gardens and would have ignored Mark had he not been a part of her friends at Exed. She became a ploy that kept him safe from the neighborhood boys. They had graduated to fist fights rather than childish sissy jeers. However, when he got his job, Suzie became irrelevant.

He began hanging out with Ann-Marie and Janelle, two sophisticated working class girls. Ann-Marie was a teller and Janelle a receptionist at a travel agency. They were cousins he met at one of the infamous Immaculate Conception High School fetes. He had gone with Brian, who had planned to meet Gillisa.

The girls lived in Patrick City and worked in New Kingston. They shopped together, worked out at a chic gym on Knutsford Boulevard, went on dates with older, wealthy men, and spent weekends at popular nightclubs in New Kingston. Mark felt grown in their company. They met after work for happy hour and spoke about grown up things like sex and men, although they lived with parents.

Mark arrived with his friends at Jonkonuu Lounge, a trendy nightclub at Wyndham Hotel in New Kingston. He felt good in his stylish work clothes. He was ready for a good time. Ann-Marie sat by the poolside bar with Janelle, waiting for Orville, her married boyfriend. Mark was inside the club with a glass of rum and coke, circling the ice cubes with his finger.

The club was packed with people trying to talk over the music. Mark saw a group of guys he assumed were tourists and locked eyes with one he found attractive. He was undeniably handsome - tall and lean like a swimmer, with hazel eyes, full lips, and a square jawline. His wavy brown hair hung over his forehead. He reminded Mark of a popular actor of the time. His stone-washed jeans hugged his thighs tighter than other guys. His fitted shirt hinted at a defined chest. Mark drifted in his thoughts and the same desires he felt when he was around Brian resurfaced.

Cheers brought a crowd to the dance floor. His heart raced when the deejay played "Boom Bye Bye." The guy caught him staring and Mark shifted in his seat. He smiled and Mark felt exposed. He knew staring at a guy could put his life in danger, regardless of being in New Kingston. He wanted to leave the club or find Ann-Marie and Janelle to evade suspicion. As the guy approached, Mark weaved through the crowd, stepping on feet to get away. The guy followed and met him at the exit door.

"Hey dude, are you leaving?"

Mark's face fell to the floor.

"Wat?"

"You wanna have a drink?"

Mark glanced at the doorman.

"I'm Bruce."

"Cool it a lickle. Yuh inna Jamdown."

Mark motioned to go outside away from the club, where he wouldn't be recognized.

"Wi can hab a drink a de hotel crass de street."

"Cool, I'm staying there."

Bruce led Mark and slid a guest card through the locked entrance. They passed the lobby and sat by a poolside bar.

"I'm glad we can be together," Bruce said. "Maybe we can have some fun."

"A wah yuh mean by dat?"

"I'm here on spring break to have fun."

Bruce smiled and flicked his eyes from Mark's chest to his crotch.

"Wah kine a fun?"

Bruce smiled.

"You know?"

"Tell mi bout yuh self."

"Not much really to tell. I'm twenty-four. I'm a senior at Michigan State. I'm going to law school next year. Here with a few friends. Maybe I'll get in a little trouble… I like you … You're cute."

Mark blushed and glanced at the people at the bar, some stumbling away and disappearing into rooms. He didn't want anyone to hear their conversation. He stared at Bruce's chest then at his crotch. Bruce reclined on the chair and pushed his hips towards Mark to show off his erection.

93

"A wah yuh a duh?" Mark asked. "Yuh waan dem beat wi up?"

"Take it easy. It's okay," Bruce said. "No one will bother us here."

Mark doubted his optimism.

"Let's sit by the pool."

Mark stood and Bruce smiled when he noticed that Mark also had an erection. He sat at the edge of the pool and rolled his jeans to the knees then dipped his legs in the water. He leaned back on his arms, his hair grazing Mark's chest. Mark flinched and looked around to check if anyone saw. He was filled with excitement, but terrified. He fidgeted and Bruce realized he was nervous.

They collided into an uncomfortable silence unsure of what to do. Bruce thought if he appeared aggressive Mark would lose interest. Mark wasn't sure how to interact. They looked at the moon's reflection and back into each other's eyes. They listened to music as the bartender announced "last call for alcohol." They waited for the other to make the next move, say the next word. Bruce remained silent, moving his legs in the water. Mark anticipated his gestures, wishing he could find the right words.

The awkward silence was interrupted by a sunburned girl wearing a neon bikini under a white peasant dress. Her beaded cornrows danced over her shoulders. She gave Bruce an intoxicated grin.

"Hey you! We're gonna watch the sunrise. Are you good?"

"Oh hey, Lisa. Yeah, I'm good. I'm going to bed soon."

"Suit yourself. Don't do anything I wouldn't do."

Lisa reached in her pocket for a joint, rolled it between her fingers and stuck it behind her ears.

"A who dat?"

"Lisa. She's a big fag hag on campus."

"Mi tink shi was yuh girl."

"Why would I be here with you?"

Mark jabbed Bruce's shoulders and smiled.

"It late. Mi hab fi guh back ahn meet mi fren dem fi a ride a mi yard."

"You can stay over if you like," Bruce said. "Leave in the morning."

It was what Mark wanted to hear. He followed Bruce inside the hotel and to an elevator. When the doors closed, Bruce pulled him to his chest, splashing the drink on the floor. Mark closed his eyes. His lips trembled.

"Are you nervous?"

"A lickle," Mark said. "Mi nevah kiss a bwoy before."

Bruce was surprised. Mark's inexperience was refreshing, almost unbelievable. He sucked on an ice cube and his cool tongue entered Mark's mouth. Mark was flushed, his palms felt clammy, and he began to sweat. Bruce held Mark's arms around his waist and pinned Mark against the elevator. Mark's hardness rubbed against Bruce's thigh. Bruce ran his arms over Mark's back and held him closer. They collected themselves when the doors opened.

Inside the hotel room, Bruce flipped on the light and held Mark for another kiss.

"Tun aff de lite," Mark said.

The room was illuminated by the full moon. The blinds cast lines on the floor. The two silhouettes fumbled in the dark. Fingers moved through hair, unbuttoned shirts, caressed chest, pulled zippers, threw trousers on the floor, and explored their nakedness. They moved slowly through the sheets, legs curling between the folds, hips meeting and grinding. The air smelled of sweat and alcohol.

Bruce's wet lips explored Mark's salty body. His tongue lapping the contours. He held Mark's erect cock and rubbed it against his cheeks. Mark moaned when Bruce slipped his cock in his mouth. He moved around the bed captured by Bruce's touch. His motion was rhythmic like a skilled lover, moving with Mark's hips. Bruce curled his tongue around Mark's cock and licked the shaft. Mark held his head and pushed him into his loins. Bruce's hair matted with sweat. Mark shivered and collapsed on the bed when he came.

Bruce was laughing on the phone with Lisa when Mark awoke. She told him about her night at the beach with a *Rent-a-dread*. She bragged about her conquest and poked him to tell her about his.

"He's still here," Bruce whispered.

Mark pulled the sheet up to his chest.

"It late. Mi haffi go home."

Mark began to dress.

"Hold on a minute."

Bruce hung up the phone, took off his brief and wrestled Mark under the sheets.

Mark left the hotel room a few hours later. He was overwhelmed with guilt. He couldn't believe he had sex with a man. He wanted to run away. He felt like the soiled sheets left on the floor.

He sat on the bus trying to erase the previous night from his mind. The taste of Bruce's lips and tongue moving over his body lingered. It was like he was waiting for that feeling all his life and it answered an obscure question, an unrealized awareness. Brushing aside the guilt, it felt beautiful.

When he arrive home, the neighborhood boys gathered at Mr. Crawford's front gate, causing a commotion. He ignored them and ran to his bedroom. As the noise travelled, he heard that Mr. Crawford's washer woman had found blood stains in the son's underwear and accused him of being a homosexual. A mob entered the house and dragged the screaming boy into the street as his father looked on in support.

When the police arrived, he was badly beaten. His clothes were drenched with blood. The police released the lifeless boy back to the mob for another beating. They left his unconscious body curled up on the doorsteps. The door was shut by his father. The neighborhood boys cheered when they heard the boy died in the hospital, knocking fists and chanting, "Batty bwoy fi dead." A chill swept over Mark. He thought the dead boy could have been him.

Brian was covered in grease. His sweaty and the overalls he wore to work were soiled with dirt. His work boots were muddy and ripped at the soles. Mark was surprised to see his preppy rich friend - the heir to a manufacturing plant - covered in filth. He had imagined him in an upstairs office at an oversized desk, approving deals and signing contracts, with assistants buzzing around him. Brian knew that life was coming in a matter of time. Until then, he was learning his father's business. He didn't protest rolling up his sleeves and starting at the entry level, because he was reassured his corner office was waiting with his pick of the best looking secretary.

Brian hadn't seen Mark since high school. He thought Mark looked grown up and professional, dressed in his work clothes like he was someone important.

"Mi hear seh yuh hab ah big jab."

"It okay. Mi jus killing time till mi guh a farin fi gud."

97

Brian looked at Mark and sighed.

"No weh no betta dan yard."

Brian had visited America on vacations, but had no desire to migrate. Jamaicans migrated to America - some illegally - for a better life. His life was already secured.

"Gud fi yuh!" Brian said. "Wah yuh ah guh duh deh?"

"Mi nuh know yet," Mark said. "Ah fi de bess."

"Yuh hear bout anybady fram skool?" Brian asked.

"Nat really," Mark said. "Yuh hear bout Georgette?"

"Mi si har," Brian said. "Yuh wudda nevah believe who a de baby fadda."

"A who?" Mark asked.

Brian frowned, shook his head, and frowned again.

"A marrid man," Brian said.

"Lawd. Mi nevah know sey shi stay suh," Mark said.

"Ahn Tessa ah veggietarian. Shi nuh deh wid fi har man nuh more," Brian said. "Dem bruk up ova six monts ago. Shi seh shi a go back a Mobay."

Mark felt rescued from a miserable fate. If he had decided to stay in Jamaica he would have gone to the University of the West Indies and maybe become a lawyer. He wondered what kind of life he would have had with a secret he couldn't hide. He was relieved he no longer coveted Brian's life. He just couldn't stop his heart from racing when he saw him.

Mark told Brian he looked good and that was as far he could go to let him know he had loved him all those years. Brian realized what Mark was trying to say, and it made him uncomfortable. He talked about getting serious with Gillisa. He wished Mark the best and ended their conversation.

Part Two

Chapter Six

Mark's second trip to America meant permanence. America became his new home and although everything was familiar, nothing was the same as before. Daphne rented a shot-gun apartment on Maple Street, across from Norwalk Hospital, after Aunt Kitty complained that Russell's children never visited and wondered why she wasn't paying rent.

It was a quiet part of town, with the exception of the sirens all night and the train tracks behind the building. The car-lined street saw very little pedestrians, aside from the walkers who came for their medical appointments, and a small population of mothers jogging with their babies in strollers. Mark missed the big house on Bayview Avenue. Daphne's one-bedroom apartment made him feel like he was naked before a crowd. She disturbed him in the mornings while he slept on an air mattress in the living room. He felt exposed to a woman not prepared to relate to him as an adult.

Mark journeyed to Hartford to meet the man said to be his father. His sole reason was to secure a check to cover his first year's college tuition - a promise Manuel made while his papers were being processed. All he knew about Manuel was what Daphne said about their dispute over selling the house. He didn't even have a picture of him nor did he know what he looked like. He vaguely remembered the man running down Barbados Road soaked in his mother's piss.

When Mark met Manuel at the bus terminal, his affable expression was an attempt to conceal his disappointment. Manuel gave him a quick hand shake, then patted his shoulder, unsure if a hug was expected. Mark swung his bag over his shoulder and blocked Manuel from inching towards him. He made a face and gasped.

Manuel looked old and used. His gaunt body drooped, burdened by an unsightly large gut. He reminded Mark of one of those starving children in Ethiopia seen on television with flies around their mouth, clinging to Sally Struthers. He smelled like a mildewed closet. Mark dumped his bag on the backseat of the car and tried to overlook his coarseness. Manuel's eyes were guarded like he had lost trust in the world and anyone associated with Daphne.

"Yuh madda seh yuh a guh a callege."

"Yes, Howard University."

"Wey dat deh?"

"Washington, DC."

"A weh yuh a guh get money fram fi guh deh?"

Mark almost bit his tongue. He realized Manuel was going to be difficult. His week-long visit was to test his gratitude to a father who never gave him anything, but a second-hand toy. After all the years of Manuel being a constant visitor in his mind - the father who left him - he was expected to be cordial and bow down if necessary to not risk him reneging on his promise.

Mark could feel himself turning inside. He hated his predicament, and was nauseated by the musty smell in the car. He studied Manuel, looking for something that would make him proud. He wanted to step away from the hate his mother had embedded. He didn't blame Manuel for leaving her, but he despised him for cutting off financial support to spite her.

Manuel opened the front door to his three-story house and Mark noticed six mailboxes. The image of a slumlord came to mind. The familiar foul smell from the car sunk into his pores. As he followed Manuel up spiraling carpeted wood stairs, each step felt like he was descending into a place frozen in time. Cat hair covered the carpet, some areas so old the hair melted into an alien layer. Manuel's home looked like a 1979 relic preserved for historical purposes. The faded yellow wallpaper peeled at the edges, exposing the messy workmanship of unskilled painters.

The walls were decorated with photographs. Mark recognized Manuel and his sisters and a photo of himself propped on a towel at Hope Gardens. There were pictures of other children and families, people at church, amusement parks, and weddings. He saw children at christenings, birthday parties and graduations. He wondered who they were, and if their lives were better with Manuel's presence.

The living room had a feminine presence with fake flowers, figurines, and porcelain dolls perched around a television on a table. Two fake leather couches covered with plastic and a crochet doily gave the impression no one ever sat there. A Bible was on a corner table with a waxed statue of Jesus Christ fixed above a water fountain, which doubled as a lamp and fly catcher. The tiled floor sloped in the passageway leading to the kitchen. Area rugs overlapped with stained plastic runners. The radio was on a religious station with the preacher screaming to honor thy mother and father. Mark rolled his eyes and went to relieve himself in the bathroom.

He was ready to return to Daphne's air mattress when he saw the bedroom. The lumpy mattress was covered with a comforter, smelling like mothballs. He found a can of air freshener to eliminate the funk. Another weeping crucifix hung over the bed with a Bible on the night stand. The dresser was covered with dust.

"Delores cook chicken. Eef yuh waan dinna, help yuh self," Manuel said.

"Gudnite."

"Yuh goin' to yuh bed a ready?" Mark asked. "A only 8 o'clock."

"Wah wrang wid dat?"

"Nothing. Mi jus' saying."

"No run de TV too lang."

Mark sighed and walked to the back balcony to smoke a cigarette. Down in the backyard, tenants' cars cluttered the driveway and a dilapidated wire coop was overcrowded with fat rabbits and guinea pigs. A small garden with cabbage and callaloo competed with overgrown weeds for survival.

"A wah smell likka cigarette suh?" Manuel asked. "Yuh ah smoke?"

"Yes!" Mark said. "Yuh hab a problem wid dat?"

Mark spun around and saw Manuel dressed in a wife-beater stretched halfway over his belly. His black socks was rolled up to his knees with pee-stained bed slippers. His shriveled penis stuck out from his plaid boxers. Mark was disgusted the man before him was his father. He flicked the cigarette over the balcony and set off down the precarious wooden stairs.

"A goin' to Beverly shap."

"No cum back too late. Mi a guh church inna de marning."

"Yuh can leave de key inna de letta box."

Manuel grumbled something, went to the kitchen to put the lukewarm chicken in the refrigerator then turned the lights off before returning to his bedroom.

Beverly's salon was closed. Next door at Marvin's jewelry shop, a woman resembling Beverly was chatting on the phone. A group of Rastafarians sat in economy cars with flashy silver rims, sipping beers in brown paper bags, smoking weed, and listening to dancehall music. He felt like he was back home in the ghetto. He monitored the way he walked past the men and asked the woman for Marvin. She told him Marvin was in jail and Beverly went to Jamaica for a funeral.

"A who yuh is?" She asked.

"Beverly cousin," Mark said.

"Oh raahtid! Yuh grow suh big!" She said. "Mi a Bev sista, Merle, Lionel wife. Yuh nuh 'memba mi. Mi did live inna Canadah. Yuh madda know mi."

"Wen Beverly a com back?"

"Nex' week or suh. Shi ahn de pickney dem."

Mark left the shop and returned to Manuel's house. He sat before the television with frustration. He tried to ignore Manuel's snores coming from his bedroom.

Winsome drove up in her brand new Nissan Maxima on Edgewood Street and invited Mark to her apartment in Windsor Locks. She wanted to show him how successful she was. It had been six years since she migrated to America. She had been working at Hartford Insurance Company for four years. Mark wondered how Eileen was doing in North Carolina with her track star husband, Ronnie.

Windsor Locks looked like the prototype of a future community - an idyllic neighborhood built on a bulldozed forest with semi-detached homes on evenly manicured plots. It was a place for model white couples to raise happy white children.

Mark was impressed with Winsome's manufactured apartment in the suburbs. Everything in her home matched like a JC Penny catalog. The drapes matched the carpet and couch. The bathroom towels matched the rugs, which matched the toothbrush and soap dish, and the potpourri in a bowl on the toilet. The bedroom walls matched the comforter and the sheets, which matched the lamp shades and the crochet doilies on the nightstand. The apartment was a Pepto-Bismol colored monochromatic bore. He was pleased it smelled like Pine Sol.

Mark spent days watching *The Sally Jesse Raphael Show*, excited that Winsome had tickets for an upcoming taping in New Haven. He ate microwave snacks, vigilant not to spill or drop a crumb on the furniture or carpet. He watered the lawn for an excuse to go outside to watch the only black family in the neighborhood. He feared if he walked on the street the residents would call the cops to report a suspicious prowler.

Winsome took Mark to an INXS concert. She got tickets because Ziggy Marley and the Melody Makers were the opening act. The white audience sang along to the popular "Tomorrow People." Mark joined, but felt self-conscious by the stares recognizing his accent. During the intermission, concession stands hawked artist memorabilia. "Things Jamaican" stands sold Bob Marley T-shirts and caps, and cassette tapes with reggae and dancehall music. Mark saw his culture for sale and being ridiculed by patrons. He wanted to be far away from being Jamaican. When INXS returned onstage, he pretended he knew the words to "Need You Tonight."

The next day they drove to New Haven for the double taping of *The Sally Jesse Raphael Show*. The first show featured Lola Falana and her battle with multiple sclerosis. It was billed to be a tear jerker and boxes of Kleenex were on hand for the guest and her sympathizers. Lola Falana spoke about her triple threat career, Las Vegas cabaret shows, and movie gigs. After years of being seduced by show business, she said she found God at a time when her career was over and she was diagnosed. The empathetic audience made interchangeable sound bites, but were more interested in the sordid details of her affair with Sammy Davis, Jr.

The second taping was aimed to increased ratings. On one side of the podium was a morbidly obese white man with a southern drawl, representing the KKK, and on the other side, an angry, black man with a pick sticking in his afro, representing the Black Panthers. The audience was mixed with people who supported both sides. Midgets waved confederate flags and girls in dashikis chanted, "Black power!" Sally Jesse Raphael peered through her red-rimmed glasses and calmly questioned the guests between threats and character assassinations. After the taping, no one remembered Lola Falana; they all wanted to hurt each other.

At the end of the week, Manuel went to his credit union and reluctantly handed Mark a check payable to Howard University. He said it was his life savings and thought the money was payment for twenty-one years of being a deadbeat father. Mark pardoned his absence and promised to keep in touch when he was away at college, even though he knew he wouldn't.

Mark spent the day in Manhattan sightseeing. He bought clothes with the fifty dollars Daphne had given him. At the corner of 42nd and 7th Avenue, Mayor Rudolph Giuliani's "clean-up" campaign was in full effect. Police manned corners on bicycles and horses. The porn shops with neon marquees and sweet offerings for a quarter were closed, evicting drug dealers and sex workers. Graffiti tags were repainted and Madame Tussauds and other tourist-friendly establishments moved in. Time Square took on a Disneyland appeal. Overweight, middle-aged tourists from Middle America dressed in Abercrombie and Fitch and deck shoes, swarmed the streets.

They snapped photos and sat on stools waiting to be sketched by Asian street artists.

Mark had seen Jennie Livingston's *Paris Is Burning* and wanted to meet anyone like "the children" from the documentary. He wondered what it was like to attend a gay ball. He took the C train to West 4th and walked down Christopher Street to West Side Highway, in search of a community he thought would accept him.

The scene changed. The fence was removed and replaced with concrete boulders. The area was under construction for what was to be a new millennium park.

Gay boys loafed, listening to house music and voguing. Mark sat and watched, assuming they were in one of the "houses." They talked about a ball in Harlem. Mark asked to go along. They looked at him with indifference, scrutinizing his clothes.

"Honey, you can't go to a ball lookin' like that," one of the boys said.

"Mi jus waan fi watch."

"Your look isn't polished. You look tore up from the floor up."

"Mi can get si'ting a de store."

The boy rolled his eyes, trying to decipher what Mark had said.

"Where you live girl?" he asked. "Run home and change."

"Mi here fi de weekend," Mark said. "A live in Con-necki-cut."

"Oh really, what parts?"

"Wess-port."

It got their attention. The other boys gathered around him.

"Chile, I guess you don't have to *mop*," the boy said. "Just swipe your cards."

Mark smiled. He had no idea what he meant.

"Okay honey. We're gonna eat first. You ever pull a stunt?"

"A wat?"

The boys laughed and ran around in circles. They screamed at the top of their voices and pointed at Mark like he was a circus act.

"Okay, Miss Westport, you have a lot to learn."

"Can I cum?" Mark asked. "Pleaze."

"Ok. That's Angel and Kiki. Miss Thing there with the fucked up mug is Tyrone. She walking tonite. We in the house of Escandala. I'm Queen Bee, their mothda."

They nodded when introduced, posing like actors in a pantomime.

"And I'm de one ahn only Marcia Pendavis. Jus kiddin,' I'm Mark."

"You should walk in the butch queen first time at a ball category."

"A caan vogue, but a can runway."

They shrugged. Queen Bee waved his hand at Tyrone who sat next to the boom box. Tyrone turned up the volume and found Paul Alexander's "Walk for Me."

"Bring it to the runway, bitch!"

Paul Alexander uttered, *"Take to the catwalk, walk for body, walk for face and snatch first place."* Mark stepped back on the pavement with an attitude, stood tall, posed with his hand on his hip like a teapot, and crossed his right leg. His walk was graceful. He crossed his legs with each step. He spun around and kept walking. When he got in front of the boys, he stopped and spun in the opposite direction down the pier, switching his ass. Queen Bee waved his index finger in the air as they cheered.

"You betta work!" Queen Bee said.

"It's over for you!" another boy said.

Mark followed the boys to the West 23rd Street diner, at the corner of

111

9th Avenue. Queen Bee surveyed the room before using the restroom. They ordered hamburgers with fries, chicken wings, and large sodas. When Queen Bee returned from the restroom, he looked worried.

"Well looks like we have to skip this one, okaay."

"Why girl?" Tyrone asked. "I'm hungry."

"Look over dere in the back cubicle honey. It's the po po!"

The boys turned in their high chairs and saw two police officers nursing their coffee. Tyrone recognized the officers from one of his open misdemeanor cases. Before their orders came, they left the diner and gathered on the sidewalk.

"Wat is it?" Mark asked.

"I ain't fixing to go to jail honey," Queen Bee said. "Not tonite!"

They took the subway to Harlem and exited at Central Park North. Queen Bee's third-floor apartment was on 113th and St. Nicholas Street. The refurbished loft had exposed brick walls with a new coat of paint. A queen-size mattress was on the floor. At the window by the fire escape, were a sewing machine and a mannequin covered with patterns and fabrics. Books, magazines, and shredded fabric were scattered on the hardwood floor. Queen Bee was working on a wedding dress for his design class at The New School. Mark waited for them to dress as they fluttered in and out of the closet and bathroom, changing their minds and making last minute alterations.

Kiki changed from polo shirt and cargo shorts into a long sleeve, burgundy satin dress with ruffles at the hem and a plunging neckline. A red wig cascaded down his back, matching his clutch and pumps.

"Butch queen up in pumps, okaay." Kiki smiled. "I'm snatching de trophy tonite!"

Tyrone took off a stripe shirt and Levis and changed into a wife-beater, khaki Fubu shirt and black Dickies shorts. Plaid cotton Ralph Lauren boxers sagged on his ass. He tossed a baseball cap to the side of his head to cover a scar. He slipped on a pair of Timberland boots and cupped his testicles.

"Butch queen thug realness. Whaz up?"

Angel made-up his face like a geisha. He replaced the T-shirt and jeans he wore to the pier with a white sequin dress. The rhinestone accented hem dragged on the floor. Around his neck was a metallic Turkey feather boa. Rhinestones and glitter sparkled in his greased black hair pulled back into a long ponytail.

"I'll show you how to runway Miss Honey," he said curling his lips.

Queen Bee was the least flamboyant. He changed from his boy clothes to a fake, black Chanel skirt suit with a chain strap black purse and white stilettos.

"Legendary!" Queen Bee exclaimed. "Another year of course."

Mark felt left out of the shenanigans and asked Queen Bee to borrow something to wear. He searched the closet while they waited, reapplying makeup, nibbling fried chicken, drinking gin, smoking Newport, and listening to Frankie Knuckles.

"You been in dere an hour," Kiki said. "If it ain't cute, prepare for a reading."

"Mi jus waan fi luk presentable." Mark said.

Mark stepped out the closet in a black leather mini-dress, black boots, and large Jackie O styled shades. The dress flattered his body while the sunglasses feminized his face. He smiled and waited for their response. Queen Bee raised his brows.

113

"You look very New York, honey."

"Is dat gud?"

"Like Naomi bitch!" Queen Bee smiled. "All you need is your hair."

"And beat that face!" Kiki said.

The ball occurred in the backroom of a rented warehouse on 129th Street. It was on a block with a church, a wash and fold laundry, a Chinese takeout, a check cashing store, and a few abandoned brownstones. After long hours of categories with much excitement, Tyrone walked and won top prize. Kiki was mad for getting the runner- up trophy, but felt redeemed when Queen Bee was again named the mother of the year. Angel got stage freight and ran off the runway.

Mark met Nevia, who won the Femme Queen Sex Siren category. They said she dated a plastic surgeon in New Jersey and received surgeries as gifts. She had two breast augmentations, her eyes slanted, her forehead lifted, her hairline pulled down, and her brow bone reduced. She also had her forehead, buttocks, and hips enlarged with liquid silicone injections. She looked like the next step in the human evolution. She decided to keep the penis.

Mark slept on Queen Bee's couch after the ball and left in the evening. He promised to look them up when he returned to the city and to do it all over again, even though he knew he wouldn't.

At Grand Central Train Station, he sat on the floor in the main concourse, waiting for the last train to Connecticut. Within the moving crowd his attention was drawn to a guy, who glanced at him as he passed. The guy stopped before him and asked for the time. Mark pointed to the huge four face opal clock on top of the information booth in the center of the station. The guy felt silly and smiled.

"Going home?"

"Yeah."

"New Jersey or Connecticut?"

"Narwalk."

"It's a nice town isn't it?"

"It okay."

The guy smiled again and walked away to smoke a cigarette on the sidewalk at 42nd Street. He kept looking back. Mark blushed when he realized he was being cruised. He felt a tingle of excitement. The guy had sleepy green eyes and retreating lips. Mark thought he wasn't the best looking guy in the world, but he wasn't average.

He wore a white dress shirt, fitted jeans without a belt and black dress shoes without socks. His curly, medium-length Richard Marx's '80s mullet wilted in the humid air. He flicked the half-smoked cigarette on the curb and walked back into the station. Mark anticipated a conversation, but he passed and headed to the restroom. Mark didn't know it was an invitation to follow. The guy returned with his shirt unbuttoned to his chest and approached Mark again with his hands fiddling in his pockets.

"I'm sorry, I couldn't help but staring. What's your name?"

"Why?"

"You remind me of someone. You're cute."

"Tanks."

"I'm staying at a hotel nearby. Wanna have a drink before your train comes?"

"Mi nuh even know yuh!"

"You can get to know me. I'm Jeffrey."

"Jeffrey?"

In the news, Peter Jennings spoke about serial killer Jeffrey Dahmer, who murdered seventeen black men in Milwaukee. Mark knew it wasn't him, but the coincidence was unsettling.

"I know, I saw the news, too. No relation."

Jeffrey's calm, sensual voice dismissed Mark's fears. He decided Jeffrey would be the first guy he touched or kissed and not feel bad about it. He followed him to the Grand Hyatt hotel and they sat at a bar in the lobby. They chatted over drinks. Jeffrey complimented, and Mark blushed. He tried to touch, and Mark moved away. Jeffrey ordered more drinks, and made more compliments. Mark began to relax.

Jeffrey was a flight attendant for Eastern Airlines. He said his preference was slim, black guys. Mark wasn't sure what answer he expected when he asked why he liked him, but that response didn't come to mind, nor did he feel flattered. Jeffrey became more appealing after the third drink. He spoke about traveling all over the world. He said it could be lonely because he didn't have a boyfriend. Mark couldn't imagine having a boyfriend. All he knew about being gay was a secretive life of anonymous sex that fizzled before the light of day.

"Do you wanna come to my room?"

"Wah mek yuh tink mi wud do dat?"

"Because it's after midnight and there are no more trains."

"Shit!"

"Don't worry. You can crash with me."

"Mi haffi use de phone."

Mark stood at a pay phone in the lobby, scrutinizing Jeffrey, trying to convince himself he was doing the right thing.

"Hi Miss Jackie, hope me nevah wake yuh. Is Mark."

"Oh, hi Mark. Yuh aw right?"

"Mi still inna Manhattan."

"Yuh tun big man. Mi hardly recognize yuh voice. How ole yuh is now?"

"Twenty-one"

"Bwoy, time fly."

"Miss Jackie, mi wid a fren fram high school. If mi madda call yuh…"

"Yeah Mark, mi wi tell har yuh a stay de night wid me."

"Tanks. Its jus dat mi waan fi guh a one club with har ahn yuh know how Maa is."

A week later, Mark waited until Daphne turned off the bedroom light before dialing the Acme Dating Line. He listened nervously to the recorded voice prompts and quickly pressed number two for "Men Seeking Men."

The phone echoed in his ear. He climbed on the windowsill and stuck his head outside and listened to personal ads from guys who wanted to meet that night. A message from one of the guys was arousing. He liked the way the caller described himself. The sound of his voice was a turn on. The guy said he was in Darien and wanted to meet later. Mark was excited, but knew the Wheels bus stopped its service at seven. His only option was the Stanford bus or a train and that was a lot of effort for a stranger. He dialed the guy's number and when the stranger picked up, he said he was responding to his message.

"Where you at?"

"Narwalk, near downtown."

"You wanna come by?"

"A don't drive."

117

"I can come get you. Give me half an hour."

"Wah yuh luk like?"

"Italian. Used to play football."

"Oh."

"And you?"

"A brown skin and slenda, wid shave hair … A black."

"I know."

Mark looked over his shoulder. He thought he heard Daphne in the bedroom. He had an erection when the guy described what he liked to do.

"Are you a bottom?" Tony asked.

"Nat really. A jus wanna play around."

"Okay. That's cool."

"Wah yuh name?"

"Tony. Yours?"

"Andrew."

"I'll call you when I'm on the way."

"Eehee."

Mark hung up the phone and tip-toed to the bathroom. He washed his face and rolled back the foreskin on his penis to make sure it wasn't cheesy. He watched the wall clock with the phone in his lap. A few minutes passed and he stuck his head out the window to redial the Acme Dating Line. He browsed other profiles, then hung up and waited for Tony's call. About forty-five minutes passed and Mark lost interest. He wasn't sure if he wanted to meet a strange guy anymore. His heart raced when he heard Tony's voice on the phone.

"Where you at?"

"Yuh downtown?"

"I'm by Pathmark."

"Mi on Maple Street by de hospital. Tek Van Buren, the red building on de left."

"Okay, I'll be there in a few minutes. I'm driving a yellow I-Roc Z."

"A wat?"

Tony's yellow Camaro pulled into the parking lot. The engine barked. Mark unlocked the apartment door and ran outside to meet him before he blew the horn.

"Hey."

"Hey, what's up?"

Tony looked nothing like his description on the phone. His thirty-two inch, athletic waist was closer to a thirty-six beer belly, and his six-feet-two height looked more five-feet-ten by the way his torso slumped in the car seat. He had hair all over his body, with long curly strands peeping out from the back of his tank. At least he wasn't lying when he said he was Italian. He was nothing like what Mark imagined. He felt obligated to go with him. If not for any other reason than to get off.

Soon they were driving down Connecticut Avenue. Tony took the scenic route on Merritt Parkway. They drove in silence. Tony rubbed his crotch, motioning Mark to feel his bulge. Mark pretended he wasn't that kind of guy, not in the car. Tony pulled off the freeway at Exit 37. A few miles later he entered a dark dirt road with a house hidden by overgrown foliage. He got out of his car and gave Mark a bear hug, picking him off the ground, and pinning him against the car door. He pulled up mark's shirt and bit his nipple. Mark held him off when he poked his finger in his anus.

"Wi jus playing round, right? Can wi guh inside?"

At the front door, a black pit bull jumped on Mark and knocked him to the ground. He yelled for help. The dog panted over his chest and licked his face.

119

"Don't worry, he's not bad, jus' playful."

"Get him awffa mi!"

"That's enough Bones, stop!"

The dog ran to the kitchen and peed on the floor. Tony pulled off his shirt and wrestled Mark on the couch. Mark didn't like the rough play.

"You wanna play right?"

"Yuh nuh hab nothing fi drink first?"

As Mark sat on the couch, Tony took his belt to tie around Mark's neck. Mark wasn't sure what Tony had in mind and he didn't want to find out.

"Wah yuh doin'? Get de fuck awffa mi!"

"I'm just playing dude."

"Mi nuh like it! Mi waan fi leave!"

"Make me come first."

Mark sighed and gripped Tony's hairy cock. He pulled the shaft to hurt him, but Tony moaned with pleasure. He started to sweat and rolled his eyes. Within seconds he came in Mark's palm. Mark pushed him off and walked to the bathroom to wipe his hands. When he returned Tony's face was hard.

"Where you want me to drop you? I'm not driving all the way back to Norwalk."

Mark felt like a ten dollar whore.

"Yuh can drap mi awffa de train station. A guess."

"Hold on. I gotta piss."

Mark sucked his teeth.

"Yuh fucking asshole."

Bones returned to the living room and licked his feet. He pulled away and kicked the dog in the ribs. The dog made and horrific squeal and dashed to the bedroom.

"What was that?" Tony asked.

Mark felt stale and dirty on the train. He could still smell Tony's sweat on him. He sneaked into the apartment, took a shower, and discarded his clothes in the laundry basket. He dialed the Acme Dating line and deleted his membership.

Mark took the fifteen minute bus ride to Shady Beach in East Norwalk. He looked at the shoreline. They were only a few sunbathers; no one was in the water. He walked to the adjoining park and saw what appeared to be a father and his son playing miniature golf. There were teenagers playing basketball in the parking lot. He strolled into the video arcade to play Ms. Pac-Man. He grew bored and headed back to the bus stop.

A black vintage Mercedes stopped at the bus stop, and a gray hair man rolled down the passenger window and asked if he wanted a ride. Mark gritted his teeth and declined. He asked Mark if he was going downtown. Mark gritted his teeth again and nodded. He persisted. Mark declined again. He said he was on his way home to Wilton and it wasn't out of the way. Mark accepted the ride when he heard Wilton because it was one of the richest places to live in the America.

"I'm Aaron," the driver said.

Mark forced a smile.

"Andrew," he said.

"Where are you going?"

"Downtown."

Aaron looked distinguished with salt and pepper hair and a lean physique, like a washed-up actor or someone used to attention. He wore a green cashmere sweater with light blue seersucker pants and brown suede

121

moccasins. His wrinkled eyes were blue and his hands looked delicate. He had a groomed mustache and diamond studs in his ears. He smelled like expensive aftershave and flavored smoke. He opened his glove compartment, pulled out a cigar, and changed the radio station to jazz.

"Would you like to come with me to the country club? Have a drink?"

"A drink? A tree in de afternoon."

"Would you like to come anyway?"

"Nat really."

"Maybe another time?"

He gave Mark his business card that read Dr. Aaron Bloomberg, College of Liberal Arts and Sciences, University of Connecticut.

"Wah yuh teach?"

"Sociology. I'm on a sabbatical."

Mark thought of Mr. Nwosu and his unbearable crush. Aaron parked at the terminal and waited for Mark's bus to pull up. He looked at Mark with interest like he was a blank canvass, waiting for its first stroke of paint. Mark waved goodbye and promised to call.

A few days later he saw Aaron driving out from the farmer's market on Connecticut Avenue. He looked the other way, but Aaron recognized him.

"I thought you were going to call."

"Sarry. Mi figet."

"Wanna go for a drive? After I drop off the groceries."

"Sure, eef yuh pramise fi drap mi home afta."

"I promise I'll show you a good time."

Aaron pulled the top down and cruised to his house. The house was as Mark imagined - massive. He sat in the car and looked at the lake behind the backyard. He wished Aaron was thirty years younger, but knew if he was, Aaron wouldn't have given him the time of day. *It seems they aim lower when they get older*, he thought. He wasn't flattered by Aaron's interest. He felt like he was his last resort.

Aaron took Mark on a drive to Shady Beach, circled the parking lot and then to the Maritime Center. He drove past Compo Beach and stopped by the Cedar Brooks Café on Post Road. He told Mark it was the oldest gay bar in Connecticut, and the second oldest in the nation. Mark tried the Sea Breeze Aaron recommended. He liked the taste and ordered another glass. He felt giddy and their conversation was filled with laughter.

Mark thought he could learn a lot from Aaron as he was older and sophisticated. When Aaron tried to kiss him, Mark decided it was time to go home. Aaron apologized Mark told him he wasn't attracted to older guys. He told Aaron they could be friends and he would like to hang out with him again, even though he knew he would.

Chapter Seven

Howard University, by reputation, is the premier historically black university in the world. Located in Washington, D.C., it is often referred to as *The Mecca* or the "black Harvard." Its alumni roster read like a who's who in America's black history to present luminaries in every sector of society. Mark choose Howard over New York University and Yale because of the hit television sitcom *A Different World*. It painted a picture of an ideal black college where its references came from Howard. It was the answer 286 miles away from Daphne.

When Mark checked into the co-ed dormitory on 16th Street, he didn't mind that the building looked uninhabitable. The humid air seeped through the weather-beaten windows with police sirens racing up the congested streets. He sat on his twin bed on the sixth floor and it felt like a new beginning - the promise of something.

When his roommate arrived, he had an uncomfortable sense of recognition after noticing his limp wrist and switching hips. He wondered how Residence Life knew they were pairing two closeted boys as roommates, away from the self-professed thugged-out children of buppies, happy to be at Howard University after being the only black student in their high school's graduating class.

Dr. Dre's "Let Me Ride," blasted its west coast G-Funk through the dormitory. The smell of Phillies Blunt and St. Ides forty-ounce malt liquor permeated the air along with burnt microwaved popcorn and spicy Ramen noodles. Girls dressed in Hello Kitty pajamas and bunny slippers, listening to Mary J. Blige's "What's The 411" flirted with boys pretending they were the fifth member of Jodeci. They had an open door policy for anyone who could hang until four in the morning. Mark thought it was better than *A Different World*, and it was only the first weekend.

When Mark's Campus Pal realized he was older and possibly gay, he avoided him. Mark gravitated to the international student body and made friends amongst members of the Caribbean Student Association. He saw Richie, his high school prefect who gave him a detention during his Brian infatuation phase. He squashed his resentment and befriended him.

They were a group of students from wealthy Caribbean families, who could afford the doubled tuition and board payable in US currency. Although the Caribbean students came from wealthy families, they were not part of the social elite on campus because they were not American born. They had separate social activities – weekend fetes off campus, ski trips to Pennsylvania, outings to Kings Dominion and movie nights at Union Station. They had their own territories outside Douglas Hall and at the Punch Out. They were proud of their dialects and other Caribbean traits. They went home during holiday breaks, dined at Caribbean restaurants on Georgia Avenue, and maintained and promoted their heritage. Only a few assimilated.

Ritchie was a senior in the School of Architecture on a full scholarship. He had a wide network of friends from the Caribbean. He lived in a house on 13ᵗʰ Street with Howard undergrads from other islands. He was popular amongst the Caribbean students, although he spent more Friday nights building models for his Monday morning critiques, rather than going to the CSA dances at Club Cache.

Mark liked Ritchie. He was an upgraded version of Brian, half Chinese-Jamaican raised in Red Hills, a posh area in Kingston. Mark felt privileged with his green card, coming to Howard from Connecticut and not a flight on Air Jamaica. He frequented Ritchie's apartment and they would lie in bed, entertained by *In Living Color* late at night. He hung around Ritchie when he felt awkward around his American peers.

He developed a crush and when Sade sang "No Ordinary Love," it felt like she was telling his whole life with her lyrics. One night, Mark slept at Ritchie's apartment and touched him when the lights went off. When Ritchie didn't respond the way Mark wanted, he knew their friendship was over.

When Ritchie graduated summa cum laude and returned to Jamaica, Mark made no further attempts to befriend any of his peers from the islands. He wanted to shed his debilitating Caribbean skin and appear American. He withdrew from the Caribbean Students Association and disassociated with anyone Caribbean. He detested the "No problem mon" stereotype, the Jamaican Bobsleigh jokes, and anything Jamaican. He wanted distance from his culture to assume an all-round college experience and assimilate into being American for what he thought it meant.

He not only wanted to feel like he belonged at Howard University with the privileged African American students, he wanted to be amongst the popular crowd, the Homecoming Fashion Show squad - the most coveted social group and image builder on campus. Howard had long been known as a fashion school for the black elite. In the '80s, Jack and Jill girls made one leap from their debutante balls to Howard, dressed in mink coats and driving Mercedes. The new, hardcore, gangsta rap scene with its "keep it real" motto infiltrated the campus and created a dent in that behavior. However, acquiring the hip hop persona didn't come cheap. Being decked out in Mecca USA, Cross Colors and Marithe Francois Girbaud jeans with a pair of Air Jordans cost a lot of money. Not everyone could afford to "keep it real."

Mark was not athletic. The chances of being recruited by a fraternity was nil and a student government post was unheard of for a freshman. His only outlet to become popular on campus was to be a member of the fashion show squad. He thought he knew how to model. He had demonstrated his ability to cut-throat queens.

At the tryouts in Blackburn Auditorium, he was stumped when he saw the fashion show coordinators, Dean and Darren, demonstrate what was known as the Howard walk. It was aggressive and obnoxious. Their legs stomped and arms ticked like marching soldiers. It was a colorful presentation, but it was nothing from an international catwalk. It was their trademark, and soon every student was seen walking on the yard with a similar strut on their way to class.

Mark didn't make the squad his freshman year. His walk wasn't masculine enough for the two gay coordinators. His thrift wardrobe, eclectic amongst the fine arts students, was ridiculed by members of fashion show squad. They were a group with starter credit cards who purchased Ralph Lauren and Tommy Hilfiger gear. They felt better than their colleagues waiting in line for Stafford Loan checks.

The next semester, Mark began to shed his Caribbean skin and tried to assimilate. His accent shifted to a pseudo-British twang, after lying his father was from London. When the task proved difficult to keep up, he drifted towards Ebonics, explaining he grew up in Connecticut.

As he adapted easily, he was troubled by his effeminate manner and less about his sexuality. He knew he was gay and didn't want to deal with being harassed and ridiculed because he wasn't as masculine as he wished. He wasn't as successful as the other gay students who were able to monitor their mannerisms to deflect the bashing.

The first day on campus, Mark was labeled "the gay guy." A tag that meant having girlfriends who were entertained by his candor. He wasn't surprised to enter a classroom and hear something disparaging or the students snickering. He knew if he walked by the Caribbean students at Douglas Hall he was going to be called a *batty bwoy*. When in a group, he was tolerated by the boys, but none wanted to be seen alone with him on the yard, or worse, visit his dorm room. Howard's homophobic culture wasn't only perpetuated by the hip-hop presence, but the black culture in general. His existence on campus was different from the straight students' "Ain't no party like a HU party" experience. He felt alone.

The students who were gay avoided Mark because he was too obvious. They sought refuge in weekly poetry slams and hid behind ambiguous verses. They had hushed excursions to Bachelor's Mill, a gay club in North East Washington, DC.

Some of the girls made Mark's loneliness tolerable. NeFah from Chicago, was a hybrid of hip-hop and afrocentricity. Her hairstyles varied weekly from braids, afro, twists and flat iron pressed. Her sisterly qualities combated Mark's isolation. When he was desperately trying to assimilate, she was busy dropping beats on her radio spot at WHBC and soliciting students to buy tickets on a Black Star Liner prototype, for their

129

expatriation back home. Sometimes they had sleep overs and Mark performed his renditions of Sade ballads, wishing she was Richie.

Connie from California came with sunshine. She was bubbly, eager to please and the token plus size girl selected for the fashion shows. She was a Mathematics major who blended with the fine arts crowd. When Mark saw her, he didn't mind no one thought they had a romantic connection.

He made the fashion show squad his sophomore year and it felt better than his 4.0 grade point average. At the fashion show, the veterans took the spotlight. Their pictures were on the front page of *The Hilltop* and in the pages of the *Bison* yearbook. History major, Anandale Louise opened the lingerie scene straggling a guy. It made the faculty sitting in the front row seats cringe. She tested the censors and the students whistled with approval for her daring feats. Eli, the campus heartthrob, made the girls scream when he strutted down the runway in barely there Speedos.

When Mark walked down the runway, he felt like an affirmative action mandate that went wrong. The red two piece suit was too big for his skinny body and his orange hair never quite achieved the bleached blond SisQo look the dye was intended for.

Although he was overlooked, it was an official credential on campus. "Hi, I'm Mark. I was in the fashion show," was how he introduced himself. He felt like he had arrived and went on a date with Summer, a demure, dark-skinned beauty with slanted eyes and a slick cropped bob. Summer was one of the few students from Washington, DC. She wasn't the stereotypical gum popping, go-go dancing, neck shaking, easily provoked DC girl. She grew up in the city with Jack and Jill grooming.

They went to a cafe in Adams Morgan and Mark tried to impress her by being the type of guy she liked. He thought it was how charming boys behaved. They talked about their backgrounds, interests at Howard, and future goals after graduation. The most memorable thing for Mark was not his first date with a girl, but the thrill of ordering a cappuccino and feeling sophisticated. After dinner, they walked through Malcolm X Park. It was obvious that Summer's goodnight peck on the cheek was gratitude for a free meal, and it was nothing for Mark to brag about because the next day on campus she still saw him as "the gay guy."

Mark wandered off campus and discovered a world he never knew existed. Rainbow flags soared in Dupont Circle, the heartbeat of the gay scene in Washington, DC. Connecticut Avenue and P Street were the epicenter of gay bars, bookstores, restaurants, and shops catering to a gay clientele. Men walked down sidewalks holding hands. They curled up on park benches. It looked like a new world where being gay was the norm.

He was amazed by the openness of everything gay for sale at Lambda Rising bookstore - photo books of naked men, Mapplethorpe's portraits of men in fetish sexual acts, Tom Bianchi's poolside orgies, and Tom of Finland's erotic drawings. On the shelves were gay magazines with pictures of men holding hands and kissing, and commentaries from a gay point of view. Gay novels were displayed on tables. These books told about the invisible lives of gay men - their sexual conquests and escapades.

Gay men strolled in and out of the store like a leisurely early evening routine. No one looked over their shoulders for fear of being brutalized. Everyone went about their business as they intended. Mark lingered, hoping he'd see someone from campus to form a bond.

The gay strip ended at 22nd and P Street. It was a popular spot because Badlands and the Fireplace, two gay bars, shared the same block. SoHo

131

coffee shop was located between these bars and it had a strong gay following. Mark went across the street one night, heading to Rock Creek Park, and discovered the notorious "P Street Beach." By day, it was a patch of grass the size of a football field, where residents laid out towels to soak up the sun and college boys played football. At night, gay men cruised the forested paths along the river like nocturnal animals, looking for anonymous sex.

Dupont Circle became Mark's mecca. He met other gay college students who found their campuses stifling. They came from Georgetown, American, George Washington, University of the District of Columbia, University of Maryland and even a small group of deaf and mute students from Gallaudet University. On Tuesday nights, they found themselves at Cobalt Lounge for the two dollar specials.

It was there he met Aamir and Guia. They sat at the bar looking inebriated too early. Aamir was the older of the two - pushing thirty - from Afghanistan. He lived in Virginia and waited tables at a restaurant in Adams Morgan. He squandered his paycheck on alcohol and clothes. He had ended up at an after party on R Street and stumbled into Cobalt, his new hangout. He was like a teenager on a temporary high, partaking with urgency, aware it would disappear when he returned to being a suppressed man living with Muslim parents. He drank, smoked, and laughed freely and was available for the next dance, the next bump, or the next trick.

Guia was twenty-two, half Cuban and half white. His Spanish heredity was only apparent when he spoke to his family on the phone. He was cute and petite. He had been to Paris for a semester and returned with an alvedar trill and a penchant for Gauloises cigarettes. He majored in Art History at Georgetown University on a full ride thanks to his father, a faculty member.

132

Guia could get any guy, and he knew it. He was everybody's type. He had green eyes and rock star hair. His lips were always dry. He soothed them with cherry lip balm, which he was never seen without. His acne had cleared and he was looking to score drugs, get drunk or laid and make it to his ten o'clock lecture.

Aamir and Guia would never have been friends if they both weren't gay, attractive, and loved coke. They had only met a few days earlier, and were already inseparable. They understood that regardless how their night progressed, they would end up in Guia's bed, passed out or having drunk sloppy sex. When Mark spotted Aamir and Guia, he felt like a kindred spirit in their multi-national mix - the third wheel to an impossible ride fueled by sex, drugs and six am after parties.

Guia was on the guest list at every club and invited to every after party in the finest townhouses in Georgetown because he knew where to find the drugs and he kept suppliers with a steady stream of customers. Aamir and Mark were always up for the ride. Mark changed his early morning classes to a mid-day schedule, and Aamir's evening work shift accommodated the late night debauchery. They became regular fixtures at Cobalt Lounge.

On Mondays, Mark hung out with Cheng, a South Korean, burgeoning drag queen, who had a gig singing traditional Korean folk songs at a basement tea house in Adams Morgan. He studied drawing at the Corcoran School of Arts and had an apartment on 16th Street, across the street from Mark's dorm. Cheng was still learning English, and his life's ambition was to have a white American boyfriend.

Mark met Kookobird at Tracks. The first time he went to Tracks in South East DC, he was robbed at gun-point two blocks from the club. Three black inner-city teenagers made off with twenty dollars and his Perry

Ellis wallet. He never bothered to report it because he was eager to get to Tracks to be on the guest list. The wallet and cash would be long gone before a cop showed up in that neighborhood.

That night was filled with thrills. The moment Mark entered the club, he knew it was time to escape the closet and embrace his gayness. The main dance floor easily occupied a few hundred sweating dancers, with a smaller room populated with club kids. Outside, a volleyball court with sand and metal seats was next to a cement platform, which served as the third dance floor for anyone who wanted attention.

Kookobird was Demante's alter ego. A shy, skinny, black boy from Richmond that at night became a popular club kid. He was all legs and arms, and yards of duct tape. He did the rounds at Tracks dressed like a spectacle. He danced like an epileptic. He dipped and kicked like a gymnast. He wore custom made fourteen inch platform shoes. The heels were decorated with bottle caps or anything that could be crazy glued. His trademark neon hair matched whatever jacket he wore. His could be spotted within the crowd dancing from the main platform.

There were the three Chrises. The older Chris was a pale, athletic built white boy with large blue eyes. He was a psychology major at the University of Maryland. He cooked special K in his apartment and sold it in the clubs. The first time Mark met Chris, he planted a wet kiss on his lips and every time thereafter. He had an animated smile and a questioning face like he was trapped in his childhood. He orbited another world based on his prescription of oversized white T-Shirts, blue jeans, and zip lock bags. He was a friendly drug dealer with a "try it before you buy it" policy. It attracted pasty white teenagers with fake IDs, congregating at the restroom stalls. His boyfriend Kris wandered in and out of the group's psyche like a mysterious cat, showing his presence when it was time for another drink or another bump.

Christian was the sassy Latino of the group. He was a Yeoman in the Navy with a groomed, military box cut. His outfits, which he changed while speeding away from Fort Detrick military base on his way to the club, were always colorful like a nine-pointed star Mexican piñata. He always checked his watch to see if he had enough time to make it back to base, change his clothes, wash the makeup off, and duck into his dorm room before any of the military guys suspected.

Ori and Wallis were from somewhere in the Middle East. They were also undergrads at the University of Maryland, both with undecided majors. They usually arrived at the club as part of Chris' entourage with water bottles in hand and chewing gum. Ori only dated white guys, and he was very selective because his parents were wealthy. Wallis was the sluttier of the two and didn't have a preference as long as they were muscular and well hung.

David belonged to Mark's group of friends, but he had very little time for the clubs. He was a working boy kept busy by out-call from lonely men in the metro area willing to pay $200 for his pretty boy appeal. He preferred raves at warehouses and liked the Gothic underworld. He was very friendly and curious to try anything. He was the most unique kid of the bunch, but often second-guessed himself.

Petro was from Venice, Italy. He was a medical student in the international exchange program at Georgetown University. He had lived throughout Europe, attended boarding schools in Switzerland and Germany, and spoke four languages. He looked like a coked-out version of Calvin Klein model, Michael Bergin.

Mark's circle of friends all had sex with each other at one point in their friendship, but the details were cloudy. They all slurped from the same drink and shared bumps in the restroom stalls. They all went to after-parties at stranger's houses and it turned into an orgy. They participated in each other's lives, accepted and loved each other, and were on the same path of self-exploration and discovery.

It was dubbed the "Storm of the Century" or the Great Blizzard of 1993. Classes were suspended and the snow was twelve inches in some areas. Everywhere was impassable except the metro. Mark was dressed in a ten-inch platform shoes, leather pants, a turmoil undershirt, and his favorite fake fur jacket. He was determined to walk through the snow to meet his friends and watch Kookobird perform Armand Van Helden's "The Witch Doctor."

Everyone was at Tracks. Aamir and Guia sat outside on the steps. Ori and Wallis were flexing their muscles in a game of snow volleyball. Cheng was dancing in the small room with a scrawny white guy he'd recently met. Chris, Kris and Christian were busy in a restroom stall. Mark was dancing with David's friend Lea, who was high on acid. She was one of the ravers that came to Tracks when there were no other parties. She was half white and Thai with long black hair streaked with blond and red highlights that went down to her butt. She was friendly, always smiling and flirting with the gay boys to garner a free drink or a bump.

Mark was intrigued by the way she danced with him - tossing her hair over his face, pushing her breasts against his chest, and rubbing her crotch against his thigh. Other ravers danced around them. Ashley, a blond skater boy with a swimmer's build, carried her to a corner by the speakers. He liked girls, but welcomed attention from boys. When Mark saw them kissing, he wanted to join in the spit swapping. They called him and they danced around each other, touching and kissing.

They took a break when Kookobird performed then continued on the main dance floor. Mark liked the idea of a threesome with a girl and guy. Kissing Lea felt like the thing you did with a girl, which he thought would have been less appealing if Ashley wasn't there. While they danced she slipped a tablet on her tongue and coerced him to take it. He obeyed, and she did the same to Ashley. Mark wished he felt this way sober. They left Tracks and headed back to his dorm room - slipping in the building when the security guard left his desk.

They listened to Ashley's mix tapes and finished a bottle of vodka before passing out. When Mark woke up, Ashley and Lea were making out. Ashley made an unskilled attempt to undo Lea's bra straps. Mark moved his arms around Ashley, released his belt and pulled off his shorts. Lea smiled at Mark kissing Ashley, then played with his hair and kissed the back of his neck.

They devoured each other. Ashley pulled down Lea's panties. She kneeled on the floor and he entered her without force. Mark stood next to Ashley and unbuckled his pants. Ashley slipped his mouth around Mark's cock. Lea moaned as Ashley pounded in her. Mark held Ashley's head and kept his mouth steady. He kissed Ashley then Lea as she shook like a leaf in the wind. Ashley pulled out and came. Lea fell flat on her stomach. He fell on top of her and Mark held them close.

They were silent. Sunrise brimmed the horizon. The air conditioner hummed. Lonely cars crawled up Georgia Avenue. The drugs slowly lost its hold and in their nakedness they weren't sure what had transpired or what led them there. Lea grabbed her skirt and stumbled to the bathroom. Ashley wiped his face and followed. Mark waited for them to return and made an attempt to clean up the room. He heard them laughing in the shower. He joined, and they washed themselves to sobriety.

The next semester, Mark began to flaunt his gayness on campus when he won the bid to coordinate the homecoming fashion show. It was a title he wore with pride because it meant the students elected to maintain Howard's conservative regime were giving him the opportunity to express himself, under the watchful eyes of a censored Homecoming Steering Committee.

Mark was going through his club kid phase. His wardrobe changed drastically. His twisted hair began to lock with the tips bleached blond. Vintage plaid pants and ripped jeans became a daily staple, along with T-shirts and an assortment of fake fur jackets. When he wanted a little more attention, he wore his ten-inch platform shoes and showed off in front of the fine arts building.

He skipped hanging around his peers at Howard. The people he coveted during his freshman and sophomore years were dismissed. He preferred the multicultural pseudo-family he saw every night. He no longer cared about being the token "gay guy" they tolerated. Like his Caribbean background, he shunned his black skin with mild doses of self-hate, rejecting black men that found him attractive. His one-night stands were usually with men that looked nothing like him.

A crowd stood in line for hours to purchase tickets to the homecoming fashion show. By mid-day, the show was sold out and the student population was on edge because the rehearsals promised a different fashion show from what was expected. With Mark at the helm, they weren't sure what was in store for the campus.

The fashion show's theme was "Make Your Mark," and its objective was to challenge the status quo. It wasn't about fashion. No attempt was made to showcase a designer's forthcoming collection. The clothing came from department stores that catered to Howard's demographics - independent designers from the DC metropolitan area, and shops on Georgia Avenue that needed the publicity.

The curtains rose to a freestyle dance with two oiled, muscular, male models dressed in black spandex, waving tree branches amongst a group of scantily clad female dancers with masks. Nubia opened the show to Lords of Acid's "The Most Wonderful Girl." She lip-synced, *'I'm fucking beautiful! I'm the greatest thing I've ever seen! God I love myself!"* She flashed her long ponytail weave and stomped down the runway. Her outfit, which looked like it was on sale was insignificant to her attitude. Her face conveyed a "Don't fuck with me" message Howard women were known to deliver.

The girls walked in unison, posed with precision and turned according to the choreography. The first timers and veterans shared the spotlight. Mark's freshman muse, Juliana, a moon-face, brown skinned girl from California, dazzled the crowd. Her walk was effortless like she was gliding on air. At the end of the scene, Mark grabbed a microphone backstage and echoed the song's phrase, *'I wanna touch myself!"* Vonette joined in. They mouthed sounds alluding to masturbation. The audience shifted with discomfort.

In the second scene, the girls were atypical to the model ideal. They were shorter, rounder and quirkier looking to be considered models, but Mark made them shine. Vonette ran through the aisles of Cramton Auditorium dressed in a wedding dress like a hysterical bride of Frankenstein. The

139

audience was amused by her dramatics. She stumbled and rolled when she got back onstage. The techno beats transcended a state of chaos, but the message was lost. The students were more interested in seeing friends that had finally made it in a fashion show.

The general mood was Mark knew how to make the girls look beautiful. He had demonstrated it in the way he taught them to walk, pose, and turn. They were uneasy about what he would do to the guys. Were they going to be emasculated? Were they going to become something unlike the Howard man - the strong black *brotha*?

The mostly female audience was filled to capacity. When the curtains parted, they roared at the models' transformation from boys to men. The guys walked with a cool, machismo air like matinee idols to Sinead O'Connor's "I Am Stretched on Your Grave." The girls and some bold-face boys screamed with delight.

The swimsuit scene brought the crowd to their feet. Blood boiled as they gazed at the toned bodies. Joel made the muscles in their chest dance to the girls delight. Ana's curves caused the boys to sweat. The models had devoted hours to rigorous workout routines to achieve the impressive results. Models with firm asses, six packs and defined chests abounded. Madonna's "Bedtime Stories" played to Mark's direction alluding to sex positions. The rumor that the girls would walk topless down the runway to Grace Jones' "I'm Not Perfect (But I'm Perfect for you)" was put to rest.

The scenes calmed fears in the audience. They were relieved they weren't exposed to anything taboo, but Mark had a surprise the censors could only sit and watch. The models were warned if they did anything risqué the head of the homecoming steering committee would pull the curtain and end the show. Mark knew they were bluffing. If that happened, the upset audience would have caused a riot.

When the guys entered the runway, they were dressed in sarongs. A voice whispered, *"They were laughing, dancing. I mean screaming all over the place, riveting their bodies in total abandon. I mean it was disgusting!"* Unbeknownst to anyone, the deejay played Moonwalker's underground track featuring Ultra Nate, "10,000 Screaming Faggots."

The audience was busy cheering and scrutinizing bodies. Mark burst onstage wearing a dress. He had a mask on his face a held a leather whip. In the song, a flamboyant voice facetiously declared, *"I am not a homosexual!"* Mark removed the mask and laughed. He rolled on the floor and touched himself. As the guys flooded the stage, the song continued, *"Faggies here! Faggies there! Faggots everywhere!"* Mark watched with glee as the homophobic crowd gasped with disbelief. Backstage, the models were amused. They thought it was a stunt only Mark could get away with, and not risk the threat of a retaliation.

At the show's finale, Mark recreated what happened at Tracks on any given Sunday night. Nine Inch Nails' "Closer" played. The models dressed in black leather attire, danced, touched, and flirted, gyrating their bodies to Trent Reznor shouting *"I wanna fuck you like an animal!"* Girls clung to each other with suggestive poses. Mark's off-campus gay friends walked down the runway with their arms around each other. Meanwhile, he stood center stage hugging Aamir and Guia, acting as ring leader. He encouraged them to do more than what was tolerated.

A faculty member stormed out the auditorium. Mark crawled on the floor and lay on his back, gyrating his hips in the air. The crowd booed. They cheered when a girl mounted him. He removed a microphone from his crotch and moaned *"Do you like?"*

The next day the campus was abuzz by what they witnessed. Some said it was the best homecoming fashion show they had ever seen. Mark felt like he was floating on the clouds. The students regarded him as "the talented gay guy," and his opinion was no longer overlooked. *The Washington Post* feature on Howard's homecoming highlighted the fashion show. The review said the show pushed buttons, but it was entertaining. Mark felt like a star.

The Homecoming Steering Committee and faculty members who saw the show had another opinion. They thought Mark's risqué direction threatened Howard's image. He had to be reprimanded. The contacted coordinator's stipend was retracted and he was barred from living in the dorms. No one complained that the fashion show had grossed an all-time profit, and it was the highest grossing event throughout the money making week.

At the end of the school year, Mark flunked his senior classes and failed to graduate. He watched Carol collect her diploma and took pictures at her graduation dinner. She played "Everybody's Free to Wear Sunscreen" and smiled like she was going to conquer the world. Some members of the fashion show squad also moved on. Anandale Louise became the new talk show host at BET. Lena graced the cover of *Essence* magazine and Dean formed a modeling agency. Vonette got a part on a soap opera. Even Patrick, the weird guy, began assisting a top fashion photographer.

Mark worked at a bookstore in Dupont Circle and moved to a quaint two-bedroom house on Bryant Street. It was owned by Dr. Bennett, an English professor from Guyana. She was Natalia's mother, the girl that straddled him in the fashion show. It got the attention of the football players. When Natalia made the rounds on campus with the athletes, she grew bored of her white, high school boyfriend.

Natalia tried out for the Ooh La La squad, the dancers who accompanied the marching band. After a night of an alcohol induced game of truth or dare, the girls divulged secrets about their sisters - secrets capable of damaging reputations, destroying friendships, and ending courtships. When she became the newest member of the squad, the incentive of hooking up with a band member seemed passé.

Her sister, Desiree, shared the house with Mark. She had an appealing fragility and a mentally challenged disposition. During rush week, she served as the pleasure doll for the new Q Dogs of Omega Psi Phi. She showed up at basketball games and flashed the crowd her surgically enhanced, double D breasts. When Mark moved in, his failed grades and recreational drug use were overshadowed by Desiree's hunt.

Desiree pursued him unrelentingly. She walked around the house in loose lingerie. She left the bathroom door opened when she lathered her naked body behind the transparent shower curtain. She made a show of being obvious during sex with boyfriends. Natalia told her she was wasting her time because Mark was decidedly gay. She then mentioned her hairdresser, makeup artist, pet groomer, nurse, and priest who were all gay, and asked Mark if he wanted to have a potluck.

When Dr. Bennett saw her daughter mounted Mark and walked out the fashion show, she couldn't hold her head up during her lectures. She worried about what people thought of her and Natalia. She visited her second house on Bryant Street before heading home to Bethesda, hoping to have a talk with her daughter. Natalia avoided her mother. She ignored

143

her calls and emails. Dr. Bennett knew the students had forgotten Natalia's antics, but the faculty were less forgiving.

The next semester, Natalia was alarmed when she didn't receive her tuition waiver because her mother discontinued her enrollment. Dr. Bennett delivered the same treatment. She avoided Natalia. Natalia was enraged. She blamed Mark. She kicked open his bedroom door and demanded that he smooth things over with her mother.

Mark was taking an afternoon nap before going to work. He was more annoyed than frightened. He refused and her screams weren't enough. She threw objects at him. Mark mocked her Guyanese accent. When she grabbed a kitchen knife, he realized she was serious.

They fought like rabid animals. Natalia spat, slapped and kicked. She used anything she could get her hands on. Mark punched her after a defensive wound. He didn't want to fight a girl, but Natalia was acting like one. He regretted moving into the house and befriending her. He thought she had only accepted his friendship because he was another means for her to be popular on campus.

The neighbors called the police. Mark left the house before they arrived to avoid another confrontation, and fearing he would be arrested. He spent the night with his friend Tina, a graduate student with a baby, who he often ran to when he was in trouble. She made him dinner and tried to ease his discontent with her poetry. When Mark returned to the house the next day, the locks were changed and his clothes and other belonging met him at the curb.

Chapter Eight

"Roommate?" David asked. "Sure."

"Oh tank God!" Mark said.

"For how long?" David asked

"Jus a few week," Mark said. "A expecting money. A will fine a apartment."

"Okay, can I borrow your platform shoes?" David asked.

"Of course! I'll be dere in a few hours," Mark said.

Mark boarded the G2 on Bryant Street to Dupont Circle. He walked with a garbage bag of clothes to David' apartment on Massachusetts Avenue. He rang the intercom and waited for David to poke out the window of his studio on the sixth floor. David had received a call from his escort agency. He handed Mark his keys while munching on a cinnamon roll and muttered he was on his way to meet a "friend" at The Fireplace. He fed a squirrel the roll, puffed on a cigarette while singing - *"The boy with the cold hard cash is always Mr. Right"* and headed to P Street.

Mark walked into David's studio and pulled the blinds to let in sunlight. A bed in the corner was covered with a threadbare black sheet with sketches of Peter Pan. A small boom-box sat on the mattress with a folder containing about fifty CDs. The light brown carpet had stains and cigarette burns. On a table by the wall was a small microwave and an electric coffee pot. The

145

kitchen sink was piled high with dirty dishes. The refrigerator door was decorated with party flyers. Inside, it contained two ice trays and a bottle of ketchup.

Mark stood at the window looking at cars racing up Massachusetts Avenue. He lit a cigarette and gazed across the street at the American flag blowing in the wind. He drifted in his thoughts, feeling uncertain about the future. He killed the cigarette in a can on the windowsill, pulled the blinds, and lay on the bed. He gazed at the ceiling, followed the cracks, and closed his eyes and fell asleep.

David returned after midnight and flicked on the lights. He rummaged through Mark's garbage bag and found his platform shoes. He played his Madonna CD and danced around the apartment. Mark woke up disappointed that his life wasn't just a bad dream. David seemed relieved his meeting went well.

"Hey girl! You're not goin' out?" David asked.

"Nat really," Mark said. "I'm exhausted."

"Ori and Guia coming over. We're going to a party on U Street."

"I'll pass."

David danced unbalanced in Mark's platform shoes. He walked into the bathroom to change into his favorite black jeans and black lace shirt. He looked like a vampire. He slicked back his hair and painted his thin lips black.

"You see my rings?" David asked. "They were on the bed."

Mark opened his tired eyes.

"My silver rings!" David said. "They go with my outfit."

"Where yuh left dem?" Mark asked. "Yuh know I wouldn't take dem."

Mark found the rings under the sheets and tried to return to sleep. David spun around waiting for Mark's appraisal. His thin body was swallowed up by the shirt. His bony shoulders held it up like a hanger. Mark smiled and waved him off.

"Yuh luk fierce girl."

"Can I borrow your black fur vest you wore at Tracks last week?"

"It might be dirty."

David had fished it out and returned from the bathroom for another inspection.

"Yuh going to be hot."

David smiled.

"I'm hot! I know it!"

Mark rolled his eyes.

"A hot mess."

Aamir and Guia were downstairs, shouting in the intercom.

"Heeeellllooooooooo!"

"Hold on."

David pranced around in the room then returned to the bathroom and checked his outfit. Mark hadn't seen Aamir in weeks. Guia said he went to Afghanistan with his parents for the summer and had a surprise. Before David open the door, he stood before Mark for a compliment.

"Yuh luk good girl!"

Aamir entered the apartment with Guia on his back and dropped him beside Mark on the bed. Guia placed a wet kiss on Mark's lips. Mark tried to smile. He knew revealing that he was kicked out and crashing with David wouldn't look good.

"You would never guess what happened?" Guia said.

147

"Wat, yuh guys got marrid?" Mark asked.

They laughed. David looked on, playing with his hair. Mark wasn't in the mood for laughing. The noise was swallowed up by his stern face.

"No, but Aamir did!" Guia said.

"To who?" Mark asked.

"A real live fish!" Aamir said.

"Are you kidding?" David asked.

Aamir said his parents arranged a marriage between him and a girl named Shari. Mark was shocked. He said his uncle accused him of being a *bacha baz* and it offended his parents. He agreed to the marriage because Shari's visa would take a year, enough time for him to tell his parents he was gay and save enough money to move out.

Mark asked why he went through with it. Aamir said his uncle was prominent in the Taliban, and didn't want anything to do with the family until his suspicions were addressed. He warned if Aamir didn't marry, he faced the risk of being publicly executed for engaging in sodomy. It was a family reunion, but they decided on the arranged marriage because Shari's family made a lucrative offer.

"Suh, how was de wedding night?" Mark asked.

Aamir raised his hand to cover his mouth.

"The worst! Her father got us a honeymoon suite in this posh hotel, the size of the Taj Mahal," Aamir said. "After dinner, we just sat around looking at each other."

"Didn't she know?" Mark asked.

"She didn't believe I was gay," Aamir said.

Mark's face grew a light smile.

"Not me, I can spot a fag a mile away," Mark said. "Before him opens him mouth. Before him know it himself."

"Tell it like it is," David said.

"Tell him the other part about your trip," Guia said.

"Dere's more?" Mark asked. "Wat happens when shi get here?"

Aamir smiled.

"I'll be long gone."

Mark made himself more comfortable on the bed.

"Yuh betta save yuh coins," he said. "And stop buying Guia Jägermeister shots."

"Okay. You know what Afghanistan is known for right?" Aamir asked.

"Wat? Sand niggers," Mark said.

Aamir followed David into the bathroom.

"No stupid, snowball," he said.

"Wat?" Mark asked.

Aamir returned to the living room with a glass pipe.

"You know. Dragon, china white, chiva, as in heroin," he said.

"I'm not shooting anything in my arm!" David said.

Guia looked up and grinned.

"You don't have to," he said. "You smoke it like moonrocks."

"You want some?" Aamir asked.

"How yuh get dat?" Mark asked. "How yuh bring it back?"

Guia laughed.

"He shoved it up his ass."

"There wasn't a cavity search, helloooooooooo," Aamir said.

"And you know Aamir," Guia said. "His ass can hold a few eight balls."

"That's a little more than what I want to know," David said.

David was the only one who lived in Dupont Circle. His apartment was their meeting point. Soon Chris, Kris and Christian showed up then Ori and Wallis. The small apartment felt like a restroom stall at Tracks with a cloud of smoke hovering under the ceiling. It was after two in the morning when Ori opened the vodka bottle and Wallis ran downstairs to the vending machine for juice.

Aamir pulled out the heroin and stuffed a few particles into the glass pipe. Mark frowned when he passed it to him. Guia took a pull and coughed. David took a pull. So did all the other guys. They were all talking at once - rambling about the boys from the clubs, who slept with whom, who had no fashion sense, who was sick, and who was doing way too much drugs. Mark sat up in bed and took the pipe from Ori. He took a light pull. In minutes, he was gone.

Mark was in a trance in David's apartment when he heard Gianni Versace was murdered. David came home and they shared lines of coke. A few weeks later, Princess Diana was fatally injured in a car crash in Paris and they did more coke. When Mother Theresa died, they did coke and laced it with heroin. Soon time was consumed by white lines and glass pipes being passed around. The days merged into each other. Mark didn't know when one ended and the other began. He wore the same clothes for days. He barely ate. When he did, it was takeout pizza or Chinese food. He quit his job at the bookstore and only left the apartment to buy cigarettes from the convenience store on the ground floor. The blinds remained closed, and the room was in a constant state of darkness.

Running to the restroom stalls at Tracks for bumps, then dancing it off for another, was modified to comfortable crawls to the cabinet hanging over the bathroom sink. There was no need to go clubbing. The clubs came to him. The boom box played non-stop. David slept like a rock. When awake, he ran around the apartment, dancing and checking himself in the mirror.

Their friends visited throughout the night and early morning. Some left within minutes, while others lingered for days. The world outside was depressing with everyone dying. Mark retreated in the room and found solace. It was the summer he wished never happened. His gaunt body felt weak. He couldn't remember being awake before mid-day. Seeing sunlight seemed painful.

"Mark, mail," David said.

Mark rolled out of bed and walked to the window. It was dark outside. He received a Stafford Loan check, but had forgotten to register to finish his remaining classes. It would have been his second year being a senior. He was embarrassed.

"Yuh wanna go to New York?" Mark asked.

"When?" David asked. "You got coins?"

"Wah yuh tink?" Mark asked.

"Holiday! Celebrate! Holiday!" David shouted.

Mark joined in and they laughed themselves silly. He thanked David for coming to his rescue and promised to show him a good time.

Mark cashed the Stafford loan check, rented a town car, and rounded up his closest friends. David, Aamir and Guia sat comfortably. They listened music, chatted, smoked cigarettes, and drank vodka cocktails. Aamir cruised a restroom in Delaware and caused a fifteen minute delay when he got lucky with a truck driver.

Mark paid for two rooms at The Chelsea Hotel for the weekend. They separated in pairs. Mark and David sat in the lobby and ordered drinks at the bar. Aamir and Guia decided to explore Chelsea. There was an interesting cover story in *The Village Voice* about a missing club kid that got Mark's attention. It had the picture of a Hispanic guy with prosthetic angel wings. He was distracted by the bodies moving in and out of the hotel.

Aamir and Guia returned and they had more drinks.

"So what's up tonight?" Aamir asked. "Where're we going?"

"Two words ..." Guia said. "The Limelight."

"Yes!" David said.

The Limelight was located at West 20th and 6th Avenue. It looked like a Gothic church. The mid-19th century concrete monstrosity was guarded by gargoyle statues perched on the roof. Inside looked like a creepy movie set adapted from an Ann Rice novel. It was the place to hear techno and score the best drugs in the city.

"Closed!" Mark said. "Wen did dat happen?"

"Busted!" said a guy, who heard the news earlier.

"Wat gud tonight?" Mark asked.

"Honey Trap," the guy said. "Michael's new party."

"Where's dat?" Mark asked.

"Midtown," the guy said. "Or try Cheetah where the Sound Factory was."

"Where's Junior?" Mark asked.

"Twilo," he said.

They agreed on Twilo and hopped in a cab to West 27th Street. Inside Twilo, they ordered drinks and shopped around the dance floor looking for boys and drugs.

"Hey, is Angel here tonight?" Guia asked a guy that looked familiar.

152

"Huh? Haven't you heard?" the guy asked.

"Heard what?" Guia asked.

"I know. I'm hurting too," the guy said. "He had the best shit."

The rumor Angel was murdered was confirmed when his decayed, mutilated body washed up on Staten Island. Michael Musto's story in *The Village Voice* alluded to his roommates Michael and Riggs' involvement. Michael fled the city and was captured by the police in a New Jersey hotel. He stated he was so high on drugs his memory was cloudy. He said Angel attacked him and demanded payment for drugs. Riggs hit him with a hammer and Michael smothered him with a pillow then injected him with Drano. The body started to smell in the bathroom. After hits of heroin, Michael cut off the legs, put them in a garbage bag, stuffed the rest of the corpse in a box, and threw it in the Hudson River. It sounded like a bad B movie, but no one was laughing.

Apart from the scandal, the weekend was a break from the gloom. Mark woke up before noon for the first time in weeks. He had the free continental breakfast and walked through Central Park to clear his head. Since drugs weren't accessible because they didn't know or trust anyone, they did things that seemed normal. They rented bicycles and rode to the Brooklyn Bridge. They hung out on Christopher Street, went to art galleries in Chelsea, and shopped in SoHo. Mark and his friends felt like a big fish in a much bigger pond, which was pretty much the sentiment shared by every gay boy in Chelsea. They left the hotel around noon on Sunday and saw the early showing of *Rent*, hoping to make it back to DC before midnight to finish the remainder of the weekend at Tracks.

The drive back to DC was chaotic with bumper to bumper traffic in Lincoln Tunnel. The temperature dropped to thirty degrees and it rained.

153

Mark turned on the heat, but the car got hot. He rolled down the windows, but the wind blew in the rain. David slept the entire trip.

When they drove past Baltimore, their spirits lightened. They blasted the radio, checked the weather, and called around for who would be at Tracks with drugs. Aamir didn't want to go home for the heroin he stashed. Mark wanted coke, Guia and Aamir wanted Special K, and David didn't care, as long as he got high. Chris called and said he had supplies for everyone. When they headed up 16th Street, they agreed it was a good trip, but the night would be better.

The apartment felt like home when they arrived. Everything was in its familiar place and nothing seemed odd or new. David pulled the blinds and the moonlight illuminated the room. He felt energized from his nap. The others were anxious for a bump. Mark dressed in jeans and T-shirt, while David wore his usual all-black, lace and leather attire and hopped into Mark's platform shoes. He stood firm. He sang along to his Madonna songs and buzzed around, checking himself in the mirror. Guia and Aamir didn't change their clothes. They weren't concerned about their appearance. It wasn't a special night.

Chris and Kris were already in line. Mark waved and got ahead. Kookobird stood at the door blowing air kisses, bobbing his head in every direction. He shone brighter than the spotlight beaming in the sky. He bent to kiss anyone he recognized, slipped them drink tickets, and served his vicious candor. David got out the line and walked to the front, smiling in Kookobird's face.

"What lovely eyes," Kookobird said.

David curtsied like a prima ballerina.

154

"Why thank you."

"How many honey?"

"Six."

Kookobird made a fan with six drink tickets like a geisha and pecked David's forehead, leaving a purple lipstick stain.

The crowd was contained to the two dance floors. The areas outside were closed for the night because of the rain. After giving shade to a few regulars on their way to the main room, they stopped at the restroom and crammed into a stall. Kris entered last.

David reemerged, his flush face and ready to dance. He stood outside the stall agitated. The others trickled out slowly, checking their face in the mirror. David swung open the restroom door and stomped through the crowd, heading to the main dance floor. Jean Philippe Aviance's "Work This Pussy" played. Soon they all joined, trying to outdo each other for attention and accolades.

David danced the entire morning, stopping to powder his nose. Ori and Guia disappeared for a long period. So did Chris and Kris. Mark waited for David, who wanted to dance to the last song. When he walked off the dance floor, he was drenched with sweat like he had fallen into a swimming pool. The boys gathered at the club's exit door, smoked cigarettes, and tried to see if they could find anyone to take back to David's apartment.

At the apartment, Aamir and Guia peed then found a clear space on the carpet and curled up together. Soon they were snoring. David took the music box to the bathroom and closed the door. Mark smoked by the window, squinting at the sunrise fighting through the overcast clouds. The music played as they slept.

Aamir's alarm went off at four in the afternoon. It was his wake up call to get to the restaurant by five. Guia pulled his hair over his eyes and poked him to turn it off. They slept another hour until Mark crawled to the bathroom, rolling his eyes at David lying in the floor.

"It's almost six David."

David didn't answer.

Mark ignored him and went back to the room. Aamir and Guia fumbled around on the carpet. Aamir called his boss for the day off and they slowly made an effort to begin another day, deciding to rest for the night.

Guia got up and saw David still lying on the floor.

"Girl! Are you hungry?"

David didn't respond.

Guia washed his face. He closed the cabinet and read the black lipstick scribbles on the mirror. David had written I love you Mark. Their stash of coke was missing.

"Where is the blow?" Guia asked.

David was on his stomach with his eyes open.

"David!!!"

The noise ricocheted through the apartment. It brought Mark and Aamir running into the bathroom.

"David!"

His face was turned to the side. A thick froth of vomit settled around his mouth. He wasn't breathing. He was dead.

They were crying and walking around the bathroom in confusion. Mark cradled David. He wiped away the vomit and closed David's eyes. His heart ached when he read David's message on the mirror.

"What are we going to do?" Aamir asked.

"Wah yuh mean?" Mark asked.

"He overdosed." Aamir whispered.

"Call the police?" Guia asked.

"No!" Aamir said.

"Yuh wanna call de manager?" Mark asked.

"No!" Aamir said.

Mark was flustered. He wanted to shout.

"Wat yuh waan mi fi do?" Mark asked.

"We have to leave " Aamir said.

"Why?" Mark asked.

"We can get in big trouble," Aamir said. "He's underage."

"Oh Jesas!" Mark said.

"We can't just leave him here like that!" Guia said.

"He's already dead," Aamir said. "We can't do anything about it."

Mark kissed David's forehead and placed him back on the floor. He stuffed his clothes in a garbage bag while Aamir and Guia paced the room, fretting in silence. He didn't know what else to do. He was overwhelmed his best friend for a couple of weeks was dead and he had nowhere to live.

They went to Guia's apartment in Adams Morgan and called Pietro. Pietro said David must have choked on his vomit. Mark waited two days before they decided to call the manager of David's apartment. He lied that he hadn't heard from David in a few days and asked the manager to check the apartment. He discovered David's body on the floor in the bathroom and called the police. When the police arrived, the manager contacted David's family in Ohio and his body was taken home.

Guia's cold never went away. He was always coughing. The medicines weren't working and he was scared. He couldn't remember the last time he had sex sober or used a condom. He was accustomed to going to the clinic for a shot to stop his penis from dripping or to ease the burning. He knew it was something more serious and he dreaded going to get another HIV test. It had been over a year since his last test. He stayed in his apartment for a week and worried.

The tight cold invaded his life. He was embarrassed to cough. It made sex unpleasant. He couldn't walk up a flight of steps without running out of breath. When he found out he was HIV positive, it was a relief from the uncertainty. He told the boys and they were alarmed because they shared the same fuck buddies.

Mark fell into an adaptive state of helplessness that irritated everyone. He lay around Guia's apartment all day. Halloween came and he missed David. Thanksgiving passed and he had slept through the festivities. A few days before Christmas he walked along the river to Georgetown. He ate a slice of pizza at Pizzeria Uno and went back to Guia's apartment to lie on the couch.

"You wanna go out?" Guia asked.

"Why?" Mark asked.

"You've been lying around all week," Guia said. "You're not the one that's dead."

"A don't feel like it."

"It will make you feel better."

"Where yuh wanna guh?"

"Tracks."

"Is Sunday?"

158

"Kookobird is having a Christmas show. He's going to do a tribute to David."

It was a somber night at Tracks. Mark and his friends were dressed in black. Kookobird closed his Christmas show with a melodramatic interpretation of Madonna's "Oh Father" and the deejay began to plat a two-hour set of back-to-back Madonna songs as a tribute to David. They sat in the small dance room, sipped on drinks, and chain smoked. No one spoke. They gave each other hugs and grieved.

Kookobird broke the gloomy mood with a more upbeat performance. His familiar kicks and twirls returned. After simulating a graphic child birth, he pulled out a platform shoe from under his skirt and named it David Junior. The boys laughed. It had been a long time since anyone laughed. Kookobird continued his gimmick and talked about David and his friends. He read everyone and it caused more laughter.

He told the clubbers that Michael in New York City had plead guilty to manslaughter, and was sentenced to twenty years. He urged the crowd to celebrate their life and not take it for granted. His message sunk in after he relayed the demise of being imprisoned. Soon Aamir and Guia were pulling Mark to the dance floor. Kris was the first to offer a bump. They filed into a restroom stall unsure who would go first. Mark waited outside, but was pulled in to avoid attention. They all had a moderate amount of coke in their pinky fingernail and made a quick sniff without feeling the effect. Aamir and Guia felt cheated, but didn't complain. They stood outside the stall waiting for someone to say something.

After the Madonna set, the deejay dropped a hypnotic dose of house music that lifted their spirits. Mark noticed a guy staring at him. He thought it was Ashley, but the guy was taller and Ashley was blond. He welcomed any feeling beyond the ones he felt for weeks. He smiled bashfully and waved the guy over to dance.

"Hey!"

"Wat yuh name?"

"John."

Mark took his hand. They were warm like summer. His blue eyes were fixed on him. Mark was flattered.

"Sorry about your friend."

Mark forced a grin.

"Yeah."

"How old was he?"

"Twenty."

"So young ... what a shame. Where was he from?"

"Buenos Aires ... A mean Ohio."

"What was he doing in DC? Was he in school?"

"Nat really."

"How did he die?"

Mark shot him a look. He didn't want to talk about David anymore.

"Sorry. You wanna drink?"

They walked to the main bar and Mark ordered a Sea Breeze. John decided on bottled water. Aamir and Guia came over to introduce themselves. They added another round of questions, curious about John because they had never seen him before at Tracks. They smiled cordially until Mark pulled John down to his lap and wrapped his legs around him, signaling that this one was his. They understood and went back to dance. Aamir returned. He wasn't certain if he wanted John to be in their clique or if he was willing to leave Mark alone with him.

"Hey. You have anything?" Aamir asked.

John smiled.

"Like what?" he asked.

"Coke," Aamir said.

Mark glared at Aamir as Guia approached

"You know anyone with any?" Aamir asked.

"I can get some," John said.

"From who?" Guia asked. "You have to be careful. It could be baking powder."

"Naaw, it's good," John said. "I get it from a friend of Kookobird."

Guia scanned the club looking for Chris.

"Aamir. Where's Chris?" he asked.

"I think he's in the other room," Aamir said.

"Yuh waan mi get him?" Mark asked.

"No … it's cool," Aamir said.

"A don't feel like doing anything tonite," Mark said.

"Why not?" Aamir asked.

They scrambled for their wallets and came up with ninety dollars together. They needed ten more for an eight ball. He knew Chris would give him a better price. They settled on three dime bags. John got up from Mark's lap and walked to the door then flicked open his cell phone. Within minutes they were surrounded by men who quietly placed them in handcuffs and ushered them into the club's security office. Mark fought back the tears. He didn't want anyone to see him crying as he ducked his head to enter the paddy wagon.

Mark fell asleep on the jail floor with his arms tucked under his T-shirt,

161

to ward off the freezing air conditioner. A rancid bologna sandwich with a box of milk rested by his head. His throat was scratchy and sore like he had been screaming the whole night, but he didn't remember screaming. Aamir paced in silence. He kept his hands in his pockets to keep his pants from falling. Guia sat on the bench with his legs crossed and arms folded. He eyes looked bloodshot like he had been crying all night.

They waited for hours until they were asked to mouth off their date of birth. They were then placed into a colder holding cell with more men. Someone said they were weeding out the felonies from the misdemeanors. They were mixed with drunks booked for disorderly conduct, vagrants caught trespassing, and others who had violated their probation for one reason or another.

They waited another hour - which seemed longer - until they were allowed a phone call. Aamir and Guia called their fathers and told them the bond was $1000.00. They reverted to Spanish and Hebrew for privacy. Mark had no one in the area to call, so he returned to sleep. The next day Aamir's and Guia's fathers posted bail. Mark remained and he was worried sick.

Another day passed and he was issued the standard green uniform, and transferred out the holding cell to a large open dormitory housing eighty-five first time offenders and hardcore career criminals. Mark feared for his life, but when another night became his fifth, he became acclimated to his surroundings. He slept the entire day and only left his bunk for head counts, chow, and to relieve himself when the bathroom was empty. At night, he read whatever he could find to pass the time. He was disgusted by the sporadic burst of snores, coughs, and farts.

The older men were remorseful for their treacherous past. They were kinder and more inclined to help with their knowledge of the criminal justice system. They called Mark, princess. The younger boys were wild and boisterous. They reveled in any attention. Their trips to jail garnered bragging rights. Those with the least severe crime acted like mafia dons. They called Mark slurs like punk, fuck bwoy, pussy nigga, or whatever hateful epithet came to mind.

On the second, Mark was lined up for "fresh air break." He felt the sun on his body and stretched like it was a blessing. He wiggled his toes from the rubber flats and absorbed the mild winter heat. The men exercised, played basketball, jogged, and walked around the barbed wire enclosure. They told Mark it took twenty-eight days for an arraignment unless he paid the bond. The Stafford Loan check was spent and he was broke.

He hoped Aamir and Guia would come back to get him. He thought about their trip to New York City he had paid for and the times he bought them drugs. He hoped they didn't forget him. They never came and suddenly sleeping for twelve hours, playing spades, and trading mustard for ketchup, no longer seemed like a novelty.

At his closed circuit arraignment, he was advised to look in the camera and answer to the best of his knowledge to the judge. His rehearsed defense wilted into monosyllables, head nods, and silence when he was questioned. He wasn't sure what he had agreed to, but he remembered hearing he had the choice of a six month residential treatment, joining the military, or deportation.

Chapter Nine

When the plane landed, Mark's stomach ached from diarrhea. He wanted to throw up the turkey sandwich he ate on the flight. It was after midnight, and he wasn't in the mood to meet a drill sergeant. He saw passengers lining up at the main concourse at Chicago International Airport. A guy a few years Mark's junior was shouting at them like they were hard of hearing. Mark walked over to introduce himself.

"Is dis where yuh meet for boot camp?" he asked.

The guy knitted his brows and looked at Mark like me was going to bark.

"Seaman Recruit!" he said. "Get in line and stand at attention!"

Mark rolled his eyes and thought, *who de fuck yuh talking to?*

The guy glared at him. Mark realized he had made a great mistake.

The drive to the Recruit Training Command at the Naval Station in Great Lakes was in utter silence. Mark pressed his lips shut and glared at the other recruits. He saw his life as an out of control, carefree, civilian dissipate within minutes. He wondered if rehab would have been better. He knew it would be the hardest six weeks of his life. He wept because he felt there could have been another way.

He stood with the group of terrified teenagers in front of the Recruit In-processing Center at Camp Moffett on the verge of shitting his draws. He was lead through a round of inoculations. He had a medical and dental screening, and a psychological evaluation. The administrative process lasted seventy-two hours, and he was not permitted to sleep. His hair was shaved to the scalp and his civilian attire replaced by Navy gear known as smurfs - a reminder he was at the bottom of the totem pole.

The P-Day week was said to be the most challenging. Mark's division of seventy-six recruits looked like they were already scared straight and ready to go home. They stenciled their names on dungarees and underwear and watched the instructor demonstrate how to make a bunk so tight a quarter could bounce off it.

During the first PT at four in the morning, Mark fell to the deck out of breath after fourteen pushups. He jumped from a ten feet diving platform into a swimming pool. He learned to shit, shower, and shave in five minutes with a group of acne infested juveniles without dropping the soap or paying attention to the recruit standing watch at the head while he squatted.

The Recruit Division Commander yelling, "Reveille, reveille, all hands on deck!" before sunrise replaced rolling out of bed at mid-day. The Uniform Code of Military Justice was distributed. When Mark failed to know about the ranks and ratings or the Navy's core values, he had to *drop* and do twenty pushups. When he was heeled by the recruit marching behind him and he stepped out the marching line, he was punished with more pushups and jumping jacks until he slipped in his pool of sweat. When he threatened the recruit who called him a faggot, he was sent to another division a week behind.

The division assembled on the asphalt for a drill. It felt like a hundred degrees. Beads of sweat covered their foreheads. The petty officer started his cadence and eight rows narrowed to four as they increased their steps.

"I don't know what I've been told," the petty officer said.

"I don't know what I've been told," the division repeated.

The petty officer motioned to the A-Roc to continue.

"One, two. One, two. One, two, three, four," the A-Roc chanted.

"One, two. One, two. One, two, three, four," the division repeated.

After ever twos and fours, the division's steps were synchronized. Their fists swung behind their back and they face had a mean look.

"Everywhere we go," the A-Roc yelled.

"Everywhere we go," the division mouthed.

"People wanna know," the A-Roc said.

"People wanna know," the division repeated.

"Who we are," the A-Roc yelled louder

"Who we are," the division roared.

"So we tell them," the A-Roc's voice cracked.

The cadence died as the A-Roc commanded "heel to toe" before they entered a classroom for the firefighting lesson. The recruits stood close together, breathing down each other's neck. Mark cringed when he felt a hard bulge against his butt.

After taps, a recruit with a southern drawl whispered to his bunkmate another cadence he learned from his father who was a marine.

"I don't know, but I've been told, Eskimo pussy is mighty cold."

His bunkmate chuckled, urging him to continue.

"I don't know, but it's been said, southern women give good head."

He smiled like he knew it as a fact.

Mark was relieved when some things worked in his favor. He wasn't

167

assigned a four-hour watch, his pay rate was higher because of college credits, and he received a limited duty chit for two days, when his wisdom tooth was pulled. Seven weeks later, he passed the physical fitness assessment with ninety pushups and survived the tear gas chamber and firefighting drills. It was the final test of endurance, strength and teamwork to become a sailor.

He loved the uniforms, especially the sixteen button, bell bottom polyester pants. It hugged his hips and girthed his *bottom* like a harness. He loved the dog tags. The way they rested on his chest and clicked when he moved, seemed like a calling card for civilian gay boys.

During the Pass in Review the chain of command sat on comfortable seats in the stands with parents and well-wishers cheering on. Mark marched with the hundreds of seamen. Instead of a salute, he gave a quick finger to everyone who thought he would fail. The sailors yelled, "Ooh rah!" and gave each other high fives and bear hugs. Mark was exhausted. He was glad boot camp was over.

He felt better about the relatively relaxed change at the three-week seamanship school. There were no drills or inspections. There was a wreck hall to play pool and videos games, a movie theater, and a nightclub on-base. The seamen had more freedom. They congregated at the smoking areas and spit buckets after chow and before taps. Mark knew his mannerisms were suspect, so he avoided socializing. If he went to the nightclub, he stood in a corner away from the crowd and sipped a beer. He guarded the way he stood or moved his hands.

Although he had received a high test score and was the top student in the seamanship class, he did not choose a *rating*, unaware of its detriment. He was offered an *A school* to become a Submarine Yeoman, but the thought of being confined to Navy personnel in a submarine seemed paralyzing. The recruits warned he was making a mistake because he would spend his Navy career swabbing decks. Mark ignored them because the Navy was never a choice he made in pursuit of a career, just a bad choice to avoid rehab or deportation.

After graduation from seamanship training school, Mark earned two weeks of leave before reporting to his assigned ship in San Diego. He stuffed his backpack with *skivvies* and hopped on the train at Great Lakes and headed to Chicago. He wore his navy blue pea coat and dress blues and tried to re-socialize himself with civilians. He walked to the center of Grant Park and sat by Buckingham Fountain then past the Art Institute of Chicago and fixed his eyes on the Sear Towers, which seemed to follow him everywhere.

As the chilly evening approached, he was bored with sightseeing. He had long forgotten how it felt to have a guy down on his knees before him and he wanted to make up for missing it. His fanned down a cap on Michigan Avenue and told the driver to take him to Boystown.

The cab zipped up North Lake Shore Drive. Mark rolled down the window and stuck out his head like a happy dog, soaking in the air. When the driver pulled onto West Belmont, Mark asked for a reasonably priced hotel and the driver suggested the Best Western on North Broadway. The front desk clerk swiped his Armed Force Bank debit card and checked him into a cozy room for the weekend.

Mark pulled back the sheets and jumped around for a few minutes, making sure he left the sheets soiled and wrinkled to defy his boot camp indoctrination. He ordered room service and wolfed down a chicken and rice dinner with urgency. He showered and changed into tight jeans with a

169

gray shirt he picked up while strolling around the business district. He flipped through a magazines on the nightstand and found nothing of interest. He went to the lobby and asked the front desk clerk about the nightclubs in the area. The clerk winked like he was addressing the newest member of a private club and suggested anywhere on North Halsted.

Mark walked two blocks west as the street hustled and bustled with activities. He was filled with excitement, glad to be amongst a crowd of local gay hipsters. They were walking in and out of bars, coffee shops, and restaurants. Rainbow flags were posted from every business on the North Halsted strip, with stickers on glass entrances boasting their establishment's gay owned and operated status.

He was lured into Sidetrack Glass Bar by smiling faces and colorful drinks being poured into tall glasses. He ordered a Sea Breeze and smiled willingly at anyone that looked at him. He wasn't there for just a few drinks. He wanted to meet someone for sex. He wanted to forget about the Navy or anything that reminded him of it.

The bar was busy with groups of gay guys. Mark didn't feel like having a conversation. He listened to the gay bar's high drama chatter and decided to try another venue. Three blocks along the gay corridor was Cell Block, a sleazy leather bar. It was still early with only a few guys were on the dance floor. He didn't feel like dancing. He picked up the weekly fag rag and flicked through the pages for something interesting, something different than what he had done before.

An ad got his attention. It had a glossy picture of a shirtless Latin guy showing off his physique with a white terry cloth towel tightly tucked around his waist, revealing a massive bulge. He had seen many of those ads before. They were the staple to advertise a gay party. But it wasn't for a dance club. It was a different type of club. He tore the page from the magazine and quicken his steps to find 3246 North Halsted Street, the location of Steamworks Baths.

He was nervous when he took out his Department of Defense issued military ID, but he felt important when the attendant gave him a respectful smile. The attendant asked if he wanted to pay for a one-time pass or the popular "Frequent Fuckers" membership. Mark smiled and agreed to the one-time deal. The attendant took his money, handed him a white towel, and two keys on a rubber band. He pointed Mark to a jar with condoms and lubes.

When he entered the club, he felt a rush of blood to his loins triggered by the inescapable sexual energy. The masculine space was filled with loads of men waiting around. Mark entered the locker room and stripped down, pulling the towel around his waist and securing his clothes in his locker.

He passed the gym and stepped into a dimly lit communal shower. There were guys masturbating in the showers, their soaps spinning around in a whirlpool of water at their feet. Mark smirked, realizing if he dropped his soap, no one would care because man to man interaction wasn't only accepted, it was encouraged.

There was a fat white guy with hair on his back, sucking a skinny, bald Latin guy. A small crowd watched and touched themselves as he sucked him to completion. They pulled their towels around their waist and roamed the rest of the club.

There were naked men everywhere. It felt like an open season fuck-fest. They were kissing, masturbating, and sucking and fucking in the hallways, the gym, the sauna, the pool, the porn rooms, the glory holes, and their private rooms. Mark joined the attractive groups and came like the rain, showering his sticky semen onto nameless faces, pulling out of anonymous asses, and shoving his cock down waiting mouths.

Mark took a break, slept for a few hours, then returned to the shower to do it again. He followed guys to their rooms and invited them to his. He cooled off in the heated pool, only to be enticed by another guy. The circuit music pounded in his head, daring him to continue his reckless sexual adventure. He finally left in the morning when the staff closed the wet area for cleaning.

Mark spent the rest of his leave shopping at Marshall Field's and hanging out at coffee shops. At night, he danced until the wee hours. He called Guia and his number was disconnected. He also called Aamir's job. His supervisor said he had moved to New York. He returned to the bathhouse another night and decided if the shipmates asked what he did during his leave, he'd respond he wasn't at liberty to tell.

The flight from Chicago to San Diego was uneventful. Mark readjusted and quickly went back into the closet. When he arrived at the San Diego naval base, the principal homeport of the Pacific fleet, he took a deep breath, not sure if he was prepared for this next phase in his life. He reported to the USS Peleliu (LHA-5), a Tarawa-class amphibious assault ship that deployed to the Persian Gulf.

The first week on the ship, Mark was disappointed. He felt like a fool. What the shipmates in seamanship school had warned him about was exactly what happened. He reported to the Deck Division and the first two months he was assigned to the galley as a kitchen aide. It was a fifteen-hour shift. He mustered out a bunk - the size of a coffin - with two shipmates above him. His workday began at four in the morning to prepare the crew's

172

meals. He peeled potatoes, served food, and swabbed the deck. When he was late or gave too much lip he was punished with *deep dish* - washing dishes and scrubbing large pots and pans in scalding water until he saw his reflection. His quitting time was at dusk and it depended on how fast he gathered the trash to the dumpsters on the pier.

One evening, Mark was covered with grime from the day old trash and at the mercy of ravenous seagulls hovering over his head. The captain stepped out his Mercedes and walked down the pier. Mark pretended he didn't see him. He was chewed out by his petty officer because he failed to render a salute. Mark held his tongue and the impulse of rolling his eyes was curbed. Instead, he apologized.

He retreated to the hull of the ship after his shift and locked himself in the mooring line storage. No one went to that part of the ship when it was docked. He knew he wouldn't be bothered. He lay on the greasy ropes, and cried himself to sleep. He listened to Fleetwood Mac and Sarah McLachlan CDs, and pretended he was somewhere else.

When he was around the other sailors, he crawled into himself and his voice disintegrated to a murmur. He lost his confidence and felt weak around a population of low functioning, egocentric sailors. His took cigarette breaks on the starboard side of the ship and became invisible.

The shipmates in the Deck Division were full grade, certified and stamp approved morons. Seaman Eddie was a twenty-seven-year-old E-2 from Detroit. He was a sturdy brute and as stupid as they came. He dreamt of using his GI Bill to go a community college to study construction. He looked like the stereotypical black guy in prison movies serving two life sentences that wanted to make you his bitch.

His white counterpart, Seaman Davis, came from a long line of Gomer

Pyle carbon copies from Back Swamp, North Carolina. His dream was to buy a truck with his reenlistment check and hunt possums.

The two *Chucks* were all brawn and no brain. They reveled in their stupidity. Mark despised them because he felt like the third stooge in their work crew. He was infuriated to have the same menial duties they had. If he failed to do a good enough job swabbing the deck or wiping down the *bulkhead*, he would be chewed out by the supervising petty officer, a high school dropout from Wyoming. He reminded them of his college education, but they only laughed. They thought if he went to college, he would have been an officer and not an enlisted seaman.

The ship was in port for the holidays and Mark remained onboard in his bunk. He avoided exploring the ship. He skipped the special Thanksgiving dinner on base. When Christmas came, he saw a movie at the cinema in the Gaslamp District. He searched for a weekly fag rag and discovered Hillcrest, the gay neighborhood. The coffee shop next door to Rich's nightclub was the only place it was acceptable to linger for three hours while sipping on a cup of chamomile tea.

There were jocks, twinks, leather daddies, and dizzy queens rubbing shoulders with transsexuals, butch dykes, and lipstick lesbians who stopped in for a beverage on their way to one of the nearby gay bars. The coffee shop was a popular hangout for underage gay kids. After closing, they went to the beach and sat around bonfires where alcohol and drugs were generously shared.

Luis was a flaming Latin queen - the kind reporters got camera men to film during gay pride parades to scare straight viewers. He was born in Mexico and grew up in San Diego. Mark noticed his glitter-based lip gloss

174

and pink acrylic nails spread around his cup like a starfish. He had arched eyebrows and violet contacts. His hair was bone straight, and feathered around his shoulders. Mark smirked when Luis said he was cute. He warmed up to him when he saw him dangling the keys to a Volvo.

After talking to Luis for an hour, Mark filed Luis into the friends with benefits category because he was not attracted to him. Luis invited him to Rich's and they danced until the club was closed. He was impressed Mark was a sailor, and gave him a ride back to the base.

When he pulled up at the security check point and waved at the guard, Mark pulled his cap over his face. Luis suggested a weekend trip to West Hollywood for what he described as the opportunity to consummate their friendship. Mark suggested a day-trip to Tijuana because Luis was fluent in Spanish.

After New Year's Day, the ship was scheduled for a four-day replenishment to transfer fuel, munitions, and stores from another ship. Mark's galley duties remained from four in the morning to six in the evening, and he was expected to be on a four-hour watch. The Marines were on-board and the airmen were busy with flight exercises. The junior crew met to learn at sea protocol along with firefighting and man-over-board drills. Mark hated the man-over-board drills, but saw them as an unofficial smoke break once everyone sounded off.

He was looking for a diversion from the grueling long hours. He confided in a cook in the galley who winked to him, pointing out gay suspects in the chow line. It became a game between them that never went beyond an eye roll from Mark signaling he wasn't interested.

When the Marines came through the line, Mark gazed at a guy who reminded him of Taye Diggs. He was a sergeant with a defined body and a less dangerous face. The cook said he was a DL brother. Mark wasn't sure what he meant, but soon realized. Daniel caught his wandering eyes one morning and gave him a discreet nod. He was elated. The cook said he worked out in the gym in the evenings. Mark visualized his face and body whenever he had the energy to masturbate in the shower.

The second day at sea, the ship met a sister ship forty miles in the middle of the Pacific to carry out the underway replenishment. The Deck Division's duty was to hold the mooring line while supplies were transferred a hundred feet over the ocean. Mark, the weakest in the division, was put at the front of the line.

The rope slipped through his fingers like a slippery snake.

"You better pull your weight boy!" the petty officer said.

Eddie and Davis looked angry. The held the rope at the end of the line. They thought Mark was embarrassing them before the entire crew. The supervising white petty officer stood over Mark. The ropes burned like alcohol on an open wound.

"I said you better pull your weight boy!"

Mark stuttered below his breath.

"It too hard for mi to handle … Yuh fuckin' asshole!"

"What was that boy?"

Mark panicked and let the rope go. The petty officer pushed him against the bulkhead and threatened to strike. Eddie moved in front and kept the line steady.

"I'll see you at Captain's mast, Chuck!"

"A didn't seh anything."

"Shut the fuck up and go back to the galley! You pussy!"

Mark knew the punishment of being on restriction - confined to the ship for sixty days and subjected to whatever humiliation his supervisors could think of - was more than he could bare. He knew no one would defend him when the master of arms investigated. Later that night, he slept in his bunk dreaming of another life. He was awakened by cold water being splashed in his face. He was told to suit up and report to his four-hour watch.

Mark shook when he saw the captain on the navigation deck. He traded the other three hours to stand watch at the stern of the ship. Alone, he stared with wet eyes into the dark ocean as the ship ripped through the waves. It was peaceful. He followed the constellations and thought if he jumped, no one on the ship would care.

When the ship docked, Mark was released from his mooring line duties on the pier and remained in the galley. When he went back to his bunk some of the shipmates in his division avoided him.

"You done do yourself in," Eddie said.

"Why yuh seh that?"

"The shit backed up to your mouth," Eddie said. "You goin' to captain's mast."

"A didn't seh anything."

"It's your word 'gainst a petty officer"

When the bell rang for weekend liberty, Mark grabbed his backpack and went in search of San Diego's gay bathhouse. He didn't care if he was seen. He flicked his military ID nonchalantly to the front desk help and asked for extra sheets. He slept through the eight-hour session and extended his stay. He woke the next day and saw a movie in the Gaslamp District. He walked the mall aimlessly trying to feel better, and found a twenty-four hour coffee shop with pool tables and vagrants playing chess. He went inside and sat amongst them to listen to their conversation.

Justin was an all-American boy, blond and blue, six feet, and ruggedly handsome. He looked like the lead singer of a boy band in his burgundy jacket, brown paisley shirt, and dark brown corduroy pants tucked into cowboy boots. He commanded everyone's attention when he played pool. Mark watched the girls swarming around him. Justin smiled and revealed his pearly whites. Mark sighed, thanking a higher power for the chipped front tooth because it made Justin a little less perfect.

Mark went looking for Justin the following week. He wished he knew how to play. He would have joined Justin in a game, but he watched as he did before. Mark sat near the pool table and listened to Justin's group of friends. He realized Justin was also in the Navy - on a cargo ship a few piers from his.

Mark was free of his galley duties and reported back to the deck division. The officer in charge of the division was transferred and replaced by a Filipino ensign who had recently graduated from the academy. She was lost in her position and took advice from the senior chief petty officer under her management who had sixteen years of service under his belt. Her newness to Navy life and superiority over the men was a mockery of the rank and status order. They corrected and schooled her about the duties of the Deck Division. Even nincompoop, Eddie, gloated when he showed her the many ways to tie a mooring line.

Mark waited for Justin to show up at the coffee shop. He introduced himself as a fellow sailor. After a brief chat, Justin relaxed his ego. They realized they both hated the Navy and wanted to be far away from base when on liberty. They talked for hours. Mark lingered around while Justin played pool or took a smoke break. In the morning, they had breakfast at Denny's before Mark returned to the ship. Mark felt a rush of life injected into him when Justin laughed. Justin was intrigued because he had never met anyone black and foreign.

Justin invited Mark to crash at his hotel room because he didn't want to go back to his ship. He brought a girl he picked up from the coffee shop, and after shots of vodka she straddled him on the bed as Mark watched from the bathroom door. When Mark entered the room, Justin didn't object that Mark saw him naked and having sex with the nameless girl. Mark smiled, and Justin smiled back.

Later that night, Mark told Justin he was bi sexual. Justin suspected differently. Mark joked that one night maybe they could get drunk enough and explore the possibilities. When Justin didn't object, he felt like the cloud over his head had shifted. Mark endured the ridicule from his shipmates and counted the days for his weekend liberty to be with his only friend, Justin.

One evening, he waited for Justin on base to play pool at the recreation building. Justin never showed up, but he saw Daniel. When he left and headed back to the ship, Daniel followed. He ducked behind a building and waited. Daniel approached with his pants unzipped and began to fondle himself. Mark couldn't believe what was happening. His heart raced. Daniel motioned for Mark to touch his cock. Mark brushed his lips against Daniel's cheek.

"I don't kiss," Daniel said.

"Wat yuh wanna do?" Mark asked.

"Take out your dick," Daniel said. "Let's jerk off."

Mark came in seconds.

When he returned to the ship, he felt less sorry for himself and had a smile on his face when he crept into his bunk.

179

The next evening, Mark saw Daniel in the chow line chatting with other marines. Daniel looked through Mark like he was a ghost. When he left, Mark followed him to his bunk. Daniel glared when he saw him.

"What the fuck you doing? It was just that one time!"

It took Mark a few days to get over Daniel's humiliation. He didn't know what to make of his behavior. He watched Daniel with his marine buddies, and was angry. Mark knew he didn't have the courage to call him out before his peers because it wouldn't be in his favor. Daniel was masculine and perceived straight while he couldn't fool anyone. Mark sulked as Daniel pretended he never existed.

Mark resented the Navy's "Don't ask, don't tell" policy. It created a hotbed of deceit amongst gay men in the military too scared to be themselves, living a life of lies. He fine-tuned his *gaydar* and realized he wasn't the only gay personnel on the ship - he was only the most obvious. He then thought one day his gayness would work in his favor.

Weekend liberties kept Mark from being depressed. He saw Justin as often as possible and their friendship developed with an understanding that when they were together, whatever they did was a secret. They went to Tijuana, West Hollywood, and as far as Las Vegas together - anywhere away from the base to explore Mark's attraction and Justin's curiosity.

A few months later, Justin's four year enlistment was about to end and he had no intention of reenlisting. He began counting the days. Mark missed him already. Mark moped when they were together. Justin had enjoyed the friendship, but he had never thought of anything in the future that included Mark. Although he experimented with Mark - touching and masturbating - he didn't feel the same way Mark did. He wasn't sure how he felt now that he was re-entering society as a civilian.

The ship's master of arms began probing into Mark's alleged insubordination. Mark's fears returned. He no longer wanted to be in the Navy. Up to that moment, he had not thought of getting out. Justin's discharge stirred in him the desire to leave because he thought he was in love. When the ship began preparing to deploy to East Timor as part of an Australian lead peacekeeping taskforce, he decided he wanted to leave the Navy before it left port.

"Tell them you're gay," the cook said.

It had been four months since Justin left the Navy. Mark was alone. The sailors in his division teased he was going to captain's mast. His supervising petty officer increased the demeaning tasks. He felt like the ship was closing in on him. He decided to go to the Chaplin when the master of arms told him to report to his office.

He missed the morning muster and hid in the hull. After breakfast, he knocked on the Chaplin's door to beg for help. A frail, well-aged man ushered him in as he spoke on the phone. His voice was calm and free of any military jargon. He smiled at Mark when he placed the receiver down.

"I wanted to talk to yuh about my situation."

"What's bothering you?"

Mark sat before the Chaplin and crossed his legs for the first time in months. He stared at the Chaplin and bawled. More noise than actual tears. His was convincing.

"I don't feel comfortable on de ship."

"And why is that?"

"I'm gay."

The Chaplin raised his head and looked squarely into Mark's face. He

181

was silent. Mark tried to read his face. His expression had not changed. The Chaplin crossed his legs as well and Mark's gaydar went off like a siren.

"Well, you can still be in the Navy. Keep it to yourself. Not on the ship."

"But I feel threatened!"

"We can address those issues. There are protocols."

"I don't tink they can be addressed on dis ship."

"Would you like to be transferred on base?"

"No."

"Are you asking to be separated?"

"Yes."

Ten minutes later, Mark signed papers and packed his belongings to be transferred on base to wait for his honorable discharge. He had a broad smile for the first time when he returned to the Deck Division.

"Where you going?" Eddie asked.

"Home!" Mark said. "Awffa dis fuckin' ship!"

A Latin petty officer parted the curtain for his bunk and glared.

"What did you say?"

"Did I stutter? Yuh heard me … yuh fuckin' wetback!"

"I bet you don't run your shit when you have me to deal with for sixty days."

On his way off the ship, Mark stopped by the galley to say goodbye to the cook and waited for Daniel to enter the chow line. He smiled when he saw him. Daniel ignored him. Mark walked over to Daniel and brushed against his thigh. The crew in line looked suspiciously at Daniel.

Mark called Justin and told him he was being separated. He tried to convince Justin to let him visit. Justin agreed when Mark said he had nowhere to go and that he missed him. Justin told his parents a different story. Two weeks later, he was requested to select a destination anywhere in America for his free one-way ticket. Mark called Justin again and told him he was on the way.

Justin lived with his parents in Kirkland, Washington, a suburb of Seattle. It was an upper-middle-class town with private dirt roads leading to large houses, surrounded by lush landscape, pine trees, moss growing on rocks, and visits from nocturnal wildlife. Kirkland had its moment in the limelight when the 1982 National League team won the Little League World Series. Since then it had remained a nice place to live for well-to-do white baby boomers.

Justin's parents were '60s hippies. They grew up on The Grateful Dead, The Mamas and The Papas and Jefferson Airplane. They smoked pot, dropped acid and protested the Vietnam War. They evolved into '90s straight laced yuppies with six figure incomes, a vacation home in Lake Tahoe, and stock portfolios. Justin's mother managed a bank and his father owned a maritime company. They were upper middle class and predictable. They weren't happy to hear their only son was involved in a gay relationship and with a black guy.

When Justin returned home, he received a pamphlet on conversion therapy, another from the Church of Jesus Christ of Latter-day Saints, and an intervention. He was sent to Salt Lake City for two months to change his sexual brokenness. During therapy, he was told his lust for boys was because he was abused as a child, or he had a psychological disorder dealing with mixed up gender roles, or he had played with Barbie and had an absent father. After a series of aversive conditioning techniques that included genital shocks, nausea-inducing drugs, psych therapy, prayers, and an ultimatum to either change or be disinherited, Justin later recanted and testified that he was heterosexual.

When Mark arrived, Justin regretted inviting him to his parents' house and warned him to act more masculine. He said he was engaged to his high school sweetheart because it was the right thing to do. He didn't know what came over him when he was in the Navy. He blamed being away from his family and friends as the reason for being tempted to live an ungodly lifestyle.

Mark realized there was no future with Justin or being in Kirkland. He was a civilian again and if living with Justin at his parents' house didn't work out, he would try Seattle. He knew he couldn't go back in the closet, not after suppressing who he was on the ship to carelessly indulge on weekends. He wanted a sense of normalcy.

After living with Justin for a week, Mark noticed a drastic change and decided to let him go. He bought a used Nissan Stanza, piled his belongings in the trunk, and drove to Seattle. He parked on a side street near Volunteer Park. Hidden from the craziness of Capitol Hill, Mark slept in his car and ate one dollar burgers from Jack in the Box. When his money began to run out, he signed up with an employment agency.

He got a job at Amazon.com and worked in the warehouse as a book picker for eight dollars an hour. There was nothing to look forward to, besides pulling book after book from storage shelves and placing them into shopping carts, and traipsing up and down the warehouse floor repeating the task as often as the grunge manager requested before the bell rang. With his first paycheck, he rented a room in Capitol Hill. He shared a bathroom in a hall with six tenants.

Mark was desperate to forget his upended life. He visited his co-worker in Queen Anne - a redhead, freckled face girl - who reminded him of a good time. Her black boyfriend was in Tacoma and she was bored. They sat around her apartment smoking a blunt, drinking beer, and gossiping about the buff Latin guy he cruised between the shelves at work.

When he returned to his room, the streets were blocked by police cars. Mayor Paul Schell had imposed a twenty-four hour curfew and a fifty-block "No-Protest Zone" from the convention center to avoid disturbance to the World Trade Organization Ministerial Conference. Mark showed his room key before a police officer allowed him in the building. Soon the protest grew violent. Police gassed and arrested the demonstrators. Fearing Armageddon, Mark shook in his bed from the hysteria.

The world didn't end, so to get away from the misery he drove to Vancouver for the weekend. He listened to some of his favorite tunes and cried. About sixty miles from Seattle, he got off I-5 and took Chuckanut Drive. He gazed at the vistas of Puget Sound and the San Juan Islands. He felt numb to the beauty around him, and was overwhelmed with feeling rejected and working a dead-end job to pay for an overpriced room. He was slipping into depression without realizing he was broken.

Mark arrived before dusk and explored Davie Village, the gay area in Vancouver. He drove to Stanley Park and followed the seawall path. He parked and looked at the totem poles, read the commemorative plaques, and got back into his car then drove over Lions Gate Bridge simply for the sake of doing it.

He went back downtown and parked off Davie Street and walked to The Oasis Lounge. He ordered a Sea Breeze and watched the Canadians trickle into the club. Nothing and no one interested him. He went outside to the heated patio and was surrounded by a group of shrieking drama majors from University of Vancouver.

The music in the club changed from top forty to deep house. Two shirtless twinks dancing on a podium were replaced by two muscled go-go boys with slicked back hair, looking like Greek statutes. They entered a glass shower and the steamy water splashed on their hairless bodies. They stripped off their underwear and stroked their cocks. The crowd came alive. Mark ordered another drink and fixed his eyes on the dancers enticing the spellbound audience.

He stood on the dance floor looking at the men. He saw a blond guy he liked and moved closer to dance with him. Mark brushed his crotch against the guy's hand. The guy smiled and kept dancing. Mark guided the guy's hand to his erect penis and smiled back. The guy moved closer so Mark could feel he was hard as well. Mark pulled him off the dance floor and headed to a restroom stall. Before the door closed, Mark slid his hands down his pants and grabbed his cock.

It happened too fast and Mark came too quickly. He wanted another guy. He gulped down another drink before closing. The trick asked if he was going to an after party. Mark told him he was going to sleep in his car then drive back to Seattle before sunrise. The guy said he would enjoy what's left of the night at F212 bathhouse.

F212 was only two blocks from the club, so Mark decided to walk. He felt seasoned when he entered. He knew what to expect, even if it was in another country. He skipped the tour and headed to the room of the first guy that cruised him. After a quick blow job, he went back to his room and slept. The music interrupted his dream. When he awoke, a tall, muscular Latin guy stood by the door stroking his cock. He made room for him on the bed.

He slept past noon. When he returned to his car, the back window was smashed and the clothes he had piled in the backseat were in disarray. His camera was stolen. The heroin junkies he saw roaming around the previous night were also missing. He sucked his teeth and thought, *There goes my dream of being a photographer.*

Before he left Vancouver, he stopped at Wreck Beach. It was a clear, beautiful day and the air smelled like suntan lotion and marijuana. The beach was a wasteland with tree trunks emerging out the sand like haunting tentacles reaching for the sky. It was covered with naked bodies in all stages of middle-aged deterioration. Fat women with rolls and lumps, and skinny women with bones and humps, lay in the sand with sagging breasts and wild hair like a Jim Jones revival. The men were equally repulsive. Few separated themselves from the batch by having a slightly defined youthful body, an attractive face, or a bigger cock. The sunbathers looked like society's leftovers who lived on the outskirts, coming up to the surface in less threatening spaces.

A topless girl wearing a peasant skirt combed the beach with a basket of homemade cookies. She was taking subscriptions for the monthly nudist newsletter. Mark bought two cookies. After the fourth bite, all the bodies on the beach became appealing. The cookies, laced with LSD were euphoric. For about half an hour -which seemed longer - he thought he was floating on the clouds when he rolled around in the sand. He heard harps, saw faces morph into animals and was amused by strange thoughts running through his mind.

He woke up when the sun was golden over the emerald green ocean, and wanted to fuck again. He noticed guys cruising the undergrowth trails. He found a tanned, muscular guy and followed him along the trail. They hid under a shading tree. Mark felt the blood rushing to his cock. He had never been this hard, or horny. It felt like something pent up wanted to escape. No words were exchanged. Mark's movements were feverish. The guy sweated profusely as he sucked Mark's cock. When he came, he thanked him for the release and headed to his car.

The trip to Vancouver was only a temporary relief. Mark felt like a desperate version of himself. He wanted to unravel his latest mistake. He spent the nights parked along Alki Beach and stared at Seattle's skyline. He was disillusioned about his future.

No one in Mark's family knew where he was and what he was going through. He had not spoken to his mother and sisters since he dropped out of Howard University. Eileen had moved to Fort Lauderdale and Daphne followed. Winsome moved to Boston after marrying a pilot. He thought Daphne would throw his distress back in his face. Eileen wasn't the nurturing sister from his youth. She had become a bitter and intolerant woman. She was the last person he wanted to know he was suffering.

Chapter Ten

Mark emailed Carol and begged for help. They didn't hang out at Howard University, but their passion for photography spawned a friendship. She would sometimes come to his room in The Towers with her "Rise and shine, Sunshine!" wake-up calls to get him to wipe the sleep out his eyes after another night out. Mark liked her spontaneous laughter and optimism. She wore her hair in long braids, flipping the strands when she walked. She wasn't attractive. She never tried out for the homecoming fashion shows, but her afrocentric presence resonated well with her peers. She had a wild streak that made her indulge. She smoked marijuana in her dorm room with her boyfriend, sealing the door with wet towels.

After graduating from Howard, she moved to New York to live with her sister Kendra. They shared a moderately sized two-bedroom on the second floor of a brownstone in Park Slope. Kendra was the prominent black lesbian on the block. While Carol dated men in between the women she loved, Kendra hated men - especially if they were black.

She was a multi-media artist. *Essence* magazine selected her as one of the future "Thirty Women to Watch" after the notoriety of her first solo exhibition at HERE Arts Center on black women lynched in the south. Galleries across the country requested a traveling show. She appeared on DYKE TV, was featured in *SHE* magazine and held a symposium at The

Lesbian Herstory Archives. When she became famous, her twisted hair developed into dreadlocks and a former black girlfriend was replaced by a media friendly white woman.

Carol said Mark could stay at their apartment until he figured out what he wanted to do. She warned him about Kendra's new fame and her vision of a world without men. Mark thought his non-threatening gayness would have made him a fellow queer. He wasn't sure where he fit in with her definition of things, and it was the last thing he wanted to worry about. He knew New York City was tough.

He stood on the steps at King Street Station in Pioneer Square exhausted before his journey. He had doubts. It didn't feel like the right decision, but he was desperate to leave his misery in Seattle. He wondered what was next. When the four-day cross country commute ended at Penn Station, he sighed and walked out the station with his bags at his sides and headed to Carol's office at Rockefeller Center.

She met him in the lobby and was surprised how gaunt he was.

"You're here, Markie!"

"Hi Carol."

He forced a smile and lightly kissed her cheek.

Carol looked different. Her hair was a brown, wavy bob matching her complexion. She wore makeup and a skirt, unlike when she was an undergrad. She looked harder with a city toughness, but more womanly. Her wild laughter was subdued and her face looked like she was thinking about ten things at the same time.

He remembered she was always busy and living in New York City made her harried. She was busy being busy. She found things to fill her schedule after work. She took a class at the International Center of Photography and

190

met with a poetry group on the Upper West Side. She did cardio at the gym, and met a girlfriend for a movie or a play. She went to jazz bars and comedy clubs, the farmers market in Prospect Park, had tea at Rising Café, the lesbian bookstore next door, and met friends at Excelsior. She divided her time between Manhattan and Brooklyn. Her Manhattan friends were a diverse group of people she met at work or in a class or seminar. Her peers in Brooklyn were "sisters" from "Dyke Slope." When she was dating, her weekends were consumed with sex and staying in bed tackling *The New York Times* crossword puzzle.

"I can't talk long," she said, interrupting his thoughts. "Take the F to 15th and Prospect Park. I'm meeting Toni ... you remember her from HU. We're going to see *Boys Don't Cry*. Help yourself to what's in the fridge. See you later."

Mark nodded, took the keys and headed to the subway.

Blue sheets on the couch in the living room greeted him at the apartment. The bedroom doors were shut. The living room looked like a Kwanza showroom. Kente cloth were draped everywhere. There were two large wooden drums, a table with wilted fruits, and paintings of nude women. On the coffee table were feminist books and lesbian magazines. The living room suggested it was the center of heated political discussions. Mark sank in the couch and fell asleep.

Kendra came home and waved to Mark as she entered her bedroom. She made a phone call to her girlfriend and during the conversation the door was discreetly closed. Mark overheard her saying that Carol had invited one of her free-loader friends to stay for a few week, and she would rather not have any visitors. When she hung up the phone and left the apartment, Mark went back to sleep.

Carol came home minutes before midnight. She looked around in the darkness, her body silhouetted by the street light through the window. She breathed an air of regret when she saw Mark sleeping. She flicked on the living room light, dropped her purse on the table, and stuck something in the microwave. When the bell rang, it was time to figure out what Mark was doing with his life and why he had invaded hers. She sat on the couch and waited for Mark to open his eyes.

"Hey Markie, what are you gonna do here?"

"A going to luk for a job and find a place."

"Get the weekender and get busy."

Mark sighed.

Have you thought about what you wanna do?"

"Anything really."

"Try the village; the new shops are hiring."

Mark fidgeted on the couch and made a face.

"Yuh have any change fi de subway?"

Carol looked at Mark and rolled her eyes.

"Change? You don't have any money?"

"A kinda low."

Carol smirked and fished through her purse. She found a twenty dollar bill and nodded. Mark knew that was the first and last time she would be that generous.

"So, how's your photography these days?" she asked.

"I haven't shat anything in a while," Mark said. "Dem tief mi camera."

"I've been busy at work, traveling to different conferences …."

She paused. She didn't want to appear like she was bragging.

Mark didn't want to compare resumes. There was nothing he was proud of to talk about. He had survived the stint in the Navy and was off drugs, but those were not things to brag about to a college peer, who thought he had so much talent.

"So what do you think?" Carol asked.

"About wat?" Mark asked.

Carol grinned.

"My hair ... my new look ... the apartment?"

"It's nice."

Mark tried to fight his loss of interest in everything.

"I got a big promotion ... so excited! I feel so good about the future. I'm going shopping this weekend for spring dresses."

She laughed, the hysterical pitch returning.

Mark nodded and pulled the sheet up to his chest. Carol got the hint and smiled before closing her bedroom door. Mark looked around the apartment and cried.

He canvassed Broadway from 42nd to Canal Street, filling out job applications at every retail shop he had the nerve to be seen in. He didn't have a resume with a solid or impressive work experience, so he skipped the department stores. A few days later, he received a call for an interview.

Mark, dressed in black, blended with New York City's aesthetics. When he arrived at the store, a Haitian guy stood at the entrance. He was taking a break and looking out at pedestrians crowding the corner of Broadway and Spring Street. Mark nodded at him and went inside looking for Ming, the store manager and daughter of the owner. The guy followed with a patrolling stare and asked if he needed something. Ming came from behind the register after slamming it shut.

"You Mark?"

"Yes, I'm here for de interview."

"Yes, okay, wait here, okay, on the phone, okay."

Mark stood in the middle of the store, glancing at the designer clothes. Ming hung up in the middle of her conversation and blinked at him.

"You sell shoes before?"

Mark nodded.

"I need sales person to sell shoes, you good?"

Mark nodded.

She pointed to one of the display shoes in the window.

"Go in back, bring me shoes, size seven. Do it fast, customer waiting."

Ming looked like a reformed Asian girl who had outgrown smiling with her hands over her mouth. She dressed like a Japanese-American princess straight off a Tokyo runway in a black Yohji Yamamoto pants suit. Her straight, jet black long hair had a sharp bang above her eyebrow. She had high cheek bones, a strong jawline and a button nose. Her delicate fingers were perfectly manicured. Her face was made up with a pale foundation. Thick black eyeliner made her slanted eyes appear larger. Her lips were blood red. She smelled like cherry blossoms and talcum powder. She was no taller than five feet. She wobbled in her Manolo Blahniks pumps.

Mark studied the shelves in the storage room. There were so many boxes his head spun. The Haitian guy followed and pointed to the shoes. He thanked him and ran up the stairs.

"Wrong color! Do again, quick, customer waiting."

Mark ran back and picked up the same pair of shoes in red and darted to Ming.

"Good! Now this, size eight. Hurry, customer gonna take subway."

194

The second pair was harder to find. The Haitian guy said it was missing. He returned to Ming empty-handed.

"Bad filing. Let customer buy other pair!"

Mark smiled, agreeing with Ming. He panted from his trips to the storage room. Ming took his driver's license to the office behind the shoes boxes.

"Background check!"

Mark was hired for eight dollars an hour and a one percent commission. After a forty-hour week, he expected about $280. It was not enough for a room at the Salvation Army.

He labored at the job, running up and down the stairs looking for shoes for moody women. Some gave him one shoe at a time to look for, and purchased the fourth or fifth pair. Some simply smiled, thanked him, and walked out the store. He began to understand their habits and became a savvy shoes salesman. His previously sweaty shirt from countless trips up and down the stairs, retained its dryness. He screened customers who were more likely to buy with the least aggravation or trips. Sometimes he returned with three or four boxes of similar shoes for indecisive customers.

After work, he browsed magazine at Barnes and Noble in Union Square. One evening he picked up *Essence* magazine and was surprised the new photo editor was Andrea Wall from Howard University. They were in the same editorial photography class. He remembered he had written a story for the school paper about her burgeoning photography career. He decided to contact her.

When he returned to Carol's apartment, he told her about discovering Andrea Wall. Carol's response was like she sucked the jam out of his donut.

"Do you have a portfolio to show her?" she asked.

What remained from Mark's depleted inventory wasn't enough for a portfolio. The *American Photo* magazine publication in the annual contest and a few tear sheets wouldn't secure an internship, even if he was relying on a favor. He borrowed Carol's camera to create one.

His first model was an attractive white girl with dirty blond hair he met at a coffee shop on Christopher Street. She was always pleasant when he ordered, and one evening he asked her to be his model. She was more flattered than interested. Mark got a few awkward shots against a marble statue in Washington Square Park, but the photos looked amateur. He was disappointment with the results.

He tried an agency model after pestering the agent at Karin Models for two weeks. He received a Polaroid shot of a black Jamaican girl, who resembled Juline Samuel. He met the model in the hallway of the agency shot her on Prince Street along a black cast iron step. The photos were better, but they still looked amateur. The model's makeup did nothing for her pimples. Her short hair pulled back to emphasize her square jawline was the only striking quality about the photos. The agency advised Mark to assist a real photographer to learn the craft.

Mark decided to try again with Ming. He purchased four black and white rolls and told her to wear a white outfit. When they had no customer in the store, he instructed her to pose against a wall that was illuminated by florescent lights. She enjoyed posing in front of the camera. She almost cracked her first smile. When he picked up the contact sheets, he felt better. He studied Herbs Ritts, Richard Avedon and Irving Penn photos. He relearned about composition and lighting. He found girls from other agencies who were testing and a few weeks later he had a portfolio of twelve portraits.

The offices of *Essence* magazine felt like homecoming. Howard graduates paraded the halls. Andrea didn't share his sentiment. She was annoyed with her college peers wanting a "hook up." She was surprise to see Mark outside her office without an appointment, but gave face and waved him inside.

"Hi Mark. I heard you're staying with Carol. How have you been?"

"Okay … yuh luk good … congratulations!"

Mark remembered the last time he saw Andrea on campus after the newspaper published their story, She was so excited and grateful. She was hired by *The Hilltop* and after graduation joined *Essence* as the photo intern He couldn't answer her question without opening the floodgates, so he lied.

"I'm shooting a lot. I brought some recent photos to show yuh."

"You can leave them with my assistant. Who are you shooting for?"

Mark wanted to clear the veneer Andrea had wrapped herself in, but he felt the coldness in the office. Andrea had also changed. She collected Mark's portfolio and placed it on a pile, some with more photos in and expensive leather bound cases.

"I was hoping yuh could luk at it and tell me what yuh tink."

"I'm sorry, Mark. The issue is closing this week and I'm on deadline."

Her face made what appeared to be a smile then rolled away in her chair and opened a file on her computer. She looked at Mark, signaling their meeting was over and it was time for him to leave. He retrieved his portfolio from the pile and left.

Mark took his portfolio to work to show Ming the three photos of her he had selected. She looked at the photos and her face grew hot.

"Model release! No model release! You have no right."

"A jus using dem for my portfolio."

"No! I want negative!"

"I paid for it."

"So what? Picture is me!"

"If yuh want dem, yuh have to pay for dem."

"Give me picture or you fired!"

Ming grabbed the negatives and ran her nails through them.

"You fired, wait for check. Don't come back!"

Mark wasn't looking forward to returning to Carol's apartment and telling her he lost his job. It had been a month of sleeping on her couch and she was ready for him to leave. Whenever he saw Kendra dashing to her room or dropping hints, he knew he had overstayed his welcome. He knew he had to find another job quickly, whatever it was, and save enough money to find someone looking for a roommate or a room somewhere. He wasn't sure where there was an opportunity for him.

When he walked up the steps to the apartment, he saw his bags at the door. The locks had been changed. A note fell from the hinge.

Hey Sweetie. Sorry, but it's time for you to move on. Keep in touch. Carol.

Mark wore his last clean white shirt and khaki slacks. He bought a gray tie at a thrift store and headed to Central Park. They were hiring for the concession stand at the Shakespeare in the Park for seven dollars an hour. He ducked under the subway turnstile and hopped on the number six train.

When he arrived at the Delacorte Theatre, fifteen teenagers dressed in jeans and T-shirts were filing out applications. He stood at the far end of the counter with an application. He made up an address and made his application as simple as possible, omitting college education, internships, and other accolades he normally would have been proud to include.

He handed the application to a bubbly twenty-year-old coed. She was plump and full of life, anxious for the day her braces came off. Her bangs were pulled back with a bandana and two pigtails dangled over her shoulders. She wore loose denim and an over-sized gray T-shirt with the Shakespeare in the Park logo on the left of her perky breasts. A sticker over the logo read "Hi, my name is Becky," which she highlighted with animated smiley faces. She felt positively radiant with her first managerial assignment of hiring ten people to man the booths. She looked at Mark's application and flashed her wire teeth then giggled when he looked at her.

"Hi! Mark how are you?"

"Hi."

Mark was already annoyed before Becky opened her mouth. She reminded him of Celeste, the manager at Connpirg, he ran around with in Westport for three days knocking on doors begging for donations to save the ozone layer.

"Where's your smiley face?" Becky asked.

She batted her eyes dubiously. Mark made a pretentious wide mouth grin. Becky read his application then the job description from a clipboard. She told him about the organization. Mark's sole question if hired was would he be required to work next to her.

"Do you have a nick-name, Mark?"

"No."

"The staff is like family." She said. "Sometimes we have pizza night."

Mark cut his eyes.

"Can I reach you at this number? I'm making my decisions later. If you don't hear from me by then, you can give me a call tomorrow."

"Okay. I look forward to hearing from you."

Mark took her phone number and knew he had no other choice but to call her because the number he wrote on the application didn't exist. He decided to hang around Central Park and find a quiet area to take a nap. At the Boat House, he sat on the rocks overlooking the lake from the Ramble. Couples paddled rowboats and ducks fluttered in the water. The restaurant at the Boat House buzzed with activities.

A wedding reception was in its second hour. Mark salivated from the smell of roasted meat on an open grill. His stomach growled. He moved up on a rock under the shades and took off his shoes. He lay on his back with his shoes under his head. The wedding party danced to "New York, New York." Mark closed his eyes.

He lost his balance on the rock and woke up. The sun was going down and a group of Mexicans were tying the rowboats against a fence. The wedding party was replaced by a quieter dinner crowd. Mark wiped the saliva from his cheek. He was hungry, but didn't feel like hunting for food in the trash. He wanted to appease another appetite.

The Ramble was a wild landscape built away from the carriage and bridle paths. It was meant to be wandered through. Gay boys called it "The Racks," or "ground zero" for outdoor gay sex in New York City. On a hot steamy, mid-summer's night, you could hear Ludwig Van Beethoven, Symphony Number Nine in D minor in the background while getting your cock sucked.

Central Park closed at one in the morning, but the boys roamed until sunrise. Every type was represented with enough to go around. Whoever had the stamina could go back for seconds. Mark walked along the dirt path under the towering sycamore trees. A black bird darted from a locust tree, shaking the leaves. A squirrel raced up the willow oak and a family of raccoons dug through a garbage bin under the yellow wood. Overlooking the lake was a log shelter. Mark looked through the trees at the shadows of men floating by. He lit a half smoked cigarette and faced the lake. He wanted to sink under the water and reemerge into the life he felt he deserved. He lost the urge for sex and fell asleep.

A patrol car was parked on the bridge and a police officer stood over Mark glaring through his gold rimmed aviator sunglasses. He rested his weight on one leg and tapped Mark's feet with a baton.

"You can't sleep here," he said. "If I catch you sleeping here again, I'll arrest you for trespassing."

Mark didn't care if he was arrested. At least it would be somewhere to sleep, free from the mosquitoes. He wouldn't mind a bologna sandwich to ease his hunger. He walked over the bridge to call Becky. He found a phone at the corner of Amsterdam and 81st Street. After the fourth ring, Becky's answering machine came on. Mark was irritated. He had wasted a quarter. He went back to Central Park and sat in the grass near John Lennon's memorial. He tried to sleep again, but was restless. A few minutes later he decided to call Becky again.

"Hi Becky. Is Mark Palmer, bout de jab?"

"Hi Mark, could you hold on, I've got my soror Sally on the line."

Becky clicked the phone to the next party, but hung up instead.

"Fucking stupid bitch!!!"

Mark redialed.

"Hi Mark. Sorry about that."

"A calling bout de job. Did I get it?"

Becky giggled.

"Oh, let me check the names."

Becky looked through the applications and found the list of new hires.

"Oh hi! Can you make it tomorrow at five thirty?"

"In de marning?"

Mark slept at the wood shelter the cop had warned him not to. He woke up before dawn and walked through the Ramble to a trail overlooking the lake to the Bethesda fountain on the other side. He saw a few gay boys leaving. He cleared away the overgrown grass and curled up behind a cluster of bamboo foliage and tried to sleep before the sun came out. He woke up after two in the afternoon and walked to a public restroom to wash the sleep out his eyes. He gargled and brushed away the fallen leaves and twigs stuck to his clothes.

Bird watchers and courting couples, ignoring the condom wrappers scattered on the ground, were walking through the Ramble. He waited at the theatre with the new hires for Becky to arrive. She had a pile of T-shirts and caps with sticker tags on a clipboard. The new hires were dressed in Shakespeare in the Park T-shirts and stickers with their names. There were no smiley faces by Mark's name.

Becky assigned Mark to the booth that sold souvenir T-shirts and posters, and distributed free headphones. He had forty dollars in his till and was warned if it came up short termination was inevitable. When the theater opened, a crowd gathered at the refreshment stands. The new hires fumbled around filling cups with soda, serving potato chips and hot hogs. The line at Mark's booth was filled with senior citizens clutching walkers and resting on companions. Tourists waited to buy a fifteen dollar cotton-polyester blend T-shirt, to advertise they saw a free Shakespeare play in New York City and it made them cool.

A petulant old woman crept to the front of the line.

"Young man, I'll have two medium T-shirts and two headphones."

"Thirty dollars."

She rested on the counter.

"What?"

Mark repeated the amount.

She looked like she lived in a cramped efficiency on Avenue B, but pretended she had a penthouse on the Upper East Side. She reached into her purse and placed two twenty dollar bills on the counter. Mark looked at her reproachfully. She looked at the man beside her and mumbled.

"Yuh said something?" Mark asked.

She shook her head.

"Expensive!"

Mark placed ten dollars on the counter.

"How much was de ticket and de headphones?"

"I beg your pardon?"

"It nuh free?"

"You don't have to be so fresh young man."

Mark looked at her and rolled his eyes.

"Nexs!"

The rest of the night went similarly. The third evening, Becky pulled Mark aside and told him to be polite. Mark said he would, but when another customer complained about the black guy giving out headphones, she stepped in to supervise the booth. Mark was quiet and forced a smile.

Mark showed up to work in the same clothes he had worn for days. He was relieved the black T-shirt and jeans hid the dirt and he was able to wash up in the park's restroom. He ate anything he could scrounge, waiting for his first paycheck.

One evening Mark's till was short forty-five dollars. Becky wasn't sure where the money went. She didn't blame Mark because she miscounted the number of T-shirts that were sold. A few days later, the till was short thirty dollars. Becky wasn't aware because the two T-shirts sold gave Mark a reason to be nice.

His luck ran out when Becky's father told her to let him go because Mrs. Frances was appalled by the way he was rude to her. She had been coming to see the plays for ten years. She missed one summer when she went to Sicily to bury her father. She said she had never been treated with so much disrespect. She thought Mark needed to learn how to show respect to white people.

Mark pocketed a hundred dollars his last night and didn't return for his paycheck. He bought cigarettes and a six pack and it made him feel better about himself. He decided to go to Chelsea.

Chapter Eleven

It had been months since Mark had ventured downtown or gone to a gay club. He wanted to meet someone and crash at their place. His optimism faded after the last beer. He settled for finding a trick and returning to the park to sleep behind a tree. He hopped on the A train to 23rd Street and walked west to 8th Avenue.

There were men everywhere in Chelsea. Men leaving gyms, walking dogs, picking up carry-out, standing outside bars, jumping out of cabs, and sitting by street side restaurants. They walked down 8th Avenue with shopping bags like they were on a runway. Some acted like they had just flown in from Ibiza or wherever their diva status made them believe they were. Some had headphones - switching and bopping to music - on their way to meet friends, shrieking wide-eyed for attention.

Mark walked into Rainbow and Triangle, picked up a *HX* magazine and crossed the street to the Starbucks at the corner of 19th Street. The baristas ran around preparing drink orders. A guy in the line relayed the perils of a blind date.

"What you having, honey?"

"A grande iced coffee wid six pumps of caramel, whipped cream, ahn caramel drizzle."

The barista was used to queens ordering the usual grande skinny latte and made a double take.

"What was that?"

Mark repeated his order.

"Sure you don't want a skinny latte?"

The barista at the cash register shouted the order to the other barista, rolled his eyes then shouted "recall" and repeated Mark's order. Mark sat by the window with his drink, looking at a crowd outside the Joyce Theater. He flicked through the magazine and decided to go to Splash.

Splash was the popular gay bar in Chelsea. It had a neighborhood bar feel on weeknights, but on weekends turned into a circuit dance club. Sunday nights attracted black men and their admirers. Mark didn't like hip hop nights at any club, but he knew Splash had an international crowd with gay men from Europe on holiday. He thought he usually did well with those types, especially the ones from Germany.

Down at the video bar on the lower level, a shirtless bartender was shaking his ass to Ricky Martin's "La Vida Loca." Another bartender in a wife-beater with the Splash logo across his chest was making drinks and greeting patrons. Old gay men crowded the seats, sipping apple martinis and whiskey sours. They filled the tip bucket as the young gay boys sat on the outer seats waiting to be noticed.

Mark ordered a Sea Breeze and watched the music videos. He overheard two Puerto Ricans next to him talking about a friend they hadn't seen in weeks since he started dating a guy who lived in Hoboken. They joked that he got married. One said he wouldn't mind being with a man that took care of him, but he wasn't getting into a relationship with an old man. The other guy said old men were only good for one thing, and if they didn't have money they weren't good for anything.

Mark glanced past them to two guys making a scene in the club. A graying white man, looking like somebody's grandfather was fondling a black guy with prison tattoos. He flashed his gold grill as the old man roped his arms around his waist.

Across the bar, a guy sat fidgeting. He sang along with the music video, pausing to sip his drink. Mark lit a cigarette, and before he blew out the smoke the guy came skipping over. Mark's smirk conveyed he wasn't interested.

"What's up, girl? You have a cigarette?" the guy asked.

Mark handed him a cigarette and the match-box on the table.

"What's up?" Mark asked. "Tink it's gonna be gud tonite?"

"Suppose to. It's thug nite."

Mark looked around the club.

"You wanna go dance upstairs?"

"Nat really. A tryin' to meet somebady."

"A date?"

"No. Jus somebady a attracted to."

"Oh, my bad."

The fidgeting guy walked back to the bar and picked up where he let off in the music video. Mark walked to the restroom, hoping someone joined him in a stall. He stood over the urinal, pretending to pee, sneaking a peak at the men beside him. They came in and out, only the ones with no appeal lingered. Mark zipped up his trousers and went to the bar. He had another drink and stared at a guy next to him. He wanted to say something, but the guy walked away and met a friend. He spotted another guy walking unbalanced towards him and his luck improved.

"You want a drink?"

"A have one a ready."

207

"Wanna dance?"

"Sure."

Mark followed the guy to the center of the dance floor. He didn't feel like dancing, but it was a start. The guy glared at him like a hungry dog looking at a faraway bone. It was lust at first sight, and Mark welcomed it. The guy swung his arms and danced without rhythm. Mark thought he was either clumsy or drunk. He pulled Mark to his chest and slid his wet lips against his ear.

"What's your name?" the guy asked.

"Andrew," Mark said.

"Sebastian ... you sexy."

Mark noticed an accent and wiped his ear.

"Where yuh fram?"

"Paris."

Sebastian searched his pocket and found a little black bottle.

"Want some?"

"Wat is it?"

"Poppers. It will make you want me more."

Sebastian put the bottle to his nose and inhaled. Mark followed. He felt a rush. Sebastian plunged his tongue down Mark's throat. Mark gasping for air and moved his tongue into Sebastian's mouth. He held Mark against the wall and sucked his neck. Mark moved his hand over Sebastian's chest and ripped his shirt open. Sebastian reached up and ran his lips over the top of Mark's head and gave him little bites. Mark stuck his hand down his pants and pulled his cock. They danced all night, taking breaks to sip drinks and rearrange their clothes. Mark was drunk with him.

"Wanna come to my place?"

"Where?"

"The Bowery."

"Sure."

Sebastian pulled Mark through the crowd to the sidewalk and hailed down a cab.

"2nd and Houston."

His leg was between Mark's thighs, kissing him behind the neck. The cab driver looked through the rearview mirror then back at traffic. They cruised down 17th Street at Union Square Park and headed east. The cab stopped at the red light at The Cock on 2nd Avenue.

"Right here."

Sebastian gave the cab driver twenty dollars and told him to keep the change. He escorted Mark to a door between a wash and fold laundry and a Chinese take-out. He fumbled with the three locks on the door then guided Mark up the steps.

"Come in. I'm going to use the bathroom."

Mark looked around the apartment while Sebastian peed. A door was open and another room with ballerina slippers on the door knob was closed. A gray cat with knotted hair purred and rubbed against his leg. At a desk, the computer's screensaver displayed a purple tulips in a red neon field under pink skies. A window was crowded with potted plants by a fire escape. The unmade bed was scattered with clothes. On the hardwood floor were more potted plants and boxes storing clothes.

Sebastian looked mischievous when he entered the bedroom. He pulled Mark onto the bed and unbuttoned his shirt. Mark ran his hand through his hair and pulled his head towards his stomach. Sebastian looked into his eyes and grazed his chin against his crotch. Mark waited for him to unzip his pants and put his cock in his mouth. Sebastian gagged. They undressed and felt the heat between them when their skin met. Mark rolled Sebastian on his back and pushed his hips between his thighs. Sebastian spat on his fingers to lubricate his anus then reached for a condom on the nightstand.

"Ouch!" Not so hard."

Mark pushed slower. Sebastian inhaled and held Mark's hips, spreading his legs across the bed. Mark moved in deeper. Sebastian moaned and moved up on the bed.

"Oh Jesus!"

Sweat dripped from Mark's face. He had never been so aggressive. Maybe it was built-up frustration he wanted to expel. He slipped out and moved up inside Sebastian again. He went deeper and pounded harder. Sebastian cried out and raised his legs like Mark was changing his diapers.

"Fuck me! Fuck me hard!"

When they came, Sebastian made an uproar.

"Oh shit! Oh fuck!"

Mark exhaled heavily through his nostrils and grew quiet. Sebastian stood up, went to the shower and began singing. Mark drifted to sleep from exhaustion. Sebastian returned wearing silk boxers and curled up beside Mark to smoke a joint.

In the morning, Mark left Sebastian's bed to take a shower. Sebastian sat at his computer scrutinizing a photo of a black rose floating in a sky of red clouds. He enlarged the rose petals and painted the stems purple. Mark returned from the shower curious about the image, but decided not to ask. He studied Sebastian's far set green eyes, narrow nose, and full lips. His jet black hair was suspect. He looked at Sebastian's legs and remembered his towering height on the dance floor. They seemed shrunken wrapped around his waist. Mark was satisfied that Sebastian was attractive, although he didn't remember the night.

"You hungry?"

Sebastian turned from the computer and rolled his chair towards Mark.

"A lickle."

Mark reached down to kiss him.

"I'll make you an omelet, or I can pick up something."

"Omelet is fine."

Mark didn't want to leave the apartment.

A bony face guy peeped from behind the door and glared at Mark then smiled at Sebastian.

"That's my roommate, Gabriel."

"Hi."

Gabriel nodded.

"Makin' omelets, want some?"

"Thanks, but I have to run. Rehearsals."

"Okay. Have a good one."

Sebastian walked to the small kitchen, opened the refrigerator, and poured orange juice. He cleared away the newspapers and magazines from a table, pulled the blinds, and opened the window. The sun rays made a soft light on the wood table. He lit a candle and shuffled hand over hand a deck of Rider-Waite tarot cards.

Gabriel returned to the apartment.

"Oh, before I forget. I've got two tickets for the show."

Sebastian smiled and kept his eyes on the tarot cards. He placed them on the table and pondered. He looked up and smiled again. His eyes sparkled

211

at Mark. He went to the stove with a skillet and began pouring eggs and adding milk, cheese, mushroom, tomatoes, and green peppers. He noticed the tickets on top of the microwave.

"Wanna see a ballet?"

Mark raised his brows.

"Sure. I thought de tickets was for yuh and yuh roommate."

"No, he's in the ballet."

"Cool."

Mark was excited Sebastian wanted to see him again.

"You drink coffee?"

"Yeah, but juice is fine."

He didn't want anything to spoil his stream of happiness. He worried Sebastian expected him to leave after breakfast.

Sebastian forked into his omelet and ate in silence. Mark cleaned his plate and wanted more, but he thought it was too soon to be asking for seconds. Sebastian chewed slowly and contemplated.

"Wanna go to the pool later?"

"Yun don't work?"

"I'm self-employed."

"Wat yuh do?"

"Art."

"On really, what kine?"

"Computer art."

"Is dat wat de black rose is about?"

"Yeah, for my next show."

"Cool. A do a lickle photography, too."

"That's nice."

Mark felt patronized. Sebastian talked about his technique - using digital applications to manipulate images to create a fantasy. Mark didn't see any art in painting a rose black floating in red clouds, so he kept his opinion to himself. He thought it would have only made sense to a child's mind.

After breakfast, Sebastian pulled him onto the bedroom for another blow job before returning to the computer. Mark lay in bed browsing magazines. He wanted to say something about photography but decided not to. Sebastian was silent. Mark feared he was already bored of him.

"Where you live?"

"Huh."

"You have a job?"

Mark's stomach growled.

"Nat really."

Sebastian lit a cigarette and sat by the window, looking down at the street.

"Are you a hustler?"

Mark laughed.

"No. A was at a fren in Brooklyn, but a had to leave."

"So where you're staying now?"

"Nowhere really."

He squinted at Mark then blew smoke. He flicked the cigarette butt through the window and walked over to the bed. Mark prepared to leave.

"You wanna crash here for a few days?"

"Yuh sure?"

Sebastian wasn't sure about his offer. It had been months since he'd met someone who fucked him like Mark, and he didn't want to pass it up. Gabriel wouldn't object that he was in the apartment. He was always at rehearsals, performing, or on tour.

"You can be my houseboy. Fuck me when I want."

They spent the rest of the day poolside at The Asser Levy Recreation Center on the east side then took a cab to Chelsea and walked up 8th Avenue holding hands. They lunched at the Viceroy restaurant. Sebastian had a medium rare buffalo steak burger. Mark had smoked salmon and roasted potatoes. They browsed magazines at Rainbows and Triangle then headed to Barracuda's on 22nd for the two for one Long Island drink special.

Mark was grateful. He was oblivious to everything around him. Cigarette butts on the sidewalks were ignored. Trash bins with discarded food ceased to be a pride swallowing necessity. Everything had a sense of order and he knew it was because he didn't need to worry where he was going to sleep that night or if he had food. Sebastian calmed his worries and it felt wholesome to be desired.

Sebastian gloated like he had won a trophy. He didn't have to go out and get wasted to meet someone. Mark wasn't like one of his regulars who never called, but showed up at three in the morning for a quick fuck. He wasn't going to disappear with his wallet when he slept. He was someone decent he could make into a boyfriend, as long as the stars aligned.

"You wanna see a movie?"

"That sounds gud. Wat playing?"

"Don't know. We'll find out."

He grabbed Mark's hand and pulled him from the bar seat. They walked a block and stood before the marquee at the Clearview cinema. Sebastian suggested *The Matrix*, but Mark wasn't keen on that type of movie. He

214

decided on *All About My Mother* and it felt like a great way to end one of his best days.

After the movie, they took a cab back to the apartment. Sebastian rolled a joint in bed. Mark took a puff from the joint and sat by the window. The cat crawled down the fire escape and rubbed against his arm. Mark flinched. He thought he saw whiskers growing out of Sebastian's cheeks. He looked out the window and smiled for no reason. He felt the waves in his stomach.

"Dat is sum gud shit," Mark said.

"You like it?" Sebastian asked. "It's from Jamaica."

"Yeah."

"I know where to get the good shit."

"It been a while."

"Feels good don't it? Come here! Make me feel good, too."

Mark missed Sebastian's touch in the morning. He opened his eyes and he wasn't there. Sebastian sat by the table in the kitchen looking at his cards. His was puzzled by the reading. He came into the bedroom, sat by the computer, and looked at the black rose on the screen. His eyes darted through the room.

"You can't stay!"

Mark trembled.

"I thought yuh said a could stay for a couple days."

"I can't afford to take care of you!"

"A nat asking yuh to take care of mi!"

"I spent all my money on you yesterday."

"Yuh don't have to. A thought yuh wanted to."

"It was fun, but I can't afford it. You have to leave!"

215

"Please ... a can help hout ... a can get a jab ... a will pay yuh back."

"I don't think it is a good idea."

Sebastian still wasn't sure if he wanted Mark to leave, but he was certain he didn't need someone to depend on him. Mark thought the welcome was over. He washed his face and left.

At the Viceroy restaurant, he asked for a job application. The waiter said they weren't looking for busboys. He filled in the server position and waited. The manager told him to leave a resume. At Nisos, a few doors away, all the waiters looked like they were a part of the same family. They spoke a foreign language Mark didn't recognize. He felt it would be a waste of time, so he left.

At Caliente Cab Company Mexican restaurant, the white wait staff was busy during the lunch rush. The hostess told him to come back after four. He walked to Washington Square Park and sat on a bench. He was angry the waiters looked at him like he wasn't good enough to wait tables. He thought about going to Macy's, but an interview would take weeks. He could apply for a job at Starbucks, but it would be difficult to be so cheerful all the time, even if he was wired up on coffee.

People in the park were out and about with activities. Street performers called on spectators from a dwindling crowd. Couples sat in the grass, reading and laying around. Boys with boom-boxes break danced, and girls with shopping bags chatted on cell phones. He watched with a numbness like he didn't exist.

He decided to fill out more job applications. He thought about going to the Monster Bar to apply for a bar-back position, but he knew he wasn't brave enough to take off his shirt in a gay club. He headed to Christopher Street and saw a sign advertising for waiters. He stepped into the Riviera

Café and noticed the empty tables inside with customers out on the patio. He forced a smile and asked the bartender for an application. Her leathery tattooed skin, eighties mullet, pancake makeup and black outfit was intimidating. She returned his smile with an application.

"Is dere somebady a can talk to? De manager."

"Wait a second dude. Jerry will be right back."

She wasn't as threatening as the brownstone lesbians in Park Slope, nor did she seem to mind having him around her.

Jerry entered the bar with a box to stock the restrooms with toilet paper. He looked at Mark with his application then at his watch.

The shift change when a waiter walked in. He looked hungover. He checked his work station and exchanged small talk while folding napkins and setting the tables. Mark thought maybe between the heavy metal kid and the tattooed lesbian bartender there was a place for a skinny black queen - a label he was reluctant to embrace.

"You're a new Server?" the waiter asked.

"No. A applying."

"Where you work before?"

"Huh?"

"Don't worry, Jerry's cool."

Jerry took Mark's application to his office. He told Mark to wait until they were set up or come back the next day after four. Mark waited and was kept entertained by the waiter with the green hair. He told him what to look out for at the job. The bartender had been working at Riviera Café for two years. She said Jerry was easy to get along with and working there was fun. Mark wanted the job more than ever because he saw them as new friends.

Jerry returned and was pulled to the side by the bartender. He looked at

Mark and nodded. The interview was quick. Jerry said he had a lunch slot that he used to train new hires and if he had any dinner slots in a few days Mark would get it. The senior waiters were assigned the patio tables during the dinner shift. It was where they made the most money. Mark was happy to be hired and his placement amongst the better tables wasn't an issue.

He raced to Sebastian's with the good news. Sebastian was reading his cards. He opened the door and smiled. Mark was surprised, trying to forget his hard face in the morning. Sebastian was in good spirits when Mark told him he found a job.

Mark caught on fast as a waiter. He had no choice. It not only meant having a job, but it was his security to stay with Sebastian. The other waiters were helpful. He got random tables the second day and looked forward to when his training was completed. His duties were to set the tables, take orders with recommendations, serve and pour wine, carry two or three dishes at once, and ring up the bill with the new computer system. Mark coasted through the training. His only fear was difficult customers because he knew he didn't have the best customer service skills.

When he returned to the apartment, Sebastian made a light chicken dinner. Mark suspected he had a good reading. They had comfortable sex that night without marijuana or poppers. It felt like routine.

The third day, Mark had a section on the patio. The waiter with the green hair called in sick and the coveted spot was available. Mark had a fair estimation of what he would earn in tips judging from a couple who ordered burgers and beer, leaving six dollars, to a table of four who had steak, and twenty. He was satisfied because he didn't have to pool his tips with the other waiters and it would keep Sebastian stable.

His first table arrived earlier than the regular dinner crowd. An older man and what appeared to be his daughter, seemed predictable, so Mark wasn't worried. They ordered Caesar salads and he quickly returned with bread and water. He buzzed around pouring Pellegrino and cleaning bread crumbs. Jerry's eyes were on him. Another set of patrons landed in his area. The four Chelsea boys looked like well-aged teenagers. He braced himself for the challenge. As the noise of their chairs settled, they exchanged kisses and compliments. One of the men waved for service.

"We'll have a Mai Tai, vodka with OJ on the rocks, and two Heineken."

Mark forced a smile and bolted to the bar. The kitchen rang for the salads to be picked up. Mark raced to serve the two-top. They asked about the specials. Mark flipped through his menu notes and recommended the Mahi Mahi. The girl wiggled her nose and asked what that was. Mark smiled and said he would check the kitchen. She decided on a medium rare burger with fries and her father agreed to the same.

As he waited for the Chelsea boys drink order, Jerry asked if he had checked their IDs. One of the men cocked his head to the side and asked how long it took to get a Mai Tai. Mark carded him and he rolled his eyes when he had to open his Louis Vuitton wallet to reveal he was thirty-eight.

When Mark returned with the drinks, he fumbled and knocked the Mai Tai on the guy's lap. He cringed like it was hot water.

"Oh my God! Oh my God! My outfit!"

The bartender shook her head. Mark reached for a napkin.

"Don't touch me! Get your manager!"

Mark rushed to Jerry, leaving the two top with their mouths slightly opened. The bartender made another drink and told him it was on the house. Mark returned without Jerry and the guy accepted his free drink, sucking it down in triumph. He took their orders and apologized. The kitchen rang and he raced for the two-top's plate. When he returned, the girl's frown disappeared when she bit into the burger.

Mark dreaded returning to the four Chelsea boys with their salads. He asked a busboy for help with the plates. It annoyed Jerry. He stood over the table grinding pepper on their salads until they dismissed him. He took a deep breath and kept a straight face in front of the bartender.

"You should see what it's like on a Friday night with the NYU kids."

The evening ended with little fanfare, but Jerry wasn't impressed. The bartender told him to give Mark a week. The next day he was assigned to the section of the restaurant that was often empty. He knew he was being watched. No one wanted to sit in the chilly room, when they could be outside on the patio and enjoy the warm summer breeze and people watch while gorging down an overdone steak.

The week got better although Mark was demoted to cleaning silverware and folding napkins. He was assigned the unpopular tables in the chilly room. It was frequented by pairs of old women in angora sweaters who complained of the heat on the patio. He had no patience with these diners. They expected to be treated like royalty. They ordered a pitcher of water with lemons and used the sweet and low condiments to make a drink. Their tips was always at the minimum and rounded off to the last nickel and dime.

Whenever a customer raised their head for service or waved because a fork fell on the floor, Jerry was there behind Mark. He felt the pressure and he began to crack. He needed to have a favorable response to Sebastian's constant work inquires.

He survived a second week, got paid, and decided to treat himself. He wanted to go somewhere he didn't have to eat humble pie. He wanted cigarettes and drinks without getting it from someone. He needed to feel good about having a job and coping with Sebastian. It was summer and he was fucking alive in New York City.

At The Monster, he stood by the piano listening to old queens singing show tunes. He hoped their festive spirit was contagious, but it wasn't. He was distracted by their stares and missed the chance to appreciate the singer's rendition of "I feel pretty."

He bought cigarettes and beer and sat by the pier. He looked in the Hudson River at the New Jersey skyline, gulping down the beer then walked up the pier. A crowd stood outside a club with flyers littering the street. Junior Vasquez was spinning at The Tunnel. He decided to go because it was free before midnight.

The Tunnel was a mega club that attracted hundreds, located in the Terminal Warehouse Company Central Stores Building. Like Twilo and Roxy, it was the trendiest place for a gay boy to be on a Saturday night, if he could drop twenty-five dollars at the door after midnight. Kevin Aviance was scheduled to perform.

Gay boys stood in line, salivating over Vinnie, the muscular bouncer with dreams of being an actor. The popular clubkids sashayed through the VIP line, sucking lollypops. Inside, Mark stopped at the unisex bathroom to refashion his waiter uniform. He rolled up his shirt and pants, tossing his mildewed socks in the trash.

The up tempo, synthesized baseline, and electronic drums were hypnotic. Rainbow lights flashed on the warehouse ravers like a police siren. Their movements looked like mild seizures. The clubbers danced with sheer ecstasy or whatever available drugs they could get while cruising the restroom stalls.

Mark sneaked into the VIP Lava lounge, trailing a group of club kids. He felt a tingle of importance when he heard it was once the stomping ground of nightlife royalties like Amanda Lepore and Rupaul. He decided to do a bump if anyone offered. No one did. He wasn't welcomed into any clique. Around two in the morning, the boys strolled to the dance floor like zombies. Kevin Aviance was ready to cut up.

A six feet five, black glamazon with bald head and a face made up like one of the girls at a Mac counter, stood on a makeshift stage in the center of the club. Long eyelashes fanned his cheeks, his white teeth flashing from his smooth dark face. His body was designed for worship. He wore a black tube dress with spaghetti straps down to the waist, exposing large nipples. He posed in a pair of stilettos that could only have been custom made for his size fourteen feet.

The crowd yelled, "Junior! Junior! Junior!" approving his nightlife protégé.

Junior played his popular summer anthem, Deborah Cox's "Who Do You Love" remix.

Kevin served like his next meal depended on it. The crowd reveled in his performance. Mark joined the decadence and felt alive for the first time in months.

It was after six in the morning when he rung the buzzer to Sebastian's apartment. When the lights came on, he heard something unsettling inside and his nerves rattled. Sebastian came down the stairs looking like he had not slept all night. He glared at Mark with bloodshot eyes.

"Where were you?"

"A went to a club afta work."

"Did you ask me if you could go?"

222

"A didn't know a had to aks yuh."

"What club?"

"De Tunnel."

"The Tunnel?"

"It was free before midnight."

Sebastian stood before the door and struck Mark across the face.

"Get out my house!"

He went up the steps to the apartment and return with a garbage bag stuffed with the few clothes Mark owned. He threw the garbage bag down the steps and slammed the door behind him.

"Don't come back! You fucking whore!"

Mark gathered his clothes and walked to the park. He didn't know what to do with himself.

Chapter Twelve

Mark slept in Tompkins Square Park for two nights then took the subway to Brooklyn to a shelter off Flatbush Avenue. He sat on the sidewalk waiting for a bed. When the door opened at dusk, he stood in line for a bunk and was issued a soap, a blanket, and sheets. He felt more afraid than when he was in jail. He went to the restroom and half of his clothes were stolen. There were fights over sneakers and food. Before sunrise, he grabbed what he had and headed back to Manhattan.

He sought help at the LGBT community center. The lesbian at the front desk asked if he wanted a free HIV test. She gave him a print out with a list of support groups. There were groups for HIV prevention, living with HIV, overcoming the stigma of HIV and every other mentionable issue dealing with HIV.

He walked the halls and read the notice boards, hoping there would be something to help a homeless gay boy. There were invitations to join recovery and transgender groups mixed in with circuit party flyers. Down the hall in a closed room, a group of octogenarians congregated for a SAGE meeting. He thought about asking a senior if they had any use for a house boy. He felt there was no help for him, so he went back to Central Park.

Mark found a spot along a wall near the reservoir, under a cluster of evergreens. He didn't return to the restaurant because he was dirty. He had spent his last twenty dollars from his paycheck. He woke up disillusioned from sleeping behind trees. His clothes were diminishing. Each outfit he wore that was soiled he threw in the trash because he had no money for the wash. After stretching the twenty dollars for three days - buying one dollar hot dogs and pizza slices - he had nothing left. He was hungry, but embarrassed to stand in line at a soup kitchen. He decided to hustle. He wasn't sure what he was doing. He didn't know how to solicit money for sex. He decided to watch and learn.

Street boys crowded Two Potato bar on Christopher Street. They walked to the porn shop, then the streets until six in the morning. They sat at the bus sheds and on steps and waited. Mark knew what they were waiting for.

Old, seedy white men touching themselves patrolled the streets. They went to the gay bars then the porn shop with their hands in their pocket. They drove past the street boys at the bus sheds and on steps. Mark knew what they were looking for.

They drove at a slow pace with their hands steady on the steering wheel. They kept their windows down, looking sideways, shopping for a boy. They decided who they wanted to pick up and what they wanted at their price. Sometimes they took a boy to a cheap motel, but rarely took them home. They never trusted the boys because they pulled stunts in their apartments, stealing cell phones, wallets or whatever they could get through the door. Some did their business in a nearby alley. They paid very little, bargaining to ten dollars for a blow job. For some boy, it was enough to buy a nickel bag or a dinner plate.

There were different types of street boys. Straight acting club boys came out earlier in the night. If they were lucky, within hours they hopped in a car and returned high before midnight. There were thugs called "gay-for-pay." They looked like they would snatch the filling out of your teeth if you fell asleep with your mouth open. They were usually high or drunk and weren't picky about which cars they went into, as long as they topped.

Transsexuals came later in the morning before sunrise. It was then what was left of the night came alive. They came out in colors. Like spectacles, they walked in the middle of the streets to the disgust of the bridge and tunnel crowd. They were Black, White, Asian and Latino. They ruled the night. The regulars had their side of the block their competitors dared not cross. Newcomers were warned not to steal their "dates" or they wouldn't work another night. Fights came with the hustle because slashing someone's face or dousing them with acid earned respect. Those who got along walked the streets together, sharing cigarettes and food, but never their drugs. They bragged about the money they made from tricks, without disclosing what they did for it. They couldn't perform or face themselves the next day without a bump or rolling a blunt.

Mark learned fast. He knew where to stand and be noticed by a passing car. He knew who amongst them would be nice or give him a cigarette. He knew the police station on 11th Avenue routinely conducted stings. He was told never to go with anyone to a motel in Queens or Brooklyn because he wouldn't come back in one piece. He didn't know where he fit in. His washed up preppy look implied he was a young twink, but he didn't want to bottom. He wasn't hard like the thugs and not as femme as the transsexuals. He wasn't sure what type of men he would attract. He hoped to find someone who wasn't going to kill him, give him AIDS, or wanted anal sex. He wanted someone clean, and fairly attractive that wouldn't let him feel like a street walking man whore. Clearly, he was choosing the wrong line of work.

He floated between types and hoped someone found him suitable. He thought he could choose who to go with, but he learned it didn't work that way. It was the ones who had the money who called the shots. It was their choice to nod their head or stop their car to make a proposition, regardless of how repulsive they looked.

Mark wore his tight jeans and navy blue polo shirt the first night. He slipped into a pair of worn out Birkenstocks and hoped to meet someone decent. His stomach growled, which he kept at longer intervals by sucking cigarettes butts.

Christopher Street was busy with its usual weekend crowd - gays from other boroughs looking for Mr. Right or Mr. Right Now, NYU coeds eating pizza, and a flow of commuters heading to the New Jersey PATH train. He passed the leather daddies at West Side Highway and crossed the street.

Down the pier, men cruised for sex. He avoided their eyes, ignoring them pleasuring each other in the openness. They were talking and smiling, touching and groping, and kissing in the open night. Some on their knees, some bent over with their trousers down to their ankles. Some stood in a crowd watching, masturbating and waiting their turn.

It was past five in the morning. Cars delivered *The New York Times*, garbage trucks picked up dumpsters and Mark was tired. He eased his hunger with a piece of bagel he found on a windowsill. He walked back to West Side Highway and headed north. On Jane Street, he strolled in the middle of the quiet cobblestones street. Three-story brownstones with open bay windows and fancy doors separated the hard tree lined street from the wealth inside.

Before crossing West 4th Street, Mark flicked his eyes at a car going around the block. The driver looked through his rearview mirror and nodded. A rush of excitement shot through Mark. He stuck his hands in his pocket to create a bulge. When the driver drove past again with the windows down, Mark stood under a tree and waited. He fanned away a street boy who wanted a cigarette before the car returned. The driver stopped before him with the engine running.

Mark nodded.

"Hey."

Mark cleared his throat and put a little base in his voice.

"Hey, what's up?"

The driver looked at him, trying to decide if he would say something or drive off.

"What you get into?"

Mark wasn't sure what to say. He hadn't gotten used to being what the man saw him as, but he knew it came with a certain crude language.

"Wat yuh looking for?"

"Do you suck? Fuck? PNP? What?"

"Just head."

The driver tapped his finger on the steering wheel.

"How much?"

"Sixty."

Mark wasn't sure if that was too much or too little.

"You wanna come to my place?"

He wanted to say yes immediately because he could take a shower and have some food, but he didn't want to appear desperate.

"Where yuh place?"

"Hell's Kitchen, off 52nd."

"Dat too far. Tryin' to make some money tonight ... by de time I come back ...."

"I'll give you a hundred, and I'll drive you back down."

Mark knew he wouldn't find another generous guy who was nearly as decent. He was tall, maybe six feet four. He spoke softly, but masculine. His green shirt and khaki pants looked like he shopped at J. Crew and was looking for something different than his boyfriend.

"A don't get fucked."

"That's cool. I don't either."

Mark got in the Ford Explorer and scanned the interior. The car was clean. It drowned out the ripe smell rising from his armpits. The driver rolled up the tinted windows and shut all the doors.

"A guess a caan jump hout or anything."

"I don't usually do this. I just feel like some company tonight."

Mark tried to relax. He wondered what the guy wanted for a hundred dollars.

He drove up West Side Highway at a steady pace. He looked like he knew Mark all his life and had just picked him up from the airport. He turned on the radio, pressing in search for music. He found nothing to his taste and turned it off. He placed his palm on Mark's thigh.

"I'm Glen."

"Andrew."

He looked over at Mark.

"That's not your real name is it?"

"It can be whatever yuh want."

"You wanna get some beer?"

"Sure. Can yuh get some cigarettes too? Marlboro Lights."

Glen pulled into a gas station on 49th Street and bailed out the car with the keys in the ignition. Mark turned on the radio and watched Glen walking away. He felt human because Glen trusted him with his car, even though driving off never crossed his mind. He was concerned about the pack of cigarettes and thinking how much he could get out of Glen during the course of the ordeal.

Glen returned with a pack of Black & Mild and a six pack without cigarettes. He found a plastic bag with a stash of marijuana.

"You wanna roll?"

"No. Where de cigarettes?"

"I have some at the house. You can have those."

Glen drove up to the curb on 52nd Street. There were brownstones amongst the warehouses and empty office spaces. The street looked deserted to be in the city. Glen held a remote and a metal wall opened up like a garage door. He drove into a dark space and lights came on. The apartment behind the metal wall looked like an art gallery in SoHo. It had high exposed brick walls with large canvasses visible by track lights hanging below the skylight. The furnishing was sparse. Two black leather sofas sat against a black table in front of a furry area rug. There were no televisions and the doors that lead to the kitchen and dining room were shut. Mark sat on the sofa and watched Glen light his blunt, filling the room with smoke.

"Sure you don't want some? It's from Cali."

Mark declined because weed made him sleepy. He needed to be coherent in case anything fishy happened. Glen fumbled around the apartment, flipped through mail, turned on the radio, and adjusted the lights. Mark wasn't sure if their arrangement was to take place in the bedroom or on the area rug in the middle of the living room.

"Hey, yuh know a need de money first."

"Why, you don't trust me?"

"Naaw. Dat nuh hab anything to do wid it."

"You have a big dick?"

"It ah-rite."

"You wanna go up to my room? I'll show you my toys."

Mark pocketed the money and followed Glen to his dimly lit bedroom.

The décor changed to a bondage den with BDSM equipment - restraints, kinky sex toys, gags, muzzles, collars, leashes, nipple clamps, slings, swings, spreaders, strap-ons, whips, paddles, and even a straitjacket.

Mark stopped at the door and glared.

"A don't get into dat."

"Relax. I just wanna eat your ass baby."

He was relieved.

Mark left Glen's apartment at dawn and walked to the diner on 42nd Street. At the counter, he checked his pocket for the money and bought cigarettes to make change. He scanned the menu, but already knew what he wanted. A waitress sat by the kitchen door reading *The Enquirer*. She didn't look up when he entered nor when he looked at her for service. Another waitress came out the kitchen with a plate of scrambled eggs with toast and a side order of grits.

"Be right with you, hun."

Mark had a light smile on his face. His first rim job he found amusing. He wondered how Glen got off on that, when he was trying not to laugh. That was an easy way for a street boy to make a hundred dollars, he thought.

The waitress placed the plates on the counter before a half asleep, half drunk homeless man. He lifted his head and opened his eyes when she poured the coffee. She smiled, flashing two rows of crooked, cigarette stained teeth.

"What you having hun?"

"Tree eggs scrambled wid cheese, hash browns, two slice a toast, potato wedge, ahn tree pancakes. A blueberry muffin ahn coffee wid cream ahn sugar."

The waitress was stunned.

"We're out of potato wedges, hun. Don't make them this early."

"Fries?"

"Okay hun, coming right up."

She placed the pen back in her hair, ripped a page from a notepad, and went to the kitchen. Mark lit a cigarette and took a long inhale. He blew the smoke over his head and sighed. It had been weeks since he had a cigarette he didn't have to bum or find on the sidewalk. He was ashamed about what he had to do to get it, but no one had to know.

The waitress returned with a pot of coffee and reached behind the counter for a cup.

"Here you go, hun. Look like you had a long night, huh."

That night, Mark wore the same jeans and sandals with a black T-shirt from the Salvation Army. He headed back to his spot. A few cars circled the block. He smoked a cigarette, walked to Jane Street then sat on a step and waited. He walked up Horatio Street, passed Jane Hotel and waited. At two in the morning, more cars appeared. Some stopped for boys, but none of the drivers paid him any attention. He walked into Two Potato Bar, ordered a Sea Breeze, gulped it down, and left. There was a drag show at the Monster Bar. He decided to hustle later.

Larissa Dumont was reading the crowd during her popular weekend show. She rolled her tongue like only a Puerto Rican drag queens could, calling the patrons from the piano bar down to the basement circus. After a few jokes, she ran through what she did in the day before her show. She mentioned an incident at Patricia Fields when she tried to move a few eyelashes and some lipsticks in her padded, boy bosom and was caught red handed by Miss Patricia Fields herself. The crowd bellowed when she relayed the details of her weekend in jail dressed in drag.

She moved to the main attraction of the night - the fifty dollar amateur strip contest. Boys in the crowd signed up. Mark knew them from the streets. When the first contestant stepped on the stage he headed back upstairs to the piano bar. Mark spotted a boy staring, checking him out. He was probably twenty-six, but no older than twenty-nine. Mark knew he wouldn't pay for sex, but if they hooked up, he could crash at his apartment for a few nights and trade his body for his roof. All kind of thoughts came to mind because he didn't want to return to sleeping in Central Park. He returned to the basement shenanigans with Larissa Dumont and stood in the back. The guy followed. Mark looked at the guy and motioned for him to come over. The guy smiled, but didn't move. Mark walked over and stood next to him.

"Hey, what's up playa?"

Mark looked the guy over to decide if he was going to go through with his plan. The guy bopped his head to the hip hop music playing. The passive looking, corn starched, white boy acted like he was in a rap video. Mark didn't buy it.

"What's up with you tonight?" he asked.

"Not as much as a want to," Mark said.

Mark massaged his penis and rubbed against the guy.

"Yuh close?"

"Say what?"

Mark raised his voice.

"Yuh live close by?"

"Naaw. Brooklyn."

"A used to live in Park Slope."

"Oh yeah. Where do you live now?"

"Uptown. But a have a roommate."

"Me too, but it's cool. You party?"

A light went off in Mark's head. Jackpot! He nodded and the boy gulped down his beer, went to the restroom, and met him outside the club. Mark didn't want anyone to see them leave together, so he agreed to meet him at the West 4th subway. He ran across the street to Stonewall, hoping to find a better offer in Manhattan. A group of girls had taken over the club for a bridal shower. He left and headed to the subway to meet the guy. At West 4th, the guy stood by a car, the driver tapping his fingers on the steering wheel. Mark rolled his eyes and went back to Christopher Street.

He was tired. He wanted somewhere to sleep. He walked into the porn shop and noticed new faces. He thought about stealing a wallet during. He went down the steps to the booths, ignoring the Middle Eastern attendant at the counter.

A door popped opened at the booth where he stood and two men came out, straightening their shirts and zipping up their trousers. They waited outside the door then left the store. Mark stood with his hands in his jeans, looking sideways at the men. A guy in a black shirt and jeans with shiny

235

dress shoes caught his eyes. He smelled of sweat, alcohol, and cologne. Mark followed him into a booth.

"Tokens! Drop tokens please!" the attendant said.

Mark zipped up his pants, pulled down his T-shirt and opened the booth. He walked over to the attendant and gave him five dollars. The attendant gave him four tokens. The guy lost interest and left the store before another guy briskly walked down the steps and stood next to Mark. He had his hands in his cargo khaki shorts, fidgeting, unsure which leg to rest on. He looked agitated like he was rolling.

Mark thought he would do as soon as he saw him. He looked like a model from an old Marlboro ad - white, handsome, and rugged with a five o'clock shadow. He looked at his crotch and brushed his hand over his cock. The guy nodded and entered the booth behind him. Mark entered the next booth.

The guy peeped at him. He dropped a few tokens in the video monitor and flicked the channels looking for something of his taste. He skipped the bears, chicks with dicks, black thugs, and leather daddy channels to settle on the Bel Amici euro twinks. Mark dropped his tokens in the machine and found the muscle boy channel.

The guy pressed a button and a red light went on in Mark's booth. He pressed it and the metal partition between the booths went up like a garage door. The guy was masturbating. He nodded his head for Mark to join. Mark hesitated, realizing he had only three minutes on the video. He decided that was all the time he needed to get off. When the guy's time ran out before his, he waited outside. Mark existed the booth and the guy whispered in his ears.

"I live off Christopher. You wanna come over?"

Mark nodded and followed.

A week passed and Mark enjoyed the pleasant sensation of a full stomach. He gorged on Big Macs, Double Whoppers and General Tso's chicken. He drank iced coffee at Starbucks and six packs from the corner stores. He bought a change of clothes from the Salvation Army, a six months membership at the YMCA, and took long hot showers. He washed the remaining pieces of clothing he owned and hid them in a suitcase under the pier. He slept on the F train from Coney Island to Jamaica Queens until the conductor noticed and kicked him off. When the sun was out, he slept under shaded trees away from the crowd and traffic. The next week he was back to one dollar pizza slices and cigarette butts.

One morning he stopped by the corner delicatessen at Christopher and Bleecker Street for a seventy-five cents cup of coffee. A white van pulled up on the curb as he sat on the sidewalk. The driver waved to the shop attendant, who came out for a conversation. Mark listened to the two Indian men and grew annoyed by their accents. He bummed a cigarette from a pedestrian.

"Hey my friend, how you doing?" one of the Indian man asked.

Mark nodded.

"Why you so serious my friend?"

Mark forced a grin.

"Okay, all right my friend, have a good day."

Mark returned gazing at the bustling foot traffic. A police pulled up and he casually finished the coffee and headed up West 4th Street.

The Indian driver was parked at another deli making a delivery. Mark walked past the van and bumped into him existing the deli.

"Sorry, my bad."

"No problem, my friend."

237

His stomach brushed against Mark and he squeezed his hand. Mark flinched. He was not expecting a proposition. He looked up and walked away.

"Where you go my friend?" the Indian man asked. "You want a ride?"

"Nat really."

"Maybe something else?"

"Wah yuh mean?"

"You know, my friend."

Soon Mark was heading up West 4th to the Meat Packing District. The Indian man stopped at Ace Packing Company on 12th Street to pick up a package of meat and threw it in the back of the refrigerated van. Mark waited impatiently, not sure what he was getting into.

The Indian man placed his palm on Mark's thigh.

"Where we do this?"

"Do wat?"

"You know? Blow me. How much?"

Mark hesitated to size him up. He was overweight with a full beard and bloodshot eyes. His white embroidery *kurta* fell below his knees. The loose fitting *salwar*, a pajama like pant, was stained with animal blood. He smelled like feet and burnt curry. His breath reeked of stale gyros.

"Sixty," Mark said.

"Oh no my friend. Too much. I give you twenty?"

Twenty dollars could buy a dinner plate, a few cans of beer and a pack of cigarettes, but it wasn't enough to swallow the little pride Mark had left.

"Naaw. Yuh can drap me aff a de corna."

"Okay, my friend, thirty."

"Forty!"

"Okay. I make delivery, few minutes then my place."

"Where's dat?"

"Harlem."

"No! Dat too far."

"Okay, okay. I know place near, my friend."

He stopped on West 23rd Street for a delivery, then stopped at a garage on 38th Street. The electric gate went up and another Indian man waved him into a space. They spoke Hindi and the joke was on Mark.

"Wat yuh doing?" Mark asked.

"Everything okay my friend. We go in back."

"Back where? In de fridge?"

"It's okay my friend."

"Wid hall dat meat?"

Inside the frosty, damp refrigerated van, slaughtered pigs hung from metal hooks. Bins with chopped meat wrapped in brown paper were set on pallets separating Mark and the Indian man from the bloody metal base. The raw meat and bleach were nauseating. The Indian man sat on a milk crate, spread his legs, and lifted his stomach. Mark wanted to vomit.

"Ah, my friend, one minute. I get it up."

Mark stuck out his hand for the forty dollars. His pulled the Indian man's flaccid penis from the webbed pubic hair. He bowed his head and inflated his cheeks like a blow fish, stretched his lips over his overbite, and grazed the Indian man's penis against his outer lip.

"Yeah. Suck it my friend!"

Mark waited for an erection then spat in his palm and rubbed his shaft.

"Suck it good my friend."

"Let mi know when yuh gonna com," Mark said. "Nuh cum on mi!"

"Yeah, suck it, suck it good."

"Let guh de back ah mi neck!"

Mark wanted it to end. He alternated sucking, spitting, and rubbing like he was milking a cow. The Indian man eyes rolled back in his head and his body jerked off the milk crate. Mark closed his eyes when semen leaked from the tip of his penis.

"That was good my friend. You liked that?"

Mark shot him a look that summarized his disgust. He spat on the floor and headed for the gate. The parking lot attendant came out as the gate opened. He smiled at Mark, hoping for a reaction. Mark waited for the gate.

"Hello my friend, what's your name?"

Mark rolled his eyes.

"Sixty dollars!"

A Puerto Rican guy stood by the bus shed at Christopher Street, looking like an angry thug. He puffed a cigarillo, checking the cars going by. Mark had never seen him before and thought he looked suspicious - maybe an undercover cop. He didn't look like a hustler. Too straight. Too street.

A slightly muscular transsexual came down the street wearing tight jeans, black tank, and slippers. Her long weave looked dirty. Her bleached dark skin appeared lighter around her face with hair stubbles sprouting around her chin like something crawled under her skin and laid eggs. She gave the Puerto Rican a hug and they sat gossiping. Mark walked across the street looking for entertainment.

The Puerto Rican said something about Rikers Island. The transsexual said something about three months. They talked about a body found in a cheap motel uptown. They smiled coldly. She said something about crack pipe and probation. He said something about dirty urine and wearing a bracelet. She called him Jugo, and he called her Peaches. They made plans to meet at Two Potato Bar or by the subway entrance on Christopher Street. They shared the cigarillo. She sat on his lap and played with the long wavy hair he kept in a ponytail covered with a do-rag.

Mark stared. Jugo screwed his face. ✴

"What's up?" Jugo asked. "What you lookin' at?"

"Noting," Mark said.

Peaches clicked her tongue on the roof of her mouth and smiled.

"Don't mess with him Jugo. Maybe he likes chicks with dicks."

Mark wasn't amused. He walked back across the street and sat on the sidewalk.

A meager black man in a limo nodded as he spoke on a cell phone. He relaxed his tie and rested it on his stomach. Mark got up and walked over to the limo.

"Wat's up?" he asked.

"Can we go to SoHo?" the limo driver asked.

"How much yuh hab?" Mark asked.

"Fifty," he said.

"Okay," Mark said. "Can I sit in de back?"

"Don't touch nothing," he said.

Mark slipped in the limo and opened the roof. The driver adjusted the rearview mirror to show off his crotch. He looked massive. Mark grinned. He turned on the radio, speeding through the amber lights. He parked at the corner of Prince and Mulberry Street, eased out of his tie, and walked to the back of the limo. Soon he was rubbing his cock, removing Mark's

241

pants, and pulling out a condom.

"A don't get fuck!" Mark said.

"What?" the driver asked. "What you do then?"

"Jus suck," Mark said.

"Not for fifty dollars!" he said. "You fucking crazy?"

Mark moved up the seat. The driver put the condom back in his pocket and unzipped. Mark gagged at the sight of his cock. It rested mid-way on his thighs.

"Okay, suck it for twenty."

Mark didn't complained. His cock throbbed in his mouth. He held Mark behind the neck and pulled him down.

"Yeah boy. Suck that dick!"

"Nuh call mi boy!"

"Shut up and suck it! I'm about to bus a nut."

He came over the upholstery, on the ceiling, and in Mark's face. Mark felt humiliated. He picked up a towel covering the wine bottles to wipe his face. The driver glared at him and he thought it a better idea to use his soiled T-shirt instead.

He gave Mark ten dollars.

Mark looked at him and cut his eyes.

"Yuh seh twenty!"

"That's all I have. Maybe next time."

"Tek mi back to Christopher Street."

He looked at Mark like he was crazy.

"Naaw, I have a client in Tribeca. I'll take you down the block."

Mark waited when he returned to the steering wheel and he moved one of the wine bottles under his shirt. He walked up Bleecker Street and detoured through Washington Square Park. He gulped down the wine hoping to get drunk before the bottle was empty.

A guy on the outskirts of the park was whistling to passing NYU students, trying to make a sale. Mark's eye burned.

The police patrol cars were making their way through the park. He left and headed back to Christopher Street. He saw Peaches walking in the middle of the street, waving at cars. He dodged her trail at Jane Street.

A few cars were still cruising at five in the morning. He passed on a twenty dollar offer from a feeble Asian guy, waiting for the stout white guy that reminded him of Walter Cronkite to return around the block. At Horatio and West 4th, the red Escalade with the Connecticut license plate stopped before him.

"How you doing?" the driver asked.

Mark smiled.

"Fine."

The driver also smiled.

"What a nice guy like you doing out here?"

"Working."

"What you get into?"

"Nat much. Jus play round."

"Like what?"

"Head."

"Where?"

"Up de block. In yuh car."

"How much?"

"Forty."

His smile vanished.

What Mark remembered when he told Jugo - who shared a cell at the precinct - was the white guy driving away and high beams flashing in his face. His tried to convince the police it was a misunderstanding, and that he was a journalist working undercover. The officer laughed and told him he should get a lot of lines from his cellmates.

Peaches and other hustlers were also booked. The officers joked about picking up one on Gay Street. They jeered the transsexuals with welcome back remarks.

"Soliciting? I didn't do anything!" Mark said.

"They got you when you said forty dollars," said. Jugo. "Don't worry, you'll be out after the weekend. R and R"

Jugo lay on the metal bench and slept. Mark watched his body move, keen on the way his Dickies sagged, but disappointed he couldn't see a dick print. Peaches and her friends in the other cells heckled the police officers. Mark wasn't worried anymore when he listened to the circus around him. He felt safe from the streets.

He stared at Jugo sleeping on his stomach, anxious to see his bulge when he turned over on his back. Jugo got up, half asleep to pee. His body was beautiful, sculpted by the streets. His arms were covered with tattoos. Mark moved slowly up the metal bench when he returned and lay in the opposite direction to get a closer view of his crotch. Jugo moved his legs when Mark grazed him, and drifted back to sleep.

When they awoke, no one knew what time it was. Peaches and her gang seemed withdrawn, almost quiet. The officer asked Mark if he wanted lunch. The peanut butter and jelly sandwich was a treat. He washed it down with cherry flavored milk, and went back to sleep.

Mark was arraigned after the weekend with a hearing in a month. He was embarrassed to return to Christopher Street. He slept on the pier for a week. He was hungry and dirty. He felt depleted. Killing himself seemed like an afterthought. He walked over the George Washington Bridge, willing himself to jump into the cold, black water 600 feet below. He was out of options. There was no one else to call.

"Mark! Is dat you?"

"Yes maaa."

"Wa'ppun to yuh?"

"Noting."

"Weh yuh dch?"

"New York."

"Wat yuh doing deh?"

"Noting."

"Yuh working?"

"No."

"Weh yuh live?"

Mark couldn't answer.

"Lawd Jesas Chrise!"

Epilogue

Daphne's hair was tied up in a silk scarf. Her house dress looked uncomfortable for the Florida heat. She stood over the kitchen sink peeling green bananas, stabbing the skin and flipping it away with a flick of the wrist. She hummed a kingdom melody song, ignoring Mark sitting on the couch in Eileen's living room. She sifted a bowl of rice. She went to the refrigerator and took out a defrosted chicken. She took a sharp knife from a drawer and reached below the sink for a cutting board. She slammed the chicken on the board, running the knives through the breast bone, ripping it into two. Mark jerked. Her hands shook nervously. She batted her eyes then wiped her hands in a dish towel. She was troubled by her thoughts. She walked to the bathroom, ran the water for a few minutes, and returned with her scarf retied.

"Yuh hot? Yuh nat hot?" Mark asked.

Daphne's features contorted as she returned to cutting the chicken. Her face was hard and impassive. Mark watched her and prepared for what was coming. He knew it wasn't going to be pleasant. Eileen had already given him a piece of her mind along with telling him he would have to reimburse her for the plane ticket.

Daphne started the flame under the frying pot for the chicken. As the oil began to heat, so did her temper. She sighed through her nostrils like an angry bull.

247

"Wi nuh hear fram yuh since yuh lef fi guh a yuh big shat Howaard Uni-varse-city. Yuh betta nuh cum yah wid yuh crasses."

Mark didn't respond.

"Nuh bady nuh hab time fi yuh bod-da-ray-shun. Mi a ole ooman now. Mi only wok two days a week fi ah lickle pittance. Mi caan afford fi yuh high class lifestyle."

Mark didn't respond.

"Weh yuh was hall dis time? If yuh nevah fine yuh backside inna trouble, wi wudda nevah hear fram yuh."

Daphne was right, but he had expected a reunion. He thought time would have softened her, but she had never been his mother - not the mother he wanted. He longed for a gentle, caring, and delicate mother, but she remained ill-tempered, domineering and judgmental, with more reasons to loathe him. She used her age, her health, and religion as weapons. He hadn't been a good son, but she was never a good mother. He thought running back to her was her victory - proof of what she had warned about and predicted had been fulfilled. Mark needed her unconditionally, but she couldn't look beyond his demise.

Daphne wasn't gloating; she was suffering. She couldn't imagine what she had done for her son to treat her the way he had. Her sacrifices were met with his ungrateful contempt. Her punishment was to see him suffer. He expected her to be consoling; instead, he had to attend to the pain he had caused.

Eileen was also not supportive. She barely spoke to him. When she came home from work in the evenings, she closed her bedroom door and remained there, eating TV dinners and watching *Lavern & Shirley* reruns.

Mark retreated to the couch. The apartment was dense with disapproval. She was divorced from Ronnie, pregnant by a guy from Trinidad - who would never marry her - completing a master degree, and managing the nursing home where Daphne worked. She had no time for him.

Mark found a temp job as a file clerk with Broward County Clerk of Courts. He left the house before Eileen woke and returned when she was in her room. One Friday night, he went to a gay club and had a one-night stand. When he got back to the apartment the next day, Eileen was livid because she suspected he had spent the night with a man. She said she didn't condone his abominable lifestyle and warned if he did that again he would have to leave her house.

After the temp job, Mark picked up a retail job at Dillard's in the Galleria Mall. His first paycheck paid his first month's rent for an efficiency attached to a house in Lake Ridge. He was eager to finally have his own place, and to get away from Daphne's word-throwing and Eileen's contempt.

The efficiency had a single bed, a side table, and a standing bathroom without a sink. The swimming pool in the backyard, free washer and dryer, and being a few blocks from the mall and beach were its strongest features. The gay landlord was quiet and unobtrusive.

Working at Dillard's and living alone in the efficiency were a relief. Everyone Mark worked with was gay, from the store manager to his supervisor, and co-workers in his department. It was reassuring to mix with others of his kind who weren't negative influences. They wore pastel shirts with bright floral ties. They showered in the latest colognes from Cosmetics. They walked delicately, smiling at shoppers, luring them to their departments for a sale. They lunched at the food court and gossiped - who was at George's Alibi in Wilton Manors, what happened in the porno room at The Copa, and who was written up for soliciting a male customer in the fitting room.

Mark welcomed their frivolous chatter and tried to remold his life from the homeless street hustler he had been. He latched onto his supervisor like a gay mother. Brad was fifteen years his senior and the top seller in the Ralph Lauren department. He had worked at Dillard's for three years after living in Palm Springs. He was polished and well-worn with soft, restful blue eyes. He was strategically friendly. His wrinkled skin and thinning blond hair had stood the test of time, and a life plagued with disappointments. He had rebuilt his life when his lover of fourteen years left. Mark thought if Brad could do it, there was hope for him.

When Jorge was hired a month later, Mark was anxious to befriend someone closer to his age. Jorge was twenty-four, from Cuba, and he looked like a young, muscular Ricky Ricardo. Apart from being gay, Jorge work-out religiously at Bally's gym and lived in Miami with his mother after breaking up with a boyfriend in Tampa. He drove a silver Mitsubishi a "friend" in Wilton Manor paid for.

Mark liked Jorge immediately, and when there were no customers, they gossiped for hours. He was anxious to hang out with him. One Tuesday night, they went to Score in South Beach, after stopping at Cactus in Hialeah to watch a drag show. The Latino gay crowd was bemused by Adora's costume. She wore a purple beehive, bouffant wig with matching vintage dress that spread around her like an umbrella. Her fingers were covered with cubic zirconia rings, the size of ice cubes. She lip-synched to La Lupe "Que Te Pedi," as the crowd threw dollar bills at her feet. She thanked them for coming after plugging her gigs throughout South Florida.

At Score nightclub, Jorge took off his shirt and jumped on the narrow stage, stealing the attention from the paid go-go dancers. The crowd was attractive. Handsome Latin men with buff bodies flirted with each other. Mark drank Coronas and danced with Jorge, reveling in the club's attention.

Jorge became his gay best friend within days. He was inspired to buy a camera and they went to Haulover Beach for a photo shoot. After a few shots, Mark took off his flip flops, wiggled his toes in the sand, and got into the warm, emerald water to let the waves crash over his body. A school of tiny silver fish swam around and pecked him on his nipples. For the first time in a long time he felt a slight feeling of happiness, and the world looked pretty.

He submitted the photos to *BLUE* magazine in Australia and received an email that they would be published in a six-page feature.

It was 2001, and he felt like a twenty-nine-year-old man child, unrealized and arrested. He felt numb to what was happening around him. He reflected on his life, yearning for something else.

Guia was in the final months of his life, living with his boyfriend in Portland. Mark smiled when he told Christian who it was on the phone. Christian had been discharged from the Navy and living in Fort Lauderdale. Christian said Aamir had moved to Baltimore after the planned marriage didn't work out. Ori was in London working at a public relations firm and dating a model from Denmark. Wallis was the co-owner of a gym in Toronto. Kris was in rehab again and Chris was killed in a drug deal gone wrong.

Mark thought about the people he knew in Jamaica. He got an email from Georgette who encouraged him to forward her religious chain message to everyone in his contact. She was in New Jersey teaching kindergarten and had only kept in touch with Gillisa, who married Brian. They had a son named Damon and lived in the best neighborhood in Kingston.

Mark wondered what he was doing at Club Coliseum on a Friday night with the under twenty-one crowd. He no longer had any interest in the gay scene. He was tired of being a spectacle - the fabulous dancing queen amusing the intoxicated, self-centered crowd. Jorge had convinced him to go; he wanted to hook up with a guy he met online.

Mark stood at the edge of the dance floor, waiting for Jorge to run out of steam. TP Lords entertained the crowd with his high energy backup dancers. Erika Nowell flirted with the go-go boys at her side. She removed her outfit to show off redesigned womanly curves with pasties covering her nipples and a fig leaf concealing her tuck.

Amongst the crowd were older men chewing gum and dressed in Abercrombie and Fitch. They were in a state of denial - diluted by their middle-age dilemma in the youth obsessed gay world. They sought younger men, living vicariously through their youth.

A guy stood in the crowd with a glass of champagne. He wandered on the dance floor like he was bored and ready to leave. He went upstairs and stood by the balcony, looking at the sea of young men then walked back to the dance floor.

He waved his glass when he saw Mark.

"You want a drink?"

"Sure.".

"I have a table upstairs."

Mark liked the way he looked. He was different. His spiked Mohawk dyed blue reminded Mark of Tracks. A tattoo of a barcode on his right

252

shoulders suggested he was unique. Ripped Diesel jeans and an Andy Warhol Campbell Soup T-shirt hinted at his taste. His green eyes were alive through tinted Christian Dior shades, balanced on a pronounced nose. His lips were unusually full. His tanned, stocky body denied his late thirties age. Mark found him appealing and welcomed the free drink. He smiled when he poured a glass of Verve Clicquot. The cold bubbles tickled his nose. The guy smiled, excited he had someone to talk to.

"A saw yuh walking round like yuh last."

"I know, I don't know what I'm doing here. It was Leslie's idea."

"Who is Leslie?"

"A friend."

"Yuh boyfriend?"

"No. Why?"

"A jus wondering."

They spoke the rest of the night with a comfortable ease. Johannes was from Austria and had lived in Florida for over twenty years, although he still had an accent. Mark said he was from Bermuda to avoid the usual Jamaican references. He was a single chef with a restaurant in Palm Beach County. Mark said he was a photographer.

They had another bottle of champagne and Mark allowed him to move closer. He held Mark's hand while they spoke and it felt like they were alone in the club. Mark followed his words like they were the most important thing he had ever heard. When the lights came on in the club, Johannes invited Mark to his house in Boca Raton. Mark gladly accepted.

"What did you say your name was?"

"Mark."

"You're pretty trusting to be going home with me."

"A feel safe wid yuh."

"Why? I could be your worst nightmare."

"Do I luk dat naïve like one a den chickens in de club? A been in many cars before."

"What's your reason for getting into mine?"

"A don't know. A like yuh. Maybe to take a chance."

"You look so young."

"A only luk young. A been threw a lat."

"Like what?"

"Yuh really want to know?"

"Sure."

Mark smiled.

"A wi tell yuh later. When yuh make mi breakfast in de marning. It's a lang story."

"Rough life, huh? I hope this will be the start of something better."

"How bad could yuh be?"

"You just have to take a chance, I guess. We could be lovers."

They waited for a valet to retrieve Johannes' car. A red Maxima pulled up and Mark walked to the door. Johannes nodded because it wasn't his car.

Jorge walked out the club with his date. He pretended he didn't see Mark, hoping he wouldn't have to give him a ride to his apartment.

The valet pulled up in a black 2002 Range Rover and handed the keys to Johannes. Mark was impressed. He immediately adsorbed the pristine leather interior and lemon smell. Johannes adjusted the seat, checked the mirrors, and turned on the CD player. Nelly's "Ride wit Me" blasted through the speakers. Johannes smiled and danced around in his seat like a giddy child. He had no rhythm.

"Yeah. It's different from inside a Range Rover."

"Wat is?"

"Life."

Johannes drove off slowly. Mark looked back to check if Jorge saw.

"You don't have to look back. Everyone knows you're leaving."

Mark smiled and held Johannes' leg tightly.

The second novel in the trilogy.

LIVE THROUGH THIS

"What sweet nanny goat ago run eeh belly"
[That that appear too good, can hurt you]

Publication date: Fall 2016

Available exclusively at

www.maxarthurmantle.net

An excerpt from **LIVE THROUGH THIS**

Mark thought Johannes was the most desirable guy he had ever met who showed an interest. What impressed him the night they met was the champagne they had at the Coliseum in Fort Lauderdale. The way Johannes filled the flute glasses and guzzled them down as they chatted, suggested he wasn't concerned they had three bottles, and the gratuity alone could have bought Mark decent dinners for a week. That moment, Mark became perennially available. Johannes looked at him like he was calling him from the depths of his soul, telling him he had finally found him, telling him he would be alright. He was so drunk that's what he wanted to believe.

When the valet handed the keys of the black pre-issued Range Rover to Johannes, Mark felt a kind of victory like he had won a prize. His told himself, whatever Johannes wanted, let him have it! Let him enjoy you, give it to him, and maybe you could enjoy what he had to offer. So he went home with Johannes without giving it a second thought that they had only met two hours earlier.

For any gay guy in his late twenties prime, meeting a decent guy, and going to his house for the expected one-night stand would have had no bearing on his future. The best he expected was a good fuck without criminal activity or catching the dreaded terminal virus. The promise to see each other might spawn dinner dates with wild and panting hook-ups until the excitement inevitably fizzled. For Mark, who saw himself as an average looking, skinny black guy with nothing to look forward to, and desperate for a boyfriend, this was it. Johannes, an attractive white guy who gave the impression he was loaded with cash was the best Mark could do. It was his chance to live a life he had imagined for himself. Johannes was his salvation.

The drive up the coast from Fort Lauderdale to Boca Raton was a trip Mark had taken many times while looking out the window of a Broward County bus alongside Haitian hotel maids, Mexican grass cutters, and other marginalized commuters on their way to dead-end service jobs. It was different inside a fully loaded 2002 Range Rover in October 2001, listening to Nelly's "Ride wit Me," and sitting next to Johannes with his hand on his thigh. Johannes was rocking like an uncoordinated white boy with an intoxicated grin. It seemed like the promise of something.

The house was off Spanish Trail Court, Boca Raton's uber rich waterfront dream community. Mark tried to subdue his elation. Johannes offered a nightcap - another bottle of champagne, and they smoked a joint. He had Ecstasy and wanted to make a night of it. He was busy all week at his restaurant preparing for the season. He hadn't had a *boy* in a long time and Mark seemed good enough. It was early Saturday morning with no reservations later that evening. He was ready for a decadent time.

He turned down the music, switching from Junior Vasquez to Buddha Bar to set the mood. He dimmed the track lights and opened the sliding glass doors to absorb the warm Florida night. They lounged on a thick faux fur, leopard print blanket on what looked like an outdoor daybed under an encompassing seagrape tree at the edge of the deck. Its branches stretched across the shallow canal like a winged creature. The moonlight glistened on the surface. Johannes was raw like the ocean. He was sweaty and aroused.

His hands felt hot on Mark's skin. Their bodies moved together like trained dancers. Everything Johannes said, Mark found stimulating. Everything he suggested, Mark complied. It seemed very simple. He wanted Johannes to feel good. He wanted Johannes to like him. The Ecstasy coursed through their inebriated bloodstreams and did as it was intended.

Johannes stripped off Mark's shirt and lapped his firm nipple. He nibbled the tip encouraged by an a cappella of erotic murmurs. He was ravenous and in some state of heaven. He unzipped his pant and led Mark's hand between his legs. Mark flinched from touching metal on the head of Johannes' cock. He felt a Prince Albert. His skin prickled from the thought of stainless steel ripping through sensitive skin. Johannes smiled and calmed his nerve. He tugged the jewelry with ease. It felt different in Mark's mouth. Something he would have to get used to.

Mark liked Johannes' kisses. The way his tongue wandered aimlessly down his throat gave him goosebumps. His lips canvassed his face. He liked the way he was held. Johannes was impatience to explore Mark's body. He had an urgency to have him. Mark felt beautiful. Desired. When he came he wanted more. He gasped from the thought of it. He saw future orgasms with Johannes, whenever and wherever he wanted him. He longed for it to happen again.

In the bedroom, Johannes fell asleep immediately, carried off into a drugged dream. Mark listened to his light snores, dreading the approach of dawn. Lying next to Johannes he felt safe, protected and chosen. He drifted in his thoughts and saw his limitations. His failed life. The overwhelming burden of being Mark Palmer. He saw a future with Johannes where he would rise above his demise. Johannes' life would upgrade his and foster rewarding possibilities. Johannes would make him better. He would become the person he had always wanted to be.

261

41543042R00154

Made in the USA
Charleston, SC
01 May 2015